9MM JUSTICE
AN OMEGA THRILLER

BLAKE BANNER

Copyright © 2025 by Right House

All rights reserved.

The characters and events portrayed in this ebook are fictitious. Any similarity to real persons, living or dead, is coincidental and not intended by the author.

No part of this book may be reproduced in any form or by any electronic or mechanical means, including information storage and retrieval systems, without written permission from the author, except for the use of brief quotations in a book review.

ISBN-13: 978-1-63696-344-0

ISBN-10: 1-63696-344-7

Cover design by: Damonza

Printed in the United States of America

www.righthouse.com

www.instagram.com/righthousebooks

www.facebook.com/righthousebooks

twitter.com/righthousebooks

THE OMEGA SERIES
Dawn of the Hunter (Book 1)
Double Edged Blade (Book 2)
The Storm (Book 3)
The Hand of War (Book 4)
A Harvest of Blood (Book 5)
To Rule in Hell (Book 6)
Kill: One (Book 7)
Powder Burn (Book 8)
Kill: Two (Book 9)
Unleashed (Book 10)
The Omicron Kill (Book 11)
9mm Justice (Book 12)
Kill: Four (Book 13)
Death In Freedom (Book 14)
Endgame (Book 15)

ONE

I WAS IN TUCSON, ARIZONA, FOR NO PARTICULAR reason, standing on a corner admiring a girl in a flat bed Ford who had slowed down to take a look at me. She gave me a wink and I smiled. The lights changed and she drove away, out of my life forever. That's the way it happens sometimes.

It was one of those Arizona days, when the sun scorches the sky to a blue that is almost white, and the palms stand motionless in tall, thin silhouettes, over broad streets of low houses. I was strolling, with my hands in my pockets and no particular direction. No particular direction had led me, without realizing it, from America's Best Value Inn, on the East Benson Highway, south to the Fairgrounds district, along South Park Avenue. I was on the corner of East Fair Street, smiling to myself as I watched her drive away, when I caught sight of a small group gathered outside Cora's Golden Café, across the road, about fifty or sixty yards away.

Like a lot of places in Tucson, Cora's Golden Cafe was set back a ways from the road, among a broad patch of dirt with a parking lot out front. Something about the group made me pause to look at them. There were four guys. Their hair was cut real short. They had the dark, olive complexion of Latinos and all four of them looked lean and athletic. I thought their attitude and manner seemed aggressive, even threatening. None of them looked much older than twenty-five.

They were talking to two girls. One of the girls was wearing jeans and a T-shirt. Her hair was long, loose, a bit wild. She seemed to be mad and was waving her hands a lot, cocking her hips and her head as she spoke. The gestures made me smile. She looked like a handful.

The other girl was holding her arm. She seemed maybe a couple of years older, though that may have been because of her clothes, and her manner. She was wearing a pale blue dress, her hair was cut to her shoulders and she seemed to be trying to reason with the boys. A small crowd had gathered outside the door to the café, watching, waiting, like people at a circus.

Before I knew what I was doing, I had started to cross the road. The far sidewalk was a strip of dirt with patchy grass growing on it. There were traffic lights and a big telegraph pole blocking my way. I loped across the blacktop and saw one of the boys move forward and push the girl in jeans. The girl in the dress stepped in front of her, blocking the boy's way. The others closed in. I noticed a couple of them were wearing hoodies. The other two had short sleeves and I now noticed they had tattoos. I had started to run. They were thirty paces away now, and I began to hear a different sound, the throbbing of ugly music played too loud in a car.

It was approaching from South Park Avenue toward me,

and without knowing why, I knew it was important, and I knew it was bad. I went from a jog to a sprint. The girls were backing away, toward a white truck. One of the boys had his hand behind his back, reaching under his hoodie. I shouted. They didn't hear me. I could feel my Sig Sauer heavy under my left arm. They were fifteen, twenty yards away, still backing toward the white pickup. I shouted again. On South Park Avenue, a customized Lincoln Continental came into view, traveling fast. I pulled my Sig and shouted again. The Continental veered suddenly, accelerating fast across East Michigan toward the far entrance of the parking lot. They all froze, staring at the car that was speeding toward them. I heard myself screaming, "*Get down! Get down!*"

The girl in the jeans turned to stare at me. She was frowning, like she didn't understand what I was doing there. Everything seemed to slow right down. I saw every detail of her face. I saw her long, unbrushed hair waft as she turned her head. I saw the small crease between her eyebrows as she frowned.

I shifted my eyes and saw the Continental screeching past behind them with the windows open. I knew what was going to happen. I screamed again, "*Get down! Get down!*" running, gesturing with my hands. But it was too late. It was like firecrackers going off inside the car. Brilliant flashes of light illuminated the cab and the diabolical faces of the men holding the assault rifles. The crackle filled the air. The small crowd scattered. One of the hoodies went down where he stood. The two guys in T-shirts ran a couple of paces before they fell. The second hoodie made it a little further and died at the sidewalk.

The girl in the jeans fell staring at me, with wide,

shocked eyes. The Continental lurched out of the parking lot and sped away, fishtailing slightly along South Park, leaving littered, scattered bodies behind it.

I stopped running, staggered to a halt and knelt by the girl, reaching for my cell. I felt for a pulse in her neck. It was a faint flutter. She blinked, panting softly. I saw she had a bullet wound in her belly, but the blood was pooling underneath her. It had gone right through.

"Take it easy," I said, "I'm calling for help. You're going to make it."

"911, what is your emergency?"

"Drive by shooting in Cora's Golden Café parking lot, corner of South Park Avenue and Michigan, six badly hurt, probable fatalities..." I glanced around me. The girl with the blue dress had gone. "Five," I said. "Five casualties."

The girl was looking at me. She was frowning again. I could see her hand moving slightly, like she was trying to lift it. I took it in mine and smiled at her.

"My name is Lacklan. I'm going to help you. The ambulance is on its way. You're going to be fine."

Her lips had gone very pale and she was trying to move them. I said, "Don't try to talk, you can tell me later. I'll be there at the hospital when you wake up."

She blinked again, with the ghost of a smile, and whispered, "Celeste, nice..." She took a couple of breaths and whispered again, "...nice to meet you..."

Then there was a slight rasp as her lungs emptied, her eyes lost focus and her hand went heavy and cold in mine. I sat and crossed my legs, holding her hand in my lap, waiting with her as the distant sirens wailed across the Arizona afternoon. Close up, she was more like eighteen than twenty. She had on a blue and violet plaid shirt and a thin string of beads around her neck. She had boot cut jeans and brown cowboy boots. Her eyes, now lifeless, had been bright and curious, and a dark chestnut brown.

Vehicles were pulling into the parking lot: four patrol cars, lights flashing and sirens crying out, three ambulances, a Ford Focus. I looked down at Celeste and realized my face was wet. I gave her a rueful smile she would never see and said, "See you in Valhalla, Celeste."

There were cops walking toward me with their weapons drawn, shouting at me to raise my hands and lie face down. I put her hand carefully back on the ground, raised my own hands and turned to lie on my face.

They didn't ask me any questions. They just cuffed me, took my weapon and bundled me in the back of a car. From there I watched how they put her in a bag, zipped it closed over her head, lifted her onto a gurney and wheeled her to one of the ambulances. I watched also, a little later, as a woman in her fifties came running up East Michigan Street and into the lot, screaming and shouting as she went. A couple of cops crowded her. She appealed to them, looking up into their faces, saying something, and they led her to a man in a blazer and chinos. He listened to her for a moment, then called over a female police officer and the woman was led toward the ambulance where Celeste's body lay. Her mother, sent to identify the body.

The guy in chinos and the blazer was walking toward me. I figured he was fifty, not in great shape, and he'd been around the block a few times—too many times maybe. He opened the car door and helped me out, then showed me his badge.

"Detective Mike Shannon, Tucson PD. You make the call?"

"Yes."

"What's your name?"

"Lacklan Walker, my driver's license is in my breast pocket."

He reached in and pulled it out, examining it. "Captain, huh?"

"British SAS."

He glanced at me, curious. "You an American?"

"On my father's side, yeah. Is that relevant?"

"I don't know yet. Tell me what happened."

I tried to keep the edge from my voice. "I witnessed a multiple homicide, called it in and tried to help one of the victims. Unless any of those things is a crime in Arizona, how about you take the cuffs off?"

"You were armed."

"Like everybody else in Arizona, New Mexico and Texas. I have a license and the weapon has not been fired. Besides, you'll find that these people were killed with an assault rifle, my weapon is a 9mm, a Sig Sauer p226 Tacops. I don't believe you have any reason to arrest me, Detective, and given that I have every intention of cooperating with you, as of right now this is a false arrest and you're breaking the law."

"Keep your panties on, Captain." He turned me around and took off the cuffs. "We have gang wars around here. You can't be too careful. They told me you were sitting beside the girl, holding her hand?" He gave it the intonation of a question and narrowed his eyes at me, like he thought my behavior was weird. I gave him a rundown of what I'd seen, then shrugged.

"She looked like she was in trouble with the guys, her friend—"

"The one in the blue dress."

"Yeah, the girl in the blue dress, she seemed to be trying to help her. I got the impression they were not the intended victims of the drive by. The boys were. I tried to help the girls, tell them to get down, but I was too late. When I got to her, while I was calling 911, she was still alive. She couldn't be more than eighteen or nineteen. She said her name was Celeste."

He nodded like he understood. "Which way'd the woman in blue go?"

"I don't know."

He frowned, sucking his teeth and staring at his notes. "You're a very observant man, Captain, the detail here is remarkable. Comes with that kind of training, I guess."

I shrugged. "Maybe."

"But you didn't notice where the woman in blue went."

"No. I was surprised. When I called it in, I said there were six victims, then realized she wasn't there."

He showed me the notebook. "I'm going to need you to sign the statement." He pointed at the crossroads. "The station house is just on the intersection."

I stared where he was pointing, then at him. "That is a damned confident drive by, on the doorstep of the police station."

He jerked his head, indicating I should follow and we walked to his car as the last of the bodies was being lifted into an ambulance and the Crime Scene team started their minute search of the parking lot.

"These kids believe they are invincible. They have more coke than they know what to do with. Take enough of that stuff, you start to think you're God. Add to that the fact that they are backed by the power of the Mexican cartels, sometimes I think we're fighting a losing war."

We climbed into the car, slammed the doors and he pulled away. After a moment, I said, "In the southwestern states, you are."

He raised an eyebrow at me. "I'd like to take every politician in Washington, D.C., and have each of them watch a son, a daughter—some loved one—die from addiction to heroin. It's not just the death." He pulled onto the road and accelerated toward the intersection. "It is the slow destruction of the person, of the mind and the character, that comes before the death. I'd like those son of bitches to have to go through that and then explain to me why we can spend three trillion dollars invading Iraq and Afghanistan, while we sit on our asses and allow this flood of death to seep through our border."

I didn't answer him. I had no answer. My answer used to be Omega[1], but with Omega all but finished, the only explanation was that this was human nature. This was the human condition. We lived in Hell, a hell of our own making, because we were too damn cruel and too damned greedy to create anything better.

He parked in the station parking lot and led me through the crowded building to the detectives' room and then to his

---

1. See *The Omicron Kill*

desk. There I sat while he typed fast into his computer and printed my statement. He handed it to me and said, "Read it, Captain, and if you agree, please sign it."

I read through it, signed it, and handed it back to him.

"I need my gun back. It hasn't been fired, so it's not part of your investigation."

He picked up the internal phone and after a moment said, "Yeah, this is Shannon, Sig Sauer Tacops p226, just brought in from the shooting outside Cora's Café..." He waited, turning a pencil over in his fingers. "Send it up, will you? No, it's not going to the lab. We're returning it to the owner. Thanks."

I'd been watching his face. Now I said, "You know who did this."

It wasn't a question and he nodded. "The four boys are part of the *Iluminados* gang. They're at war with Jesus, Pedro and Pablo Santos, the *Santos del Diablo*."

"A turf war."

"What else? They both buy heroin, coke and other shit from Mexico. They're probably buying from the same supplier. They sell it locally to the local users, and they also sell it on to suppliers in L.A., San Francisco, Chicago, New York, Washington..." He shrugged and spread his hands. "Right across the nation. It's the commodity everybody wants. Heroin for the losers and coke for the winners."

"They're making a lot of money."

"Thousands, tens of thousands every week. That's why they are at war."

"They're that hard to bust?"

"Hey, don't give me a hard time, Captain. Tucson PD thanks you for your cooperation, but I don't need lessons in law enforcement from a British soldier. Guns ain't the only thing they buy with the dough they're making. You catch my drift?" He glanced over my shoulder. "Here's your piece. Be careful what you do with it."

A uniform approached and put the weapon on the desk. I holstered it and went to stand, but stopped with my hands on my knees. "What about the girls? Do you know who they are? Were…"

"Why?"

"I'd like to pay my respects to Celeste's mother. I think she'd like to hear her daughter's last words. I'm figuring she's the woman who turned up while I was waiting in the car. Her last memory of her daughter is not a nice one right now. Maybe I can improve it."

He sighed and sat forward, leafing through his notebook. He spoke as he did it. "The girl was Celeste Martinez. Her dad was killed about sixteen years ago, shot by a cop. He was involved in narcotrafficking across the border. She and her mother have stayed clean ever since… Here, the mother is Estrella Martinez, she lives on East Michigan, eleven-oh-two."

"Thanks."

He watched me stand and narrowed his eyes at me, like he wasn't sure if he thought I was OK or a pain in the ass. "She'll appreciate it. But don't get involved, Captain. Don't turn superhero on me."

"I'm just passing through, Detective: see the sights, try the food and I'll be on my way."

I left the detectives' room feeling his eyes on the back of my head. I rode the elevator down to the lobby and stepped out into the bright, Arizona sunshine, thinking about Celeste Martinez, knowing Detective Mike Shannon was not going to punish her death, knowing her death could not go unpunished.

TWO

It was a short walk to Estrella Martinez's house, along East Fair Street and down Freemont Avenue. Hers was the third house along. It was set behind a chain link fence and a front yard that was mainly dust and scrubby grass, shaded by velvet mesquite and yellow palo verde trees.

She was not alone. There was a small crowd of women, children and young teenage girls in her front yard, all talking at once outside her door. Her door was open and I could see and hear more people inside. I went through the gate and they all went quiet and watched me as I stepped inside the house.

There was no entrance hall here. It was one room, with a kitchen in pale, faded green on the left and a living area on the right, with a threadbare sofa, a couple of armchairs and a TV. A crucifix and a Virgin Mary were both nailed to the wall.

Sitting on the sofa was the woman I had seen in the

parking lot. She was crying and had a couple of women on either side, holding her and patting her hand. They were also crying and by the looks of it, their good intentions were leading Estrella Martinez straight to hell. There were other women and young girls sitting around, looking at me.

"Estrella Martinez?"

Several of them pointed to the woman I had recognized. She looked at me, blinking and stifling her sobs. I said:

"I was with your daughter when she died. I tried to help her." They all started talking to her at once and I heard the words *es verdad* a couple of times from the young girls. They were telling her it was true.

Her expression changed. There was a hint of longing, like she thought because I had been with her daughter when she died, in some crazy way I might be able to bring her back. I took a step closer. "Can we talk for a moment, alone?"

There was an explosion of chatter then, with everybody talking at the same time, and through it all, I got the idea she was asking them to leave us alone and they didn't think that was such a good idea. Eventually they all filed out, eyeing me curiously and a little suspiciously, leaving the living room empty and the front yard full. I closed the door behind them, crossed the room and sat next to her on the sofa, half turned to face her. She spoke first.

"You were with my Celeste when she...?"

Her eyes flooded and I nodded. "Yes. Do you want to know what happened?"

She hesitated, then closed her eyes and nodded.

I told her how it had started, how I ran toward them and tried to make them get down, how Celeste had stared at me and time had seemed to slow down, how in that moment we had seemed to know each other, to live a whole life of friendship in an instant, as death had closed in on her. I found myself speaking to her, perhaps as I imagined I might have spoken to Celeste, in a way I had never spoken to anybody. Through it all, she kept her eyes closed and cried as I spoke, but it wasn't the convulsive sobbing of intolerable grief, though that was there, for sure. But rather it was the helpless weeping that comes with the emptiness of letting go.

I told her how I had sat beside her at the end and held her hand, how I had told her my name and she had told me hers, just before she went. I realized then that I too was crying, and that she was holding my hand.

I dried my eyes and my cheeks with the sleeve of my free hand and asked her, "How old was she, Estrella?"

"Just nineteen, last May, a little Taurus bull. So obstinate, so much temperament, but always laughing and happy. One minute a storm! The next minute sunshine. Such a good daughter."

"You raised her alone…"

"Yes, my husband…" She shrugged. "Better alone than in bad company. My friends tell me, 'Oh, you raise Celeste all on your own!' I tell them, 'No, I have help. Celeste help me. Celeste and Jesus help me. Now! Now, she is gone with the Angels, I am alone."

I nodded. "Did she work? Did you depend on her financially?"

She pulled a handkerchief from her apron and dried her face, then blew her nose. "I depend on her for money, to make ends meet. But she didn't know how much. Now she decide to go to college, and I didn't know how I was gonna cope, but I didn't tell her. I didn't tell her nothing. I believe Jesus would help me."

"What was she going to study?"

"Child psychology. She loved the children. Even when she was a baby, she love the babies." She stopped talking a moment, staring out the window but seeing some scene in the past. "She want to work with kids who had lived through a trauma, like her. You know, is very bad here. Here in Arizona every year there is more violence, coming from Mexico, with the drugs. Mexicans are good people, but the people who come with the drugs are bad. She don't want to know nothing about that. She want to help the victims and the children. I don't know what I am gonna do now she is gone."

She let go my hand, pulled a handkerchief from her pocket and blew her nose. I sat a moment remembering the big, brown eyes staring at me, frowning slightly, as the shape of the black Lincoln Continental closed in, as death claimed her and she became collateral damage. She wasn't even the target. She was killed because she happened to be there, in the way of their greed.

A hot coal of rage had started to burn in my belly.

"Estrella, she was with another woman, dark hair to her shoulders, a blue dress… Any idea who she was?"

She shook her head. "I don't know. Could be anybody."

I nodded, then asked, "Do you know who did this?"

Her face became drawn. What little color there was turned to gray, but she didn't answer.

I went on, "It was the *Santos del Diablo*. Do you know who they are?"

Her eyes narrowed. "Who are you? Are you *policia*? FBI?"

I smiled and shook my head. "No, I'm a friend of Celeste, and I'm mad that they took her on the day I met her. I'm not a cop."

"Don't go after them, Mr. Lacklan. Don't do nothing stupid."

I allowed my face to become reassuring. "I don't plan to do anything stupid, don't worry. I just..." I sighed and shrugged. "I just want to know."

She turned away from me and gazed out the window, where the sun was starting to stretch the shadows of the mesquite trees long across the dust. "Celeste was not involved in any of that. But everybody around here knows who are the *Santos del Diablo* and the *Iluminados*." She turned back to me. "The *Santos* are Jesus' gang. He was a nice boy, I know his mother, but when he turn thirteen he become a monster, killing dogs, killing cats, fighting with knives. When he was sixteen, he form his own gang with his cousins Pedro and Pablo, and he make this blasphemous name, the Saints of the Devil."

"Is it a big gang? Are there many of them?"

She raised an eyebrow at me and sighed. "*Ay!* I don't know. If you want to know you gotta ask the *Iluminados!* Talk to Carlitos. Maybe you can become one of them and join all the killing."

I smiled and squeezed her hand. "I have done all my killing, Estrella. I was in the army, and I am done with that."

She smiled back, but she shook her head, looking me in the eye. "You are a good man, Mr. Lacklan, but you are lying. You are still a killer, and God has chosen you to do his killing for him. You want to know where are the *Iluminados*?"

"Yes."

She stared at the carpet for a while and I thought she might start crying again. She didn't. Instead she said suddenly, in a loud, hard voice, "You go to the bottom of Freemont Avenue, where it makes a corner, there, in the bend, they have their club." She raised her face to look at me and added, bitterly, "If you go to talk to them, a *gringo* like you, they will probably kill you. Then you can ask Celeste all your questions in person."

"I doubt I'll see Celeste where I'm going, Estrella. Thank you for talking to me. I only knew Celeste for a few seconds, but I know she was a very special person, like you."

She patted my hand, I stood and left the house.

Outside, the crowd had scattered, but you could still see the odd knot of two or three women and girls gathered at their gates, talking and glancing at the house. I turned into Freemont and walked the three hundred and fifty yards to the end of the street, where it turned east. To the right there was a broad expanse of wasteland that separated Freemont from South Park, a hundred and twenty yards away. To the left there was a row of nine houses, each set in its own plot of desert. Ahead of me was a house of the same sort, but the front fence had been torn out and where the yard should have been there were half a dozen bikes and a couple of trucks, all painted with desert scenes, saguaro cacti, death's heads and cannabis leaves. They were anything but original.

The front door was open and there was a guy in black jeans, a black T-shirt and a long black ponytail leaning on the doorjamb watching me. To complete the picture, he was holding a bottle of Coronita.

To the left of the door there was a green, molded plastic table with two chairs of the same design. They were occupied by a bare-chested kid of about eighteen whose arms and face were tattooed with variations on the theme of skulls, eagles and snakes, and a third guy who'd cut the arms off his denim jacket and embroidered it with more unoriginal designs from Hollywood Mexico. They all watched me step onto their forecourt and walk to within two paces of the guy in the door.

"I need to talk to Carlitos."

They muttered obscenities at me in Spanish, then the guy with the ponytail spoke in a deep baritone.

"Fock you. Get outta here or we gonna cut you bad."

"I need to talk to him about the *Santos del Diablo*."

"What the fock you know about the Angels, *pendejo*?"

I spoke very quietly, holding his eye. "Maybe I didn't make myself clear. I didn't say I needed to talk to a long streak of bat shit with the IQ of a laxative. I said I needed to talk to Carlitos. So how about you stop playing tough guy, and you run along and tell your boss he has a visitor."

He spat elaborately on the ground and stepped out the door. He didn't put his beer bottle down and that was a mistake, because I knew he was going to smash it in my face. He was two paces away and I let him take one and a half. Halfway through his second step, when he had only one foot on the ground, I smashed the heel of my boot into his kneecap. He staggered and stumbled, making a keening noise, gripping at his dislocated knee. I grabbed his ponytail with my left hand as he went down and twisted him savagely around, pulling my Sig from under my arm and shoving the muzzle into the back of his neck.

The two guys who'd been sitting at the plastic table were now on their feet. Again I spoke quietly.

"Now, I came here for a talk. I didn't come here looking for trouble. But trouble found me. So, how I deal with that trouble depends on you boys. I don't want to hurt anybody, and I don't want to blow anybody's brain out of their face, but if that's what you make me do, then I'll do it. Only it seems a shame, as all I want to do is talk to Carlitos."

They just stared at me, waiting to see what I was going to do. Ponytail meanwhile was whimpering like a girl and doing small hops on his good leg. I jerked my head at the denim jacket and said, "Go tell your boss he has a visitor. Tell him what happened."

"I can see for myself what happened, *gringo*. What do you want?"

He was maybe thirty, slim, hard, with short hair and the kind of unremarkable face you might see at a checkout, or behind a million desks across the U.S.A. Only this one masked the mind of a psychopath.

"I want to talk to you about the *Santos del Diablo*."

"What do you know about the Saints?"

"I didn't come here looking for trouble, Carlitos. I came here to talk. Tell your boys to stand down and I'll let this asshole go. Any trouble and I'll shoot you first."

He told them in Spanish and I dropped Ponytail to the ground, where he curled up, gripping his knee and screwing up his face. A small group had gathered inside the house, behind Carlitos, and now they came out and helped Ponytail hop and hobble into the house. Carlitos jerked his head at me. "Talk."

"I saw what the Saints did to your men in the parking lot. They also killed a girl, an innocent bystander. She was only nineteen."

"So what?"

"I think they should pay."

He smiled. It wasn't a nice thing to see. He looked at his two guys sitting at the plastic table. "Can you believe this guy? He comes here, to my house, he breaks Toni's knee and threatens me with a gun, because he don't like to see a girl die." They started to laugh. "What am I, your fockin' psychotherapist?"

I let the laughter die down.

"I can hurt them. I'm a pro. It's what I do. But I need some help from you."

Now his face flushed. "Hey! *Pendejo*! Look around you! What you see? We all pros here. We kill people. Is what we do. Now do yourself a favor and get the fock out of my house before I cut you open!"

I sighed. "Come on, Carlitos! I'm offering you something here. It's going to cost you nothing but some information, and maybe the loan of a couple of your boys."

"You out of your *fockin' mind? The loan of a couple of my boys?*"

I could see I was getting nowhere. I shrugged. "Suit yourself. At least tell me where he and his saints hang out. I plan to make him pay, with or without your help."

"What the fock do I look like to you? A fockin' public information service? What the fock, man?"

Suddenly I'd had enough. Two strides took me over to

the table. I took a handful of the bare-chested kid's hair and dragged him yelping to his feet, but before he could get his balance, I had slammed my fist deep into his solar plexus and spun him around with his back to me, retching and gasping for air. They had still not reacted by the time I'd kicked him in the back of the knee, pulled my Fairbairn & Sykes fighting knife from my boot and prodded the tip of the blade into the side of his neck, over his carotid artery. He was on his knees, gasping and whimpering and holding his hands out like he was trying not to fall over. I looked at Carlitos.

"Have I got your attention? One push and the blade goes through his artery and severs his windpipe. Believe me. I don't see any pros here. Give me an excuse and I'll decapitate this pussy and shove his head so far up your ass you'll look like a fairground attraction. Now, I'm done trying to reason with you. Where do I find Jesus and his saints?"

Carlitos wasn't staring at me, he was staring at the kid kneeling in front of me. His expression was one of fascination, like he was wondering if I would really do it. Fortunately for the kid, his pal with the denim jacket spoke up.

"Don't hurt him, man. He ain't done nothing to you. They hang at Jesus' place on South Fair Avenue, by the railroad, corner of East Fairground Drive. You can't miss it. They always got their bikes and trucks parked at the side of the house." He hesitated a moment and frowned at me. "What you gonna do to them?"

"Too late. Now you'll have to read about it in the papers."

I pushed the bare-chested wonder onto the dirt and he curled up in the fetal position in a strange echo of Toni before him. Carlitos snarled at me, "You jus' made yourself a bad enemy, *gringo*."

I slipped the knife back into my boot. "Tell it to your therapist. My beef is with Jesus and his angels, Carlitos. Stay out of my way."

I turned and walked back up Freemont, toward South Park, America's Best Value Inn and my Zombie.

I was going to need my Zombie.

THREE

To look at, the Zombie is a matte black 1968 Mustang Fastback. But under the hood it has twin lithium ion batteries driving two electric engines that deliver eight hundred bhp—one thousand eight-hundred foot-pounds of torque—straight to the back wheels. It will accelerate from standing to sixty miles per hour in just over one and a half seconds, and has a maximum speed of two hundred miles per hour. She is a brutal beast, but best of all, she is totally soundless. Which is what you want if you are looking for a silent kill.

There was nobody in the parking lot when I got to the inn. I had my car sitting in the shade of some mesquite trees, backed in with the trunk to the fence. The trunk of my car is where I keep my kit bag, a habit from the old days with the Regiment, which I never quite shook off. I opened the trunk, then pulled open the bag. In it I had my spare Sig Sauer p226, a Maxim 9 and the big Smith & Wesson 500, with plenty of ammunition. I also had my Heckler and Koch

416 assault rifle, my hickory take down bow and eight out of the twelve arrows I'd had to begin with. The other four were in Sinaloa somewhere.[1]

I had a bunch of detonators, some remote and some mechanical, but no C4—that was back in Sinaloa too—and I also had a pair of binoculars and some night vision goggles. You never knew when night vision goggles might come in handy. Other than that, my kit was pretty depleted. I could have restocked it weeks earlier, but I hadn't wanted to.

I took the binoculars and the goggles and closed the trunk, pulled my Camels from my pocket, poked one in my mouth and lit up with my old brass Zippo. Then I leaned on the roof of the car, thinking. I hadn't restocked because after the hits in Argentina, Brazil and Mexico, I had decided that I'd had enough. Just like I had left the Regiment two years earlier because I'd had enough. I was tired of killing. I was tired of waging war against Omega, only to find that even as they withered and died, human evil flourished and prospered. Omega did not create human evil. Human evil had created Omega.

Yet, here I was again, checking my kit bag, making an inventory, assessing what equipment I was going to need, what equipment I was going to need to return to doing once again what I was best at—killing.

For a moment I thought of settling my bill, climbing in my car and driving north, to Wyoming, where I still had the small house and workshop I'd bought when I got back from England. Then I thought of going back to Boston, to Weston, to the house I'd inherited from my father, with my

---

1. See *The Omicron Kill*

cook and my butler and the gardener, to take charge of the family estate. I smiled. Rosalia and Kenny would be pleased. It would be peaceful. New England in the summer was a good place to be. Maybe it was time, after all...

And then I thought of Celeste, that face, strangely familiar, her eyes searching mine, that sense of a lifetime of knowing each other, passing in an instant. All she had wanted was to stem the evil and the violence that was spreading like a dark tide across the land; all she had wanted was to do something good, something valuable, and she had died because we live in Hell, and in Hell evil must always prosper.

It was not time. Not yet. I still had work to do. I climbed in behind the wheel, fired up the powerful, silent engines and pulled soundlessly out of the lot. I cruised down South Park and turned west on East Fair Street, past the cop shop and over the railway lines.

There I found myself at a broad intersection with a lot of open wasteland running beside the tracks, and stretching between one fenced off house and another. I was in the heart of the city, but I might have been in some remote town in the desert. On the right of the road there was a house behind a chain link fence, mostly concealed by trees and bushes. Diagonally across, on the corner, there was a long, low orange shack that had once been a club and still bore the name *El Sinaloa*. Now it was boarded up and covered in graffiti.

I pulled over opposite, on the stretch of dirt beside the railway track, and killed the engine. I had a pretty clear view of the house Carlitos' boy had told me was Jesus' place. It was about two hundred yards down the road, on the corner.

There were a couple of the mesquite trees that grow just about everywhere in Tucson, which would partially hide me from their view at this distance. I put the binoculars to my eyes and studied the place for a while. There wasn't much to see. As the kid had said, there were some bikes and trucks parked at the side of the building—a low, sprawling mess of a place, with a lot of junk in the yard, a couple of sheds and a long, low porch. I could see people, mainly guys, sitting around, talking, drinking, not much else. Except that after half an hour they had a visitor. Some guy pulled up in a Toyota, left the engine running, went in and came out five minutes later, then drove off.

I kept watching and after a couple of hours I'd noticed that there was a steady flow of people who would turn up like that. Some came on foot, others in cars or trucks. Once it was a couple. Most of them looked like hell and had an air of urgency about them. You didn't need to be Sherlock Holmes to deduce that they were coming for their hits.

After three hours, the sun was low on the horizon and dark shadows were stretching long through bronze light, across the blacktop and the dust. I had counted twelve visitors in that time. If they were selling Mexican brown, they were taking twenty-five bucks a paper. That was just three hundred dollars in three hours. By drug dealer standards, that was not a fortune. For the kind of turnover Shannon had been talking about, they had to have some other kind of outlet.

They did.

When the sun had gone and the dark had closed in, I crept a bit closer. One by one, six of his boys left the place, some on foot and some in their vehicles. I figured they were being dispatched to street corners and dives around the city. That would up his income by at least six hundred percent. Now we were looking at in excess of a grand an hour. That was more like it.

Among the people I saw at his house, there were three guys I noted in particular who stood out from the rest. Their clothes were a bit sharper and by their manner and the way they spoke to the rest of the gang, they had authority—were telling, not being told. They gave orders and were obeyed, and nobody sent them out to street corners. They stayed back at the house and received the cash. One had a ponytail and a goatee and was a little older, none had visible tattoos and all dressed sharp. I figured these were Jesus and Pedro and Pablo.

I spent the next three days observing them and the house, sometimes from my car and sometimes from the wooded wasteland that bordered the track at the back of the Fairgrounds shopping mall. The routine seemed to be the same every day, and the guys I had decided were Jesus, Pedro and Pablo rarely seemed to leave the place. In fact the youngest never did, and the other two rarely, except in the evenings. But on the fourth day, the Friday, the routine changed.

At ten o'clock that night, the three of them came out onto the porch and stood talking. Meanwhile, two of their boys went to one of the sheds at the side of the house and after a couple of minutes, the black Lincoln rolled out. Then one of the three, it could have been Jesus, Pedro or Pablo, I didn't know yet, skipped down the steps from the porch and climbed in the back of the Lincoln.

They turned out of the yard and headed south. I

watched the other two go inside and I followed the Lincoln. Pretty soon it pulled onto the Nogales Highway. They didn't drive fast, and from what I could make out they weren't blasting rap music either. I figured they were not looking to attract attention, but even so, it surprised me they were using the Lincoln only a few days after the hit at Cora's Café. I kept back and left my headlamps off. To them I would be almost invisible.

After six or seven miles, the city lights began to give way to the impenetrable darkness of the desert. We passed the Desert Diamond Casino and the Monsoon Nightclub, set back from the highway on the right, and then, about a mile farther on, they pulled off the road into a large, concrete parking lot that was flanked on three sides by floodlit palm trees, tall, thin and strangely eerie against the night sky.

On the fourth side there was a two-story building that would have looked more at home in Vegas than in Tucson. It was a strange cross between a Greek temple, a Roman villa and a Rococo French palace, but over the Palladian entrance there was a vast, neon image of a cowgirl in a red shirt and blue shorts riding a brown bull. She was holding a cocktail glass in one hand and a lasso in the other. The club was called the Cowgirl Rodeo and by the looks of the parking lot, it was popular.

I slowed and pulled off the highway and onto the shoulder. From there I watched them climb out of the Lincoln and go inside. When they were out of view, I drove in and parked near the exit. There I sat for a moment and thought about what to do next. Finally I climbed out of the Zombie and went into the club.

Like all clubs of that type, it was an antechamber to the

ninth level of Hell. There was a perpetual throbbing noise that made it impossible to hear anything else, and red and blue pulsing lights made it impossible to see anything clearly, except a great mass of black silhouettes with their arms in the air, jumping up and down to the infernal pulse. Dotted around the room there were retro cages, reminiscent of the discos of the '70s, where naked girls were dancing, and, in a kind of pulpit above the bouncing throng, there was a guy illuminated by electric blue light, who seemed to be a DJ.

I pushed through the crowd and found the bar, where I ordered a whiskey. As he poured it, I scanned the room and saw there was a balcony. Up on the balcony there were sofas and armchairs, and dark alcoves.

I looked around for the stairs that led to the upper level. I found them over on my right. They had a red and gold rope hung across them at the foot, and a big black guy in a dinner jacket and a bow tie who didn't let you past that rope unless you had an invite.

I took my drink and strolled over to him, leaned close and shouted, "What's upstairs?"

He let his head drop to one side, like I'd asked to get down from the table before I'd eaten my spinach. "Non o' yoe business is what's upstairs, mother focker. Now beat it."

I thanked him and returned to the bar. I didn't have time to finish my drink though. Two minutes later, the guy who was either Jesus, Pedro or Pablo came down again with his two boys. It was the first time I'd seen him closer than a hundred and fifty or two hundred yards. The two boys went ahead. One was older, maybe in his late thirties, craggy, with a moustache and a hard, wiry body. I told myself he was the dangerous one. His pal was a good ten years younger. He had a red bandana and expensive cowboy boots on the outside of his jeans. He might be dangerous in ten years, if he lived that long.

Behind them came Jesus, Pedro or Pablo. You could tell he had ambitions and aspirations by the way he dressed. He had short, well groomed hair, an expensive jacket that might have been Hugo Boss, with a collarless shirt, designer jeans and what looked like hand made boots. I wondered if he was Jesus, but decided as I watched him that he was dancing in somebody else's limelight. He was either Pedro or Pablo.

The boys opened a path for him through the crowd and they left the club. I looked around again, studying the clientele. This wasn't the kind of place you came to play with silver spoons. This was the kind of place you came for a snort. I figured right then there was probably a case upstairs with a couple of kilos of coke in it, and Jesus' right hand man was probably leaving the place forty grand richer.

He visited another couple of clubs that night, one out in the desert just past Summit, and another near Valencia West. By the time we got back to the city, the eastern horizon was turning a pale gray. I let them pull ahead and made my way back to the inn. There I fell into bed and slept like the dead for four hours.

In my dreams I could see shadowy, semi-human creatures by moonlight, inky black, highlighted in luminous blue, filtering across the border. They gathered, like a coven, around the amorphous, stygian shapes of their trucks, muttering and murmuring. They brought death with them, they cloaked themselves and everything about them in death. They were the emissaries of a vast tide, a slow tsunami of evil that was engulfing the continent.

I awoke understanding that they must have a supply line from Mexico. The most effective way of winning a battle or a war is to destroy the supply lines. I needed to find the Saints' supply line and choke it off, and then kill Jesus, Pedro and Pablo—and anyone else who stood with them. I had been watching them for four days; pretty soon they would have to take delivery and I would get a glimpse of their source of supply. Then I would plan my attack, and execute it.

It and them.

I rose, went to the shower and stood for ten minutes lathering myself and waking myself up with alternating blasts of hot and cold water. Then I dressed, had some coffee and returned to my vigil on South Fair Avenue, by the old Sinaloa Club. Nothing much happened till noon. Then I saw a white Ford truck nose around the corner and park outside Jesus' house. I put the binoculars to my eyes. Through them I saw the door open and a girl get out. She was in her early to mid twenties and, unusually, she was wearing a pale cream dress rather than jeans. Her hair was dark and cut to shoulder length. She was the girl who had been with Celeste when she was shot. Only then her dress had been blue.

She crossed the sidewalk and as she arrived at the gate, one of the holy trinity stepped out to meet her. It wasn't the guy I'd followed the night before. This one was younger, maybe in his early twenties. His clothes looked expensive, but like his pal's they were understated: jeans and a grandfather shirt. He and the girl hugged and he kissed her cheek. They spoke a moment, laughing, then went inside.

There was no mistaking the intimacy and the closeness. It was in the body language, in the way they stood together and spoke to each other. It was in the laughter. They were close.

I lowered the binoculars and sat pinching my lip. Two questions sprang into my mind: A, who was she? And, B, if she was close to Jesus, why the hell didn't Detective Mike Shannon know who she was?

I didn't have much time to think about it. A couple of minutes later, she came out of the house again, climbed in her truck and drove up the road toward me. I slid down in my seat and stared at my phone, like I was writing a message, trying to keep my face hidden, but as she passed she slowed, and in my peripheral vision I saw her staring at me. Then she drove off.

FOUR

In the end, I decided she wasn't important and dismissed her from my thoughts. But I also decided she would probably mention me to her pals, so it was time for me to move on, stop reconnoitering, and take some kind of action.

I drove around the corner, out of sight, and spent half an hour on Google. Eventually I found what I was looking for: a realtor dealing in farm property to let, and a barn about twenty miles out of town, along Ajo Way, headed west. It was well off the highway and pretty remote. I called the realtor and told him I was interested. If the place was suitable, I said, I was willing to pay cash, a year up front. He liked the sound of that much cash up front and agreed to show it to me that afternoon.

"There's just one thing: I'll be using the place to store valuable merchandise, machine parts, classic cars, you know the kind of thing."

"Certainly, but I am afraid there is no electronic security, it was just a barn. However, we can always look…"

"That's fine, I can supply my own security, what concerns me more than that is the neighbors. Is this place secluded…?"

"Oh yes, very. The nearest neighbors are at the very least a mile away. The farm itself is closed and boarded up. There ain't nothin' out there but coyotes and buzzards!"

"It sounds perfect. I'll see you there at three this afternoon."

"I'll be there, Mr…"

"Smith, John Smith."

"I'll see you there, Mr. Smith."

I pulled off the patch of dirt where I was parked, drove two blocks down Michigan Drive and up 3rd Avenue onto Ajo Way. Then I opened her up and drove fast out of the city, headed west. Pretty soon I was out in the desert, among an endless flatland of mesquite, palo verde bushes and the occasional massive silhouette of a saguaro against the misty hills in the distance.

After about fifteen minutes, I came to Postvale Road on my right. Here I turned and headed north for half a mile through more endless dust and shrubs, till I came to a dirt track with a green sign that said this was Valencia Road. I bumped and ground along Valencia Road for a quarter of a mile, until the track made a dogleg to the right, but I kept going straight for another quarter of a mile along something that could have been a track if it had tried harder.

Finally, I came to a dilapidated fence with a gate that had rotted off its hinges and collapsed to the ground, back around about the time when pudding basin hairdos were challenging convention. The farmhouse was thirty yards in from what was left of the gate. By the looks of it, it had once been a handsome home, tall, broad and well made, with an ample porch and three floors, plus an attic. Now it was slowly falling to pieces, with its windows boarded up and the doors nailed closed. But over to the side, on my left, was the barn that interested me.

I parked the Zombie out of sight, cleared the rotted gate away and walked across the dry earth to the big, faded red doors. They were held closed with a simple chain and padlock that would be easy to open. I took a walk around the grounds and as far as I could see, there were only cacti and trees for at least a mile in any direction. It was perfect.

I pulled out my cell and called the realtor.

"Hi, John Smith here, we spoke earlier about the barn on Valencia Road." He told me he remembered me well and hoped I was having a good day. I went on. "I'm afraid I am going to have to cancel. My partner has just informed me that he has found something suitable and put down a deposit. I am sorry to have wasted your time."

He sounded disappointed but said these things happened and hung up.

I climbed back in my car and made my way back to the inn. There I slept the rest of the afternoon until seven. Then I grabbed a burger and a piece of pie from the Country Folks Restaurant and returned to watch Jesus' house.

I had nothing to go on but common sense, but I was pretty sure he was going to have to take delivery of a shipment soon. He'd been selling heroin at a steady rate and he'd made several large deliveries of what I assumed was coke, but nothing had come in for almost a week.

On the other hand, I couldn't keep watching him indefinitely. For one thing, there was only one of me and I needed to eat and sleep, and for another I had been noticed by somebody who was close to at least one of the bosses.

So tonight one of two things had to happen: one, they collected a shipment, in which case I went along to see where it came across the border, or two, and this was the most likely scenario because it was Saturday, they would distribute to the clubs again. If that happened, I would make a move.

I wasn't wrong. At shortly after nine PM, the three guys I'd decided were Jesus, Pedro and Pablo came out onto the porch. There was some complicated macho hand shaking that wound up looking like an Austrian slap dance, and the same guy I'd seen the night before climbed in the back of the Lincoln and took off south again. I tailed him as I had the night before, keeping back with my lights off, but when we reached the turn off for the Desert Diamond Casino, I began to accelerate and close in silently behind him. I still had my headlamps off.

I had picked my spot. A quarter of a mile before the club, there was a long stretch of dirt, with entrances to a number of warehouses and workshops. As we approached that stretch, I put my lamps on full beam, blinding the driver, and floored the pedal. In less than a second I had accelerated from 70 MPH to 100 MPH. The G-force was powerful and I struggled to hold the beast steady. As my passenger door drew level with his hood, I slowed and turned sharply, cutting across his path. I heard his brakes scream and we both came off the road onto the side.

A Lincoln Classic Continental is a big, unwieldy car designed to look good going in a straight line. It is not designed for performance. His back end had fishtailed and he had done two full spins by the time I was out and walking to the driver's door. The first thing they knew about me was the moment the car stopped skidding and I put two 9 mm rounds into the driver's head. His pal was still gaping at him when I blew what little cerebral cortex he had out the back of his skull and all over the tinted window behind him. I guess that's what you'd call stained glass.

I leaned in and lined up the guy in the back. He was reaching under his Hugo Boss jacket, looking scared, but I smiled and shook my head.

"I don't plan to kill you, but if you do that, I will." His hand eased away. I saw he had a large attaché case by his side. "Get out. Hold the case in both hands."

He did as he was told and I covered him all the way.

"Jesus, Pedro or Pablo?"

He hesitated, then said, "Pablo."

I jerked my head at the case. "Coke?"

He nodded.

"How much?"

"Three kilos. Who are you?"

"Sixty grand right there. Go to the Mustang. Open the passenger door." He did as I told him. "Put the case in the back, then take out your piece and drop it at my feet. Do anything to make me uncomfortable and I'll kill you. Understand, I want you alive. I don't need you alive. Clear?"

He nodded that he understood and moved toward the Zombie. He opened the door, threw the case in the back and very carefully removed his weapon. Predictably, it was a Glock 19. I was a couple of yards from him. He dropped it at my feet and held both his hands up. When he spoke, his voice was unsteady and lacked conviction.

"You know what my gang will do to you for this?"

"You carrying anything else?"

He shook his head and I stepped forward like I was going to frisk him. Instead I smashed the butt of the Sig into the tip of his jaw and caught him as he sagged forward. Then I eased him into the passenger seat, went around and climbed in behind the wheel. I figured he'd be out long enough to get where we were going.

Where we were going was twenty miles away, back up the Nogales Highway and then west along Valencia Road. I was in a hurry and took a risk doing 120 MPH as far as the intersection with the Ajo Highway. Then it was a short drive up Postvale, back to the farm I had visited earlier that day.

I drove the Zombie right up to the barn, picked the lock with my Swiss Army Knife and heaved the door back, then drove the car inside and closed the door behind me. It was very dark. I put my night vision goggles on and was suddenly in a weird world of black and green. I grabbed a roll of duct tape from the trunk and dragged Pablo from the passenger seat. He was coming around, but groggy, and confused by the darkness.

There was a thick, wooden pillar holding up the roof, right about the middle of the floor. I shoved him against it, leaned close and breathed in his ear. "Do exactly as I say and you'll live. Try to fuck with me and I will disembowel you right here and now. Understand? I am not interested in you. I am only interested in what you can tell me. Play your cards right and you go home tonight. Are we clear?"

His breathing was heavy and shaky. "OK, I will cooperate. Just don't hurt me, please."

"Put your hands behind your back, around the pillar."

He did as he was told and I taped his wrists together. Then I taped his ankles, and after that I used half the roll taping him to the pillar.

I knew all he could see was blackness, with a slightly darker, moving patch of darkness within it. He was totally disconcerted and must be terrified. I took my knife from my boot and walked behind him. There I let his fingers feel the blade.

"I keep it sharp, Pablo. Sharp as a razorblade." His breathing was growing louder and faster. He was close to hyperventilating. I walked slowly around, letting him hear my footsteps. "However loud you scream, we are over a mile from the nearest person. And they'll probably figure it's a fox. Nobody is coming for you, Pablo. Nobody knows where you are."

"I told you I will cooperate."

"I know the things you do to people. I know you kill indiscriminately. I know you torture and maim. Did you know that the other day you killed a nineteen-year-old girl called Celeste Martinez?"

"Yes..."

I stopped in front of him, studying his eerie black and green face, with inhuman black eyes. "So tell me, seeing as you do all this killing and maiming and torturing, is there a single good reason I should not maim, torture and kill you?"

His face began to scrunch up. His lower lip folded in under his teeth. He started to sob. I gave him a powerful backhander. It must have been a shock, coming out of the black. He gasped and his eyes went wide. Now he was experiencing true terror. I sheathed my knife and rammed the sheath hard against his belly. He screamed and started babbling, "*No, no, no! Por favor! No!*"

"The guy with the ponytail and the goatee, that Jesus or Pedro?"

"That is my brother, Pedro."

"Where was the coke going tonight?"

"A club…"

I back-handed him again, let him hear the knife sliding out of the sheath and pressed the point against his esophagus. "Don't give me vague answers."

His voice rasped. "*OK… OK…*"

"Was it going to the Cowgirl Rodeo?"

"Yes…"

"But you delivered there already last night."

"Last night we made the deal. The *Iluminados* used to supply them. We killed their contacts a few days ago…"

"When you killed Celeste."

"Yeah. Look, I am really sorry about that…"

"So last night you arranged to take over this territory, replace the *Iluminados* as suppliers, and today you were making the first delivery."

"Yeah."

"Who do you deliver to at the club?"

"Eulogio Cremades. He owns the place."

"Who supplies you?"

"What…?"

"Who supplies the *Santos del Diablo* with dope?"

"I can't tell you that."

I sighed. "OK."

I walked behind him. He knew something bad was going to happen because his breathing became erratic and loud. I grabbed hold of his right thumb and sliced through the flesh that connected it to his index. He screamed. Then I put the heel of my hand against the joint and severed the thumb from his hand. He gave a weird, gasping groan and passed out.

I went and put the Zombie's headlamps on and removed my goggles. He was bleeding profusely from the stump of his thumb. I sealed it with duct tape, found a bottle of water I keep in the glove compartment and emptied it over his head. His eyes opened, but his pupils were dilated and he was clearly in shock. I showed him his thumb and he groaned and gasped a few times.

"You can hand it out, huh? But you can't take it. It's not too late. You can have it sewn back on. They can save it. But if you don't tell me who supplies you, I'll cut so many bits off you you'll need a fleet of tailors to put everything back on."

"Please, no, no more. The Queen…"

"The *Queen?*"

"The Queen of the Sea, they call her *La Reina del Mar*, Sandra Dorado Beltran. She brings coca from Colombia to Mexico, supplies us with coca and heroin."

"Where?"

"Rancho Grande, it's like a mile north of the border, at Sasabe. They bring it through a tunnel, like a mile west of the Sasabe border crossing."

I frowned. "Always at the same place."

He nodded. He looked like he was going to pass out again. "Jesus has it sorted with the patrol."

"Exact location of the mouth of the tunnel."

"Is covered with sand, but you can find it. Is marked by a mesquite tree, seven yards east a broad track that runs to the borderline, and fourteen yards from the border."

He was starting to slur and shiver. I patted his face and he tried to focus his eyes. "You're doing great, Pablo. Just two more questions and you can go. Who was the woman who visited Jesus today?"

He started to sob and shook his head. "She ain't got nothing to do with this, man. Don't hurt her."

"I don't plan to. Just tell me who she is."

"Luz Santos, man. She's Jesus' sister. But she is a good girl. She ain't involved in this. You leave her alone. You understand?"

I nodded. "Sure. How big is your next delivery from Sandra, and when is it due?"

"Fifty kilos of coke and fifty of heroin... Monday night. Day after tomorrow."

He told me, but even as he was saying it, he was realizing the question meant I was going to kill him. If I let him live, he would tell Jesus I had asked the question, the delivery would be cancelled and the location would be changed. His face folded in on itself and he began to sob. "Please, don't kill me, I can help you, I can be of use..."

His death was painless, as painless as death ever can be. I slipped the blade of the Fairbairn and Sykes down behind his left collarbone, severing both his carotid artery and the jugular vein. He bled out in seconds, though all his bleeding was internal.

I took his cell. It was an iPhone, so I used his thumb to unlock it and dial 911. I didn't speak, I just left the phone by his feet and drove out. I took a circuitous route along empty, country roads under a vast sky of glistening, cold stars, and made my way back to the Ajo Highway via Sandario Road. Halfway back to Tucson, I saw two cars from the Sheriff's Department speed past in the opposite direction, with their sirens wailing and their lights flashing. They'd locked on to his GPS.

FIVE

I didn't go back to the inn. I wasn't ready yet. I still had business to take care of. I went back the way I'd come, south on the Nogales Road, past the Desert Diamond and past the black Lincoln which was still sitting there, with its dead occupants in the front seats. I drove into the parking lot of the Cowgirl Rodeo, found a secluded spot beside a palm tree and killed the engine. I left Pablo's attaché case on the back seat and walked inside, to the same infernal throb, red and blue lasers and frenetic, half-naked bouncing people I had seen the night before. This time I didn't go to the bar. This time I went straight to the big guy at the foot of the stairs. He looked at me with his head on one side again and sighed, like he really didn't want to do the bad things he was going to have to do, because I wouldn't learn my lesson.

I leaned forward and shouted: "Tell Eulogio I have his six K. Tell him Pablo is dead. Tell him the sixty grand is for me." We stared at each other for a second. Then I shook my head and shouted above the throb again. "That decision you are about to take is not a decision for you. Your job is to inform your boss."

He grunted, unhooked the rope, climbed up one step and hooked it back in place again. Then he carried his massive weight up the stairs to the balcony. I pulled a pack of Camels from my pocket, poked one in my mouth and lit up with my old, battered Zippo.

A guy with pink lips and a blond fringe that flopped over his eyes tapped me on my shoulder. He had thin, white arms and probably weighed a hundred pounds dressed for winter. He leaned toward my ear with angry blue eyes and shouted, "You can't smoke in here!"

I didn't answer because a cluster of his friends, who looked as pallid and infirm as he did, came bouncing over, hugging each other, and then they all bounced off together toward the can, to snort the coke one of them had just scored.

The gorilla came back down the stairs, pulled aside the rope and jerked his head at me to tell me I could go up.

The balcony upstairs was an 'L' shape, and the stairs rose to the top of the 'L'. There were a couple of small tables up against the balustrade, where guys were sitting with girls, drinking and looking down at the throng below. In the corner, where the 'L' made a dogleg, there were leather couches, a big round table and chairs. Eulogio Cremades was sitting right in the corner, as though it was a throne. There was a blonde on his right and a dark girl on his left, like he was trying to make some biblical statement about him and Solomon: where Solomon got the pillars, Eulogio got the babes.

He was a small man who was lighting a big cigar as I

reached the top of the stairs. Up there, the throbbing wasn't so loud. I approached him along the balcony and he leaned back, releasing a thick cloud of Havana smoke. He was in his early fifties, with tightly curled, graying hair and the kind of mustache that fascist dictators feel compelled to wear.

Besides the two girls, there were a couple of guys who'd obviously spent a lot of time in front of the mirror cultivating a dangerous look. They were both wearing Wayfarers and double breasted Italian suits. There's a uniform for everything in this world, even for anarchic law-breakers. There were other guys and girls watching; some were making out, others were dancing. This was the crazy court of the little king.

I sat without being asked and looked at him and his cigar. Then I looked at the blonde who was leaning on his right shoulder. "You know, sometimes, a cigar is just a cigar."

It was a Freudian joke. Her eyes told me she didn't get it. I turned my attention to him.

"Jesus and his Saints killed four of Carlitos' *Iluminados*. That's how they stepped in to replace him and supply you. Now I've killed Pablo, I have his three Ks of coke. So if you want to buy it, you can buy it from me."

He didn't answer straight away. He removed a piece of tobacco from his lip, flicked it away and then gave me a once-over. "You got a big pair of *cojones*, coming here like this."

I nodded. "But the size of my testicles is not relevant to the deal. I'm asking the same price as Pablo. It's exactly the same coke. It's still in his attaché case." I glanced at my watch. "I only killed him… half an hour ago."

"You trying to scare me, Mr…"

"Not yet, no, Eulogio."

He shrugged, then shook his head. "I buy from you, after you kill Pablo, Jesus gets upset, it can cause problems. I have to live with my neighbors."

"For that, your neighbors need to be alive. By the end of next week, Jesus and his *Santos del Diablo* will either be dead or in the state pen. You want to deal with anybody, you have to deal with me."

Suddenly his nose was telling him there was a smell of pork in the room. I smiled. "Relax, I'm not the law. Feds aren't allowed to go around assassinating people anymore. Not unless they're presidents."

"You got a big mouth, you know that?"

"Big mouth, big *cojones*. We have a deal or not?"

"Show me the dope."

"Outside. When I die, I want to do it outdoors, not in a shit hellhole like this."

He looked at his two boys in the Wayfarers and they stood. I stayed sitting. He shrugged. "What?"

"Either of those boys carrying sixty grand? No? Then we ain't going nowhere, Eulogio."

He jerked his head again and one of the boys walked to the far end of the balcony, opened a door into what looked like an office and went in. Five minutes later, he came out with a black attaché case like Pablo's one. I said, "Open it, let me see."

He popped the catches and I made a random inspection. There was sixty grand in there in a mixture of used bills. I nodded. "OK, let's go."

We went down the stairs into the inferno below. One of

them went ahead of me and the other behind. There wasn't a lot to tell between them except that the guy in front had interesting spirals shaved into his very short hair, and the guy behind had a goatee beard with no mustache, which made his chin look like a pubic bone. Aside from that, they both looked like wannabe Secret Service.

We shouldered our way through the crowd toward the exit. On the way we passed the pallid boy with the blond fringe, bouncing frenetically with his friends. I grabbed his skinny arm in my hand and hauled him over to me. He stared up into my face with terrified eyes. I leaned close and snarled at him, "You're not allowed to snort coke in here, asshole."

I let him go and pushed through the rest of the way to the door. It was a relief to step out into the cold night, with only the desultory sound of the traffic hissing past on the highway. Goatee came out behind me and they both stood waiting. I pointed at the Zombie. "Over there."

Our footsteps echoed loud as we crossed the concrete lot, among the cars. There was no moon, and the yellow light from the tall, thin lamps obscured most of the stars. I opened the passenger door and watched them both reach for their weapons as I leaned inside to get the coke from the back and pulled it out, smiling at them.

"Relax, I want to do business with you guys, not kill you."

The guy with spirals in his hair had my case of money, so I handed the case of coke to Goatee. Now they were both holding cases. I said, "Have a look, try it. It's exactly what Pablo was bringing you."

As Goatee fumbled with the latches on the case, I took out my pack of Camels and held it up in my left hand. "Smoke?"

With my right hand, I reached under my arm, pulled out my Sig and shot them both in the head. Then I confirmed the kill.

I put both cases in the car and drove out of the lot. When I came parallel with where the Lincoln was still parked, I cut across the road and came to a stop beside it. I wiped my prints off the case, dropped the coke in the back and pulled the two boys' cells from their pockets. I kept one and, using the driver's finger, I dialed 911 again, then left the phone beside him. After that, I got back in the Zombie and headed north, for the city, and America's Best Value Inn. I was smiling, thinking what an interesting and unusual night the cops were going to have, answering all those 911s.

NEXT DAY, after breakfast, I drove through the bright, Arizona morning to Estrella Martinez's house. When she opened the door, she looked pleased to see me, though her eyes were puffy and her nose was blocked, like she had a bad cold. She asked me to come in and led me to the sofa, where we had talked last time I'd seen her. As we sat, she said, "I can make you some coffee."

I shook my head. "I just had some."

She took my hand and screwed up her face. "The worst is the nights. I cannot sleep. Thinking always, I cannot believe. I think she is gonna walk in the door, 'Hey, Mamma, you know what happen?' But she never gonna do that again." Her eyes went wide, almost surprised, she shrugged and her lips trembled. "She's gone..."

I squeezed her hand. "I know." I shook my head. "It never goes away, Estrella, but you do learn to live with it."

She stared at me a while, then nodded. "I know, you know death."

"Yeah, we're old pals."

"You lost people you love."

"Friends. Never a daughter. I can't imagine what that's like, Estrella. But one of my teachers taught me once that we never lose anybody. They just went next door for a while, and before we know it, we join them there."

She smiled. "You are not a Christian."

I smiled back. "No, but I do believe that nothing is ever truly destroyed. Whether it's heaven, the Devachan or Valhalla, life goes on. Celeste will be waiting for you, Estrella."

She patted my hand and sighed a damp sigh. "Thank you."

"Listen, I was talking with some colleagues. We were talking about funding a campaign to help youngsters in Tucson to get out of the gangs, or not join them in the first place; to help campaign against the culture of drugs. It would be a kind of tribute to Celeste. We'll begin in the City Council and maybe lobby some congressmen and women for help and support."

Her eyes were narrowed, wondering where I was going. "You gonna do this?"

"I am." I grinned. "I'm pretty well connected, Estrella. So, listen, the organization I was talking to wanted to make a donation to you. I know nothing can ever replace what you have lost, but at least you don't have to suffer the stress of money worries, right?" We held each other's eye a moment and I added, "If this money didn't come to you, it would probably be invested in drugs or weapons or some kind of criminal activity. So I figure we're all better off if you have it."

She looked at the case, then at me again, and her wise eyes knew where the money had come from. "What you done, Mr. Lacklan?"

"Me?" I raised my eyebrows in mock surprise. "Me? Did I tell you I was a captain in the army?"

"You was a captain in the army?"

"An officer and a gentleman." I handed her the case. I stopped smiling and spoke seriously. "This belongs to you, Estrella. You are entitled to it. No argument. It doesn't even begin to compensate you, but at least you don't need to worry about your rent and your bills anymore."

She opened the case and gasped. I stood and kissed the top of her head. "Don't you worry. There's a lot more where that came from, and I mean to see that you get your fair share."

I stepped back out into the sunshine and made my way to the Zombie. As I unlocked the door, I heard another door slam like a gun shot down the road. I looked up and saw Detective Mike Shannon approaching.

"Nice ride. '68?"

"The chassis is." I pulled open the door.

"Visiting with Celeste's mom. That's nice."

"She's a sweet lady. Reminds me of my mother."

"No kidding?"

I leaned on the roof. "How's the investigation going?"

"You know how it is with these gangland killings. Nobody saw nothing, nobody heard nothing, nobody was there, nobody wants to get involved."

"That's a shame."

He nodded and squinted. "The innocent go un-avenged, right?"

I shrugged. "The guilty go unpunished."

He gave a humorless laugh. "Only this time it's a bit different."

"Yeah? How's that?"

"I told you about Jesus, Pedro and Pablo, right?"

"I remember, they were biblical names."

"Well, Pablo turned up dead last night after he somehow managed to dial 911 with his hands duct taped together and his right thumb missing."

"Resourceful guy. The odds were against him, being dead an' all."

"Yeah, funny. And his driver and his bodyguard showed up in his car, twenty miles away, with their brains blown out and three kilos of cocaine on the back seat. The driver had also dialed 911 with his dead thumb."

"Maybe it's a trick they teach them at Scumbag School."

"You're funny, Captain Walker."

"I know, deep down funny, where it's not like funny anymore. Either way, at least you'll be able to get some useful forensics from all this, won't you?"

"Yeah, maybe... You know what else is funny? Two guys shot in the head with 9 mm rounds in the parking lot of the Cowgirl Rodeo Club. They were known associates of Eulogio Cremades, the owner of the club, a known associate of Carlitos Heras, whose boys *you* witnessed being shot down the other day in the parking lot of Cora's Golden Cafe. A couple of hundred yards up the road we find the car that was used in that very shooting, and the two boys in the car have also been shot with 9 mm rounds. I'm only guessing, but I *am* guessing that the rounds will turn out to be from the same gun that was used to kill Eulogio's boys. Now, stay with me, in the back of the car, there are three Ks of cocaine, and twenty miles across town, those boys' boss is found dead in a barn, stabbed in a way…" He shook his head in disbelief. "Stabbed in a way only a special ops pro could know how to do."

"That's all rather confusing, Detective Shannon. I am not sure I followed it fully. Sounds like you had a busy night. No doubt it will throw up a lot of evidence."

"Yeah, no doubt. Say, you were special ops, weren't you, Captain? Special Air Service? Who Dares Wins?"

"Ten years, Detective. Are you suggesting it might have been my Sig Sauer that was used to kill those boys? Would you like to take it in, for comparison?"

His eyes were so narrow it must have been hard for him to see. "Are you *offering?*"

I shrugged. "Why not? I have nothing to hide, Detective. It's right here, in the trunk of my car."

I unlocked it and pulled it open. I fished in the kit bag, pulled out my second Sig and handed it to him. He pulled an evidence bag from his pocket and dropped the weapon into it. As he did so, he was eyeing the kit bag.

"What the hell have you got in there? An arsenal?"

I opened it up and showed him. "Heckler and Koch 416, Smith & Wesson 500, 50 cal, kick like a mule and will blow a hole through a concrete wall. Beautiful weapon. This here is a hickory takedown bow." I held it up for him to see. "Aluminum hunting arrows, 9mm ammunition for the Sig, standard NATO 7.62x51 mm for the Heckler, 50 cals for the Smith & Wesson, nothing much else. It's all legal, Detective, and none of the deaths you told me about were caused by an assault rifle or a fifty cal—or a bow and arrow—as far as I recall." I smiled at him and he shook his head.

"Did you kill those boys last night, Captain? Are you out to avenge Celeste Martinez?"

I shifted my smile into a lopsided grin. "If I had, Detective, I would not tell you about it. But, as it happens, I didn't. I was in my room at America's Best Value Inn, watching TV. A repeat of that movie with Charles Bronson, from the 1970s. You know the one?"

He nodded. "I know the one, Captain Walker. Death Wish, about a vigilante who goes around taking the law into his own hands and killing every punk he sees."

I snapped my fingers and pointed at him. "That's the one." I closed the trunk.

"Captain Walker?"

I made a question with my face as I moved around to the driver's door.

"Your mother is an English aristocrat. In what way exactly does Estrella Martinez remind you of her?"

"You've been checking my file." I shrugged. "Underneath her cool, English exterior, my mother is a warm, loving, maternal woman, Detective."

"Right." He hesitated a moment. "You know the reruns I like the best?"

"I know you're going to tell me."

"Columbo, where the bumbling cop always nails the wiseass millionaire killer."

I laughed. "We're on the same side, Detective. Besides, I am a wiseass and a killer, but I'm not a millionaire." I grinned at him. "I'm a billionaire."

SIX

I couldn't stake out their place anymore, since I'd been seen by Jesus' sister, Luz. Besides, I didn't think I needed any more intel, not at this stage. The events of the previous night—my killing his boys and Eulogio's, stealing the coke and handing it over to the cops, were going to have a deep impact on his reputation. He was going to have to work hard to restore it. That would mean he could not afford to cancel the next shipment, or even change it. He would have to show Sandra that he was still in control. On the other hand, it would also mean that he would be armed to the teeth at the next delivery.

I drove back to the inn by way of Walmart, where I bought two disposable cells and a bottle of Old Bushmills. In the parking lot of the hotel I called Kenny, the butler I had inherited from my father.

"Sir, how pleasant to hear from you."

"Good morning, Kenny. How are things at home?"

"Nothing to report, sir."

"How is Rosalia?"

"A few aches and pains, but otherwise well. We are of course both anxious for your return…"

"I'm getting there, Kenny. I just got sidetracked in Tucson."

"As one does, sir. Do I gather you need a kit bag?"

"I never need to explain anything to you, do I, Kenny?"

I thought I detected a smile in his voice. "I hope not, sir. Anything special?"

"I have the HK, and the Smith & Wesson 500. I have my bow and the two Sigs. I could use some more arrows…"

"Arizona," he said. "Will you be operating at a distance and at night, sir?"

"Probably, yes."

"Then may I suggest the new DI MKII, mounted with an Armasight Nemesis night vision scope? The DI is comparatively short and manageable for a rifle of such high precision, and the magazine holds thirty rounds, as opposed to the usual ten, making it an ideal all rounder, should you need to switch from sniping to assault at short notice."

"Good, ideal."

"And will you be doing any demolition, sir?"

I thought about it. "It's possible, Kenny, yes."

"Tunnels, sir?"

"Are you telepathic, Kenny?"

"One follows the news, and where there is a wall, often as not, there will be a tunnel."

"True."

"I shall see to it, sir."

"Get an air taxi, Kenny. I'll see you at Richie's Café at the Ryan Airfield."

"Very good, sir. I'll let you know when I am arriving."

I hung up and climbed out of the car, then made my way across the blacktop toward my room. As I was slipping the key in the lock, I heard a voice behind me.

"Mister...?"

I turned. I'm not often surprised, but in that moment I was. She was standing ten feet from me. She was wearing the blue dress again, with white pumps. She had a silver cross pendant and her shoulder-length hair pulled back in a knot behind her head. I didn't say anything. I waited for her to speak.

"Are you FBI?"

I shook my head. "No."

"Are you a cop?"

"I'm not any kind of law enforcement. Why are you asking me these questions?"

"I saw you..."

"That's not much of an answer."

"When Celeste was killed, you were there with her. Then I saw you watching my brother's house."

I shook my head again, dismissing her. "I'm sorry. You made a mistake. I don't know what you're talking about."

I turned back to the door.

"You gave evidence to the cops. You're their prime witness..."

I paused, staring down at my key, then faced her again. "I shouldn't be, though, should I? You were there with her. You know what she was arguing about with those boys. You know who killed her, and you know why."

She seemed not to hear. She said, woodenly, "I saw you go to her mom's house. You had a black case."

"What do you want?"

"I want to talk to you."

I sighed, opened the door and stood aside for her to go in. She came forward, hesitated at the threshold and stared up into my face. She was beautiful, not beautiful like Celeste, who had an intangible innocence to her beauty, even in death, but still beautiful.

"Are you going to hurt me?"

I frowned. "Of course not. Listen, you came here, remember?"

She went inside. I put the whiskey on the dresser beside the TV and gestured her to a chair. "You want some coffee?" She shook her head. I sat on the sofa and watched her, waiting. She watched me back. She was scared. "You wanted to talk. I'm here, listening."

"Are you going to kill my brother?"

"What makes you think I even know who your brother is?"

"I've been watching you."

"That's not smart." She shrugged and I sighed. "What have you seen that makes you think I want to kill your brother?"

"You've been watching his house."

"I pulled over to answer a text message." I gave a small laugh and shook my head. "Celeste was interested in psychology. Prove to me you're not just some crazy she was interested in studying."

She didn't answer for a while. Then she pressed her hands together and slipped them between her knees, hunching her shoulders. She looked tired and her dark eyes had shadows under them.

"Celeste wanted to study child psychology. She was on a mission. I used to joke with her that she was like one of those old Wild West sheriffs, swearing to clean up Tucson. But instead of shooting people, she wanted to help the kids. She believed that if she could help the children who were victims of violence and drug abuse, she would be able to stop the cycle. She wanted me to help her."

"How?"

"We became friends a few years back. She was a couple of years younger than me, but she was very smart, older than her age. Her IQ was really high, well above average. When she was sixteen, she started coming to our church instead of her own, because she knew that a lot of kids from our parish were involved in gangs and drugs. She knew my brother was in a gang, and my cousins. She used to say to me that it was no use preaching from the pulpit. You had to get your hands dirty."

"That must have worried her mother."

She nodded, staring down at her knees. "It did. Her mother had done everything she could, after her husband died..." She glanced at me, wondering if I knew about that. I nodded and she went on. "...to keep Celeste away from the gangs and the drugs. It's not easy around here. There's hardly a family that hasn't got somebody involved somehow. I told her she was crazy. If she wasn't careful, she was going to get hurt. You know, one thing is not getting involved—I don't—but another is campaigning against them, trying to turn kids against them. It didn't help that she looked the way she did."

I frowned. "What do you mean?"

She smiled at me. "You must have noticed. She was beautiful. Jesus, Pedro and Pablo all wanted her. It was only because Jesus was my brother that they didn't take her. I begged him not to. But it was only a matter of time. Eventually Jesus would have claimed her as his."

I could feel that hot coal of rage in my belly again. "What do you mean, 'claim her as his'?"

"That's the way it works. They rule the neighborhood. A girl comes of age, they like her..." She shrugged. "They take her."

"And you condone this."

Her eyes went wide. She looked shocked. "Of course I don't!"

"But you won't go to the cops. You won't inform on them. They gunned down Celeste right in front of you. You were there. You saw them do it. You know who is responsible. But you won't inform on them."

She stared at her hands, still clasped between her knees, and after a moment continued talking as though she hadn't heard me.

"Carlitos wanted her too. I kept telling her she needed to go, get out of Tucson. She'd been offered a place at UCLA, and at Stanford. I told her she should go, go to California, but she wouldn't."

"Why?"

"Reasons." She shrugged. "She was worried about her mother—she didn't know how she would cope financially. She also said there were a couple of kids in the *Iluminados* she thought she could coax out of the gang before she left, in the fall. I told you, she was on a mission."

"That's a dangerous mission."

"I kept telling her that. But she had this crazy idea. If we kept harassing City Hall, Congress, the cops and local parents, and the members themselves, we could start a movement, a campaign, to educate kids and raise awareness. She even had a slogan: Hope not Dope."

"What makes that a crazy idea?"

Again she seemed not to hear me. "She told me if I would agree to organize the campaign in her absence, she'd go before the fall."

"But you refused."

She took a deep breath and it shuddered as she released it. "No, I didn't refuse, but I didn't agree, either. I was thinking about it. It's a hell of a thing to take on. I also had plans to go to college, you know? My brother is the head of one of the biggest gangs in the city, and they are a lot more powerful than you think. If I head up a campaign like that, not only would I have to give up on college, it could cost me my life." She paused and turned to the window. I could see light reflecting off the wet streaks on her cheeks. "Anyway, I eventually made up my mind to help her. We'd met that day to discuss it. We were having coffee at Cora's Golden Cafe. Four of Carlitos' boys came in and saw us. Two of them were the ones she thought she could persuade to leave the gang. She didn't hold back. She never held back. She went for it. It turned into a row which spilled out into the parking lot." She turned to look at me. Her eyes were pleading, like she was begging me to tell her it was not her fault. "Jesus was on a campaign, he still is, to crush Carlitos and steal his territory. Somebody must have called and told him that his boys were there, in the lot. You saw what happened next."

"Yeah, I saw."

"You tried to help."

I didn't answer.

She said, "They weren't gunning for her."

"That makes it OK?"

"That's not what I meant."

"I still don't know what you want."

"I don't want you to kill my brother, or Pedro. I know you killed Pablo."

I stood, went to the dresser and peeled the lead off the cork on the Bushmills. I found a glass and poured myself a measure. I showed her the bottle but she shook her head. I drained the glass and poured another shot.

"I told you. You made a mistake. I'm not out to kill anybody."

"You are lying to me."

"You think?" I laughed. In my own ears, it was an ugly, harsh sound. "Assuming, for the sake of the argument, that I were some kind of killer, out to get your brother and your cousin, what reason have you given me not to? He's not even a predator, keeping some kind of natural balance. He's a parasite, preying on the weak and the vulnerable, destroying lives, destroying families, using drugs and violence to enslave people. This..." For a moment I was lost for words, then blurted, "This piece of *toxic waste* murdered a good, kind, beautiful human being, for no other reason than she happened to be in that parking lot at that time. And to add insult to murder, she was there, in that parking lot, because she was trying to help two other pieces of toxic waste like him to have better, more useful lives. And her reward was to be destroyed, when she was just nineteen!"

I sat and sipped my whiskey, watching her lovely face as she stared down at her hands. I went on. "She is dead because your brother is alive. If she had lived, she would have helped hundreds of children to find some kind of happiness and meaning in life. Instead, she is dead and your brother, who is alive, will go on to destroy all those hundreds of lives that Celeste might have saved. So, give me one good reason why, if I were a killer, I shouldn't kill Jesus Santos."

She didn't answer for a while. Finally, she took a deep breath and looked me in the eye. "I can give you two reasons. The first is that you are going to trigger a gang war. My brother thinks that Pablo was killed by the *Iluminados*, and he is going to retaliate."

"And that should worry me why?"

"Because more innocent bystanders might get hurt."

I gave a single nod. "And the other reason?"

"The most important reason, perhaps: your soul. Ask yourself, are you becoming like him? Are you losing your humanity? What value do you put on human life? Do you believe you have the right to decide who lives and who dies? Who are you to make such a judgment? The decision of life and death is for God, not for us."

I gave her a smile that said I thought she was cute. "Explain that to your brother, Luz. The fact is that last time I checked, your God didn't seem to be doing much to stop all those people who think *they* have the right to decide who lives and who dies. For my part, I don't plan to sit around praying for Him to get His finger out and start doing something useful. Besides…" I studied her a moment.

She said, "What?"

"Aside from your Bible, where is it written that I can't decide who lives and who dies? I've spent the last twelve years making that decision, and by and large, Luz, I figure I've got it about right."

"You know my name."

"Yeah, I know your name."

"How did you find out?"

"Pablo told me."

"So you did kill him, and you are going to kill my brother."

I shrugged and drained my glass, then stood. "We were speaking hypothetically, remember? But even if we hadn't been, I don't see that you have given me any kind of reason why he should live, other than he is your brother and you are a nice person. Was there anything else?"

She had started crying again. It wasn't the wretched sobbing that I had seen in her cousin. Her face was composed and she was calm, but there was deep grief in her eyes. "Pablo had a family. Did you know that?"

I shook my head.

"A wife and two children."

"And he kept them in that shack?"

"Only Jesus lives there. That shack is where he and I grew up, with a prostitute for a mother and a violent *hijo de puta* for a father. Pedro and Pablo tried to get away, they moved to the suburbs. Pablo got married, had children, but Jesus, the money, the power, it dragged them back. Jesus won't leave, he refuses to leave. He could buy a beautiful house, but he says this house is what made him, and he will stay until he dies. This is the cycle Celeste wanted to break, but you will perpetuate."

"For some people it's too late, Luz…" But I didn't know

if I was talking about Jesus or me. Maybe I was talking about both of us.

She shook her head. "What would I have to do to stop you from doing this? Name it and I will do it."

I turned away and placed the glass beside the bottle. I closed my eyes a moment. "Work a miracle. Turn your brother and your cousin into something like human beings. Make the cartels go away." I opened my eyes and turned to face her. "Make Celeste's dream come true." I gave my head a small shake. "If I were the kind of man you think I am, I don't believe there is anything you could do, short of that miracle, that would save Jesus. If I don't kill him, somebody else will. We make choices, Luz. You chose to be a good person, I'm glad about that. Jesus chose to be a parasite and a son of a bitch. I won't kill him, not really, that decision will."

She nodded and stood. "I wish you too were a son of a bitch, so I could hate you for what you are going to do."

"I'm sorry."

She opened the door and I watched from the window as she crossed the lot to her white Ford pickup. As she drove away, I was thinking about what she'd said; not the bit about my losing my humanity—that ship had sailed a long time ago. I was thinking about Pedro living in the suburbs, and the gang war she said I'd triggered. She was wrong about that. The war was already under way when I'd arrived, that was why Celeste had gotten killed in the first place. But she was right about Jesus' reprisals for the *Iluminados* killing Pablo and his boys. The question was, how could I use that to my advantage?

SEVEN

I sat for a while in my room, aware of the slight scent of jasmine that Luz had left behind her, looking at the phone I had taken from Pablo's bodyguard. Eventually I picked it up and called the Tucson Santa Cruz PD station. It rang for a full minute before anybody answered. When they did, I said, "Jesus and Pedro Santos, of the *Santos del Diablo* gang, are going to hit Carlitos and the *Iluminados* gang within the next forty-eight hours. There could well be collateral damage again, and innocent bystanders could be hurt. Please notify Detective Mike Shannon."

I hung up before they could answer, switched off the phone and took out the battery. Then I called Hertz at the airport and rented the most unremarkable car they had. It turned out to be a Focus. I stepped back out into the bright sun, drove the short distance to Tucson International Airport, dropped my car at the garage parking off Los Reales, and went to pick up my nondescript Focus. It was a dull, cream color that I figured would soon get coated with dust to make it even more inconspicuous. While I was there, I picked up a Herald Tribune and a paperback detective novel about a couple of New York cops who solved cold cases. I also bought a six-pack of cold beers.

From there I drove back to South Fair Avenue, to where Jesus had his house, but this time I drove past, to the bottom of the road, where it deteriorated into a dirt track that followed the railway line down as far as East Irvington. There I parked on the sand, behind the cover of some scrub and the ubiquitous mesquite trees, and settled to watch. This time I was watching for a couple of very particular things.

I stripped off my shirt and sat on the sand, with my back against the car, reading the newspaper with a cold beer beside me, and occasionally glancing up. Through the shrubs and the bushes I had a pretty good view of who arrived and who left. No one passed that way, but if they had, they might think I was a bit eccentric, but clearly just chilling, enjoying the sun.

There was a lot of activity that day. The yard filled up with cars, trucks and bikes. I watched Pedro arrive in a gleaming red Corvette, and he and Jesus stood hugging each other and weeping at the front gate. There was no mistaking the mood or the reason for the activity. At shortly after two PM, three trucks pulled out of the yard with four guys in each one. I figured that was almost the totality of the gang. They drove fast up South Fair Avenue and crossed the railroad at the level crossing. I knew where they were going, and I was pretty sure I hadn't seen Jesus or Pedro among the twelve guys. I pulled on my shirt and threw my paper and the empty beer can in the car. Then I climbed behind the wheel to wait.

Ten minutes later Pedro, with his ponytail and his goatee, and his Hugo Boss linen jacket, came out with Jesus. This was the closest I had seen them and I was struck by how young Jesus was. They stood for a while and seemed to argue. Finally, Jesus shoved his cousin on the shoulder and extended his arm, like he was telling him to leave. It was a very Latin gesture, impatient, but without animosity.

Pedro shook his head, but made his way to his red Corvette, climbed in and backed out of the yard. Jesus climbed the steps and went into the house.

I followed Pedro at a distance onto East Michigan Drive. There he turned right onto 3rd Avenue and followed it up to the Ajo Highway. I wasn't surprised when he turned right and headed east. He wasn't going west toward Drexel Heights or Valencia. My guess was that he was going north.

I wasn't wrong. He followed Ajo Highway east as far as South Avernon Way and the Golf Links Road. We passed Roberts and took South Wilmot into North Wilmot and El Tanque Verde, where we crossed the river and turned sharp left in the Country Club Estates. We were a long way from Fairgrounds. There was no grid pattern here. There were too many pools and tennis courts to get in the way of anything so utilitarian. We wound our way among desert mansions, along meandering roads shaded by palms, jacaranda and the ever present mesquite, to Miramar Drive and San Cristobal Street. There I watched him pull into the crescent driveway of a Spanish villa. It wasn't a mansion. It was small by the standards of the area. It didn't have stables or tennis courts. But this was just his first step. This was part of his money laundering process. He would sell this one and buy another, bigger one, in a year or two. Pedro was on his way.

At least, that was what Pedro thought.

I found a quiet side street—there was no shortage of them in the area—parked and spent half an hour exploring on foot. Of special interest was the steep banks of the river that backed onto the houses along Pedro's street. After a careful inspection of the area, I climbed back behind the wheel of the unremarkable Focus and made my way slowly back to the center of Tucson, gradually building a plan in my head.

On the way I dropped Pedro's bodyguard's phone in a trash can at a shopping mall. I also bought some sleeping tablets from a pharmacy and eventually wound up at Cheddar's on East Broadway Boulevard. I ordered two sirloin steaks, one to take out, and a beer, and sat at a table in a corner wondering what had gone down at Carlitos' place, and when Kenny was going to call. I looked at my watch. It was after three.

I ate my steak with my phone on the table, drained my beer and ordered a coffee. At ten past four, my phone rang.

"Kenny, I'm glad to hear from you. What's happening?"

"I am at Worcester, sir. I have the kit and I have booked a taxi. We should be taking off in the next half hour. I expect to be with you in the next five hours."

"About nine o'clock tonight."

"Yes, sir."

"Good. I'll book you into my hotel. We'll arrange a return flight for tomorrow."

"Very good, sir."

I paid up and drove back to the inn.

Shannon was waiting for me outside my door, leaning against the trunk of his car. I parked next to him and climbed out. He watched me, squinting slightly in the afternoon sunlight.

"Where's your Mustang?"

"It has an electric motor. It's running out of charge. I left it at the airport till I can find a way to charge it."

He nodded like that was just the kind of thing that he would expect of me; just the kind of thing he would expect from a no good, smooth talking, East Coast billionaire.

"You hear about the drive by?"

I pulled my key from my pocket and went to open the door. "You'll have to be a bit more precise, Detective. Which particular drive by?"

He followed me to the door. "The one you phoned and warned me about."

He wasn't boring me at all, but I sighed like he was. I pushed the door open and turned to face him. "I have no idea what you're talking about, Detective Shannon."

"Where's the phone?"

I pulled my phone from my pocket and showed it to him.

He said, "Dickson Rodriguez's phone."

"Who?"

"The guy you shot between the eyes last night."

"Oh, that Dickson Rodriguez."

"You took his phone and called the station to warn me that Jesus and Pedro were going to hit Carlitos' gang today."

I took a step toward him, so we were barely a foot apart. "You have two things, Detective, a theory and imagination. Neither of those is worth a good goddamn. You're barking up the wrong tree and chasing the wrong squirrel. So you got a tip off that the *Santos del Diablo* were going to hit the *Iluminados*. Let me ask you something. Did you act on it? Did you stake out the *Santos*? Did you prevent the hit?"

He didn't answer.

I said, "I didn't think so."

I turned and went inside. I left the door open and he followed me in, standing in the doorway leaning against the jamb. I pulled the cork from the bottle of Bushmills and poured myself a generous slug, then I lit a Camel. I stood staring at him a moment. "Was there a hit?"

He nodded.

I said, "And instead of hauling Jesus Santos and his cousin in, you decide to come and harass me. Were any bystanders hurt?"

He nodded again. "Five-year-old kid. He's in hospital. His condition is critical."

I felt my heart rate accelerate. There was a slow burn in my belly. I felt my lip curl. "Is there some reason, Detective, why you think I am somehow responsible for that kid's injury?"

He didn't answer straight away, but after a moment he said, "Yeah, there is."

"*What?*"

"You're provoking a war between these two gangs. That attack yesterday would not have gone down if you hadn't murdered Pablo and his two boys, if you hadn't killed Eulogio's men."

I fought the desire to put his head through the window and asked him, "How about Celeste, Shannon? Who's responsible for her death?"

"We don't know..."

I held my glass like the butt of a gun and pointed my finger at him. "You are, Shannon. And you had better get with the program, or I will have your badge and your job."

His face flushed. "What the hell are you talking about?"

"How much do they pay you, Detective?"

"Why you son of a..." He pushed himself off the jamb and squared up to me.

Before he could finish, I went on. "Since when is it Tucson PD policy to ignore tip offs? You were the one who told me the killing at Cora's parking lot was the work of the *Santos*. You get a tip off today that you trace to one of the Santos' boys telephones, and you don't act on it? You could have caught both gangs red handed, but what did you do? Ignore the tip off. You want to explain that to me, Shannon?"

"You're out of your mind..." But he didn't sound very convinced.

"You want to know where I was this morning? I was watching Jesus' house. I was doing what you should have been doing. I saw the whole gang arrive and I saw them take off in their trucks, to go and attack Carlitos, wage open warfare in *your* city, and put that little boy in hospital, on *your* watch. But you know what I didn't see? I didn't see a single cop, not one. You disgust me, Shannon. Get out, and go and report to Jesus, tell him I'm coming after him, and I will kill him."

He didn't answer. He turned and walked away. The door closed, blocking him from view, before he got into his car. I drained my glass, lay down on the bed and slept for three hours. It was going to be a long night and I needed to be rested.

I awoke at eight, had a cold shower and dressed in dark jeans and a sweatshirt. Then I stepped out into the gathering night, climbed into the Focus and headed west, toward Valencia and the Ryan Airfield. The traffic was light through the city, the low, flat buildings, the small clusters of people talking, laughing, were a procession of amber-flooded stills, tableaus belonging to another world; a world that was separated from me by an invisible film, a sheet of microscopically fine, unbreakable glass. In their world, in their reality, death was a rare tragedy. In mine it was something I did, something that had become horrific not for its tragedy, but because it was banal.

I left the city lights behind me and accelerated along the Ajo Highway, into the darkness of the desert.

I arrived at the airfield at nine. It was all but deserted and Ritchie's Café was closed, so I leaned against the hood of the Focus and smoked a cigarette while I waited. At ten past nine I saw the lights coming in low over the Santa Catalina Mountains, and approaching over the distant glow of Tucson. They grew brighter, winking red, green and white and pretty soon the engines were whining loud in the night as the jet hit the tarmac and roared down the runway, then taxied slowly to the airport building.

Ten minutes later, Kenny emerged carrying a holdall and a military kit bag over his shoulder. He smiled the way only English butlers know how, showing pleasure, respect and dignity all at the same time.

"Good evening, sir. I hope you didn't have to wait too long."

"It's good to see you, Kenny. Jump in, I'm afraid we have a long night ahead of us."

"Indeed, sir. I thought we might, so I had a nap on the plane."

He dumped the kit in the trunk, turned the car around and started back toward Tucson, and the international airport. As we drove, I filled him in. He listened carefully without expression. Finally I said, "So, when we get to Tucson International, I want you to take the Focus and follow me. We'll leave the Zombie down there. I've been looking at satellite pictures…"

"Do you mean Google Earth, sir?"

"They are satellite pictures, Kenny."

"Yes, sir."

"And I am pretty sure there's a small canyon there where we can leave the Zombie, then you drive me back, and tomorrow we'll get you on a flight back to Boston."

He was quiet for a while, looking at the darkness outside the window, at the approaching glow of the city.

"May I ask a question, sir?"

"Of course, Kenny."

"Has this anything to do with Omega?"

It took me a moment to answer. "Not directly, no."

"And indirectly?"

Again I was quiet. I felt somehow almost ashamed to answer. "No, Kenny. Not indirectly either. It's just about Celeste."

"I see."

"You think I'm wrong to do this?"

"It's not my place, sir…"

"Cut it out, Kenny. I've known you all my life. You were

more of a father to me than he ever was. Tell me what you think."

He suppressed a sigh. "As I understand it, Omega is dead in the water. The war is over. What we are engaged in here is a personal vendetta." He turned to look at me. "Soldiers who kill in defense of their country, or an ideal, are soldiers. Soldiers who come home from the war and kill people they don't like, are murderers, sir."

"You think I'm a murderer?"

"No, sir, but you are treading a microscopically fine line. I think you're approaching the end of the road, and you are still in sixth gear with your foot to the boards. If you'll forgive me saying so, sir, it is time you came home and started taking over the running of your affairs." He paused, then repeated with emphasis, "The war is over, sir. People are bad, it's in our nature. You cannot kill every bad person on the planet. If you did, you would simply be doing what Omega tried to do."

We drove in silence for fifteen minutes, and as we crossed the I-19 intersection and entered the city, I said, "She was nineteen, Kenny. She was beautiful. Not just beautiful to look at, but beautiful inside. She died holding my hand, and I promised her she was going to be all right." I looked at him. "Perhaps I haven't the legal right to judge and execute people. But have we the moral right to walk away from an injustice..." I shook my head. "Not an injustice, Kenny, an outrage, like that? Am I a worse man for killing these bastards than I would be if I just shrugged and walked away, and left Celeste's murder in the hands of a justice system I know is simply going to ignore it? Am I," I insisted, "a better man if I ignore her murder, than if I avenge her?"

"I can't answer those questions, sir. I'm sorry, I will support you every step of the way, as I always have. But I can't answer your questions. All I can do is repeat that the war against Omega is over, and Rosalia and I believe it is time for you to come home."

We turned right on East Benson, then took the South Tucson Boulevard and pretty soon we were entering the parking garage where I had left the Zombie. I drove to the top floor and parked the Focus next to it. We got out, I gave Kenny the keys to the Focus and we opened the two trunks. I went through what he had brought me and smiled as I added it to my kit.

"Twenty pounds? Holy smoke! For a man who believes we are no longer at war, Kenny, you sure pack a fine kit bag."

He slammed the trunk of the Focus. "Actually, sir, I said the war is over. You, sir, are clearly still at war."

I nodded and smiled. "You made your point, Kenny. Now, let's go hide a Zombie."

EIGHT

It was a long drive, along roads I had traveled before[1]. I took the Zombie and Kenny followed in the Focus. We headed out west again, past Valencia and past the turn off for the abandoned barn where I had killed Pablo. We came eventually to Three Points; there we turned south on the Sasabe Road and plunged into deep desert. Here the sky was vast, and the stars, in a moonless sky, were like luminous specks of ice piercing infinity. But to left and right, there was only blackness, with the yellow funnels of my headlamps gouging out a narrow path along the blacktop ahead. And in my mirror, the small glow of Kenny's lamps looked somehow small and vulnerable behind me as we drove deeper into the night.

Here and there small lights winked under the irregular stencil of the mountains against the sky, or a coyote would appear, paralyzed in the passing glow, watching our passage

---

1. See *Double Edged Blade*

from among the shrubs and the small, gnarled trees. The road was pretty much straight, save for a few bends, and skirted the mountain range on our right, and after about forty-five minutes I began to slow, seeking the turn off on my right.

Finally I saw the sign, Rancho Grande, and a broad, dirt track that led away from the road, in among the hills. I killed the lights and took the turn. In my rearview I saw Kenny's lights wink out too. Now we were driving by starlight. The dusty track was a slightly luminous ribbon among the darker scrubland on either side. I followed it for half a mile, doing maybe 20 MPH, tapping my brakes occasionally so that Kenny could keep a bead on my brake lights.

After a couple of minutes we came to a kind of dirt esplanade on the right. I eased in and found another, smaller track, narrower, more of a footpath. I rolled along it for a couple of yards, then stopped, got out and walked back to the Focus. Kenny rolled down his window.

"Kenny, turn around and back in four or five yards so you're out of sight if anybody passes. Wait here for me." I handed him my Sig. "I'll be back in ten minutes."

He looked at the Sig. "Thank you, sir. I am armed."

"Of course you are."

As he backed in, I drove on, deeper among the trees and the shrubs. The path began to rise into the foothills of the mountains we had been skirting, and soon, on the right, I came to the narrow canyon I'd seen on the satellite images. I turned the Zombie around, tucked it in among some mesquite trees, collected a few items from the trunk, stuffed them in a canvas bag, covered the car with a few broken branches, and jogged back to where Kenny was waiting for me in the Focus. I climbed in the passenger seat, softly closed the door and said, "OK, let's get out of here."

He pulled out onto the broad track and we started to bump our way back toward the Sasabe Road.

"This, I gather, is where the merchandise from Mexico is delivered and collected for distribution."

"Correct."

"And there is a delivery due…"

"Tomorrow night."

"Is there somewhere you would like me to drive you now, sir?"

I shook my head. "Thank you, Kenny. But what I want you to do now is book your flight for tomorrow and get some sleep at the hotel." I glanced at him. "It's best you don't know what I am going to do for the rest of the night."

He nodded. "Carousing with young ladies, I shouldn't wonder, and drinking too much."

"Something like that."

At the hotel parking lot, he climbed out and took his shoulder bag. I climbed in the driving seat and watched him walk to reception and go in. It was just after eleven. I turned the car around and drove out, toward the Catalina foothills, and the Country Club Estates.

I cruised, taking it easy, and in a little over half an hour I had crossed the bridge and driven up Miramar Drive, to park on San Bernardino, a few doors down from Pedro's house. Opposite where I'd left the car there was the footpath I had discovered earlier in the day, which led between two of the mansions, down to the riverbank at the back of the houses. I slung the small canvas bag over my shoulder, slipped down the path and picked my way, by starlight, through the underbrush, counting the houses as I went. After five minutes I was at the back of Pedro's Spanish villa.

The wall to his garden and his pool was brick, about eight feet high. At the far left it had a mesquite tree growing up against it. It wasn't exactly pure luck. I had seen it during my earlier exploration, otherwise I would have brought a rope, or a folding ladder.

I made my way to the tree, climbed it and pulled myself onto the wall. There I lay still for a minute, listening. Pretty soon I heard, and then saw, what I had expected, since I'd seen the 'beware of the dog' sign earlier: a big, ugly Doberman, snuffling, whimpering and barking. I pulled the sirloin from my bag and dropped it down to him. He ate it greedily and, after five minutes, lay down to sleep, soothed by six diazepam tablets and six hundred milligrams of Diphenhydramine.

It was a safe bet that if they had a Doberman guarding their back yard, they would not have an alarm system triggered by motion sensors, so I dropped down from the wall and crawled on my belly through the trees as far as the back patio and the pool. There, again, I lay motionless, waiting.

There was a set of French doors that gave on to the pool. They were closed, the drapes were drawn and I couldn't see any lights flickering behind them. On the second floor, above the French doors, there was a small balcony with a wrought iron railing. Behind it, two tall windows stood open. Beside it there was ivy creeping up the wall as high as the orange-tiled roof. I thought about it and rejected it as too noisy and too risky.

I estimated the height of the balcony from the ground at

twelve feet. I was about six one; with my arms stretched up I must be about eight feet. I needed to make up three feet.

I stood and walked past the pool to where he had a white, wrought iron table and four chairs set out. I moved the chairs without making any noise, then picked up the table and carried it to place it just below the balcony. I climbed onto it and touched the iron railing with my fingers. A jump and a heave and I had pulled myself up and over the railing, to settle quietly on the balcony. Through the black portal I could see embers burning low in the grate. Everything else was inky shadows against an impenetrable background.

I crouched down, so that I wouldn't be silhouetted against the sky, and put my head around the door. I could make out the black slab of a bed, and across the room, it was impossible to tell how far, a thin sliver of hazy light at floor level: the door, and beyond it a light had been left on, probably on the landing.

There was no sound, except for the labored breathing coming from the bed. I reached in my bag and pulled out the night-vision goggles. I fitted them and the room came into eerie green and black relief: an intense green glow from the fireplace on the right, the door across the room, maybe twenty-five feet away, with the brilliant green slash at the bottom, the emperor-sized bed on the left with the pale sheet glowing a limpid green, a large, dark body in the bed and beyond it the en suite bathroom, with the door open.

Logic dictated that the man in the bed was Pedro. Luz had said that Pablo had married, not his brother; but there was a slim chance this could be somebody else—a body guard, a friend, a guest.

I pulled the Maxim 9 from my waistband behind my back. It is the ultimate firearm for a silent kill. It has a built in suppressor and a 3.5" barrel, which makes it almost as compact as any hand gun, and allows it to use full-power cartridges. It's not beautiful, but it is quiet.

I stepped over to the bed. He was on the left side, turned in, with his back to the en suite. I had a bead on his head. I could see his goatee and his hair was pulled into a knot behind his head. It was Pedro.

For just a second I hesitated. Celeste had died in pain, terrified and brutalized by this son of a bitch, but he was going to die instantly, without knowing why, without suffering, in his sleep. It seemed wrong.

Then the door opened and the room was flooded with light. I squeezed the trigger. Pedro turned and opened his eyes as the slug thudded home into his pillow, leaving a black hole and sending up a small cloud of feathers. At the same instant a girl's voice said, "What the…" and screamed, and Pedro screwed up his eyes and scrambled for the side of the bed.

I had to be in too many places doing too many things at the same time, and I had no time to think. I needed them both in the room, with no exit. I went for the girl as she turned to run. She was naked, blonde and slim. The only thing I could get a hold of was her hair as it flapped out behind her. I took a hold of it in my left hand, wound it twice around my fist and pulled. She screamed again and I yanked her toward the bed. She stumbled and fell. Pedro was sprawled out, fumbling for the drawer in the bedside table. I fired once into his hand and kicked the door closed as he screamed and rolled away, gripping his wrist.

I flipped off the light as she scrambled onto the bed and then dropped to the floor on the far side, looking at where she thought I must be over the mattress. Pedro had pulled himself into a sitting position and was hunched over his shattered hand, binding it with a sheet to try and stem the bleeding. It was a strange tableau, cast in black and green, with her eyes glimmering at me from behind the bed. I said:

"I have night vision, don't move."

For a moment I had an image of my sergeant and mentor in the Regiment, a Kiwi giant named Bradley. "The one fucking lesson you don't want to learn from experience, sir, is preparation. If you don't prepare, you'll be fucked six ways to Christmas, and six ways back again. *Prepare!*"

I hadn't prepared, and now I was fucked six ways to Christmas and six ways back again. Logic dictated I should kill them both, but as Bradley would have said, we don't make war on women and children. I reached in my bag for the roll of duct tape I'd brought along on the off chance I might need to immobilize Pedro before I killed him. Some sixth sense must have been working for him, because that was the instant he decided to roll off the bed and charge me, bent double and crouching.

Street scrappers are dangerous fighters, because they are unpredictable and they have learnt the hard way what works. Street scrappers fighting for their lives are the most dangerous of all, because their terror gives them an edge. Pedro could not see me, but he could sense where I was, and he knew he had nothing to lose. He moved fast and by the time I'd squeezed the trigger, his head had collided with my belly and we both went down.

I could hear hysterical screaming. My goggles had gone

askew. Pedro's knee was on my right wrist and his fists were pummeling my head and shoulders as he struggled to sit on my chest. I hunched my left shoulder to give what protection I could to my jaw, timing his blows as I did so. When I had his rhythm, I snatched his right wrist in my left hand. He wrestled to pull it free. But I also was a street scrapper fighting for my life and I gripped hard, snarling, and worked my thumb into the bullet wound. His screaming was added to the girl's and he stood, pulling frantically away from me.

I let him go and reached for my goggles, but suddenly light flooded into the room from the landing. The girl had wrenched the door open and was running. Pedro was screaming, "*Call Jesus! Call Jesus!*" as he ran after her.

I scrambled to my feet and went after them both, as Bradley, in my head, went crimson and bellowed, "*You couldn't organize a fucking piss up in a fucking brewery, sir!*"

They had both turned right out of the door. I followed. By the light on the landing I could see they were both naked. There was something pathetic about them in that moment and I felt a twist of pity which I had to suppress. They were on a long, 'L'-shaped landing with a wooden balustrade. She was stumbling down the first steps to the lower floor and he was close behind her. She was sobbing and screaming, and his face was twisted with panic and pain. I ran.

She hadn't seen my face yet. If she got away without seeing it, I could limit the damage. I slammed off the landing light, pulled the goggles over my eyes and went down the stairs, the Maxim held out in front of me, aiming for Pedro's head. He bobbed and weaved with every step, and she was just ahead of him. I couldn't take the shot.

Then she was in the entrance hall, but she didn't make

for the front entrance. She ran across the hall toward a closed door. Then Pedro stopped suddenly and lunged back with his shoulders at my legs. I stumbled and fell, grappling at the banisters with my hands. Next thing I was falling, smashing my back into the steps, and he was coming after me. I hit the tiles, and shafts of pain pierced my lungs. I ignored them and fired in his general direction, without taking aim. I missed and he ran across the hall on flapping, naked feet. I struggled up and gave chase.

The lights came on and the girl was standing in the living room doorway, naked and clutching her purse. She still hadn't seen my face, but she could probably identify me. I snarled, "FBI! You never saw me, *now get the hell out of here!*"

It was a forlorn hope, but it was all I had. She ran for the door and I went after Pedro down a narrow passage with a door at the end. I kicked open the door as I heard the front door close.

It was a large, modern kitchen. Pedro was standing naked by a telephone that was fixed to the wall. He had the receiver in his left hand. He screamed into it, "*En la cocina! Dense prisa, pendejos!*" He was telling somebody he was in the kitchen, and to hurry up. He dropped the receiver and picked up a huge, Sabatier kitchen knife. Then his face flushed red, he screamed like a banshee and charged.

He never stood a chance. He was fifteen feet away and before he'd taken his second stride I'd put a 9 mm lead slug through his right thigh bone. He screamed and fell, clawing at his leg. I stepped over and kicked the knife away. Blood was pumping from his leg and pooling on the gray tiles. I squatted down beside him. There was hatred, rage and terror in his face.

"Do you know who Celeste Martinez is?"

"Fuck you!" But there was a whimper in his voice.

I glanced over at the stove. It was one of those fancy iron ranges that works on gas. I went to it and opened all the taps, opened the oven and turned on the oven tap too. I took the burner cell I'd bought to call Kenny and dropped it into the oven. Then I went back to Pedro, who had crawled a couple of feet toward the kitchen door, leaving a smear of blood on the tiles.

"You're going to bleed out, Pedro. When your boys get here, I'm going to kill them, too. Now, you have a choice, I can kill you slowly, one shot at a time, or you can answer me a simple question. Do you know who Celeste Martinez is?"

"Of course I know, *hijo de puta!*"

"Good, because what is happening to you now is your payment for what you did to her, all of it, from wanting to own her, to causing her death by not giving a damn for human life. Now it's your turn, *pendejo.*"

I shot him in the other leg, so he couldn't get out of the kitchen, and left him sobbing on the floor. I closed the door, crossed the hall and walked out the front door, leaving it open an inch. I walked down the drive and out into the street. It was quiet, and there were more stars crammed into the sky than you could imagine possible. Far off in the hills I heard the ugly wail of a coyote calling to the moon. I got into my car and waited.

After ten minutes, a Jeep and a Dodge RAM came squealing up the road. I fired up the engine and, as they pulled into the driveway, I eased out and moved silently up the road to where I could see them. I had my cell in my hand

and watched as eight guys piled through the door, shouting, "*Jefe! Pedro! Esta bien?*"

The memory of Sergeant Bradley visited me again, leering, "Don't shoot, cobber, till you can see the whites of their eyes…"

I visualized them crossing the hall, pushing open the kitchen door, seeing him on the floor. They rush to him, some smelling the gas, moving to the stove, the kitchen door swinging closed… I pressed call. It rang once, twice, then the spark caught the gas.

There was a hard, nasty, flat smack of a report. I heard window glass shattering. The front door slammed closed. I waited a moment longer, until I saw the flicker of flames and a few coils of smoke. Then I hit the accelerator and moved swiftly and silently away, onto Miramar Drive and down toward the bridge, back into Tucson.

Two down, now it was just Jesus, and his supplier, Sandra Dorado Beltran. Kenny was wrong. The war was not over.

The war would never be over.

NINE

I took a roundabout route home, checking my rearview mirror to make sure I was not followed, and it was almost three AM when I got back to the inn. I parked the car at the back of the lot and crossed the asphalt toward my room. In the east, a warped blob of orange moon was oozing over the horizon. I unlocked my door and froze. The hair on the back of my neck prickled. A knowledge, primal and instinctual, told me there was a presence. Somebody was in there, in the dark, waiting.

I pulled the Maxim from my waistband and cocked it, pushed open the door and flattened myself back against the outside wall. There were no shots, nothing. I hunkered down, peered in, but there was nothing to see, either. I slipped inside and pulled the door softly closed behind me. Standing between the door and the window, I opened my bag and reached in for the night-vision goggles.

There was a sound. I froze. It was a rustle, a sigh, almost too soft to hear. Then the bedside lamp snapped on and I was standing, pointing the Maxim at Luz, who was sitting on my bed, staring at me with sleepy eyes.

"I'm sorry, I fell asleep waiting for you. Can you stop pointing that gun at me, please?"

I de-cocked the weapon, dropped the bag on the floor and went to pour myself a shot of whiskey. "What the hell are you doing here, Luz? How did you get in?"

"Skills you pick up in this barrio. I wanted to talk to you."

"Again?"

She didn't answer. I glanced at her as I sipped and she shrugged. "Something Celeste taught me: you can't give up. You have to be persistent."

I sat in the chair. "Something else she taught you, but you weren't paying attention. Some battles can't be won."

"A little boy is in hospital, he might die, because you killed Pablo."

I shook my head. "If we all followed that reasoning, we would never face up to any bullies, dictators or tyrants, for fear of reprisals. It's perverse to say that that child is in hospital because of what I did. He is in hospital because Jesus and his gang are murdering bastards."

She closed her eyes. She looked drained. "You cannot fight violence with violence. Violence begets violence…"

"The Church came up with that cliché, while they were murdering and pillaging their way across Europe, the East and South America. They also came up with the idea that poverty was good for you, while they filled the Vatican and all their cathedrals and churches with gold. Wealth and violence are the preserve of the state. The rest of us must learn to be poor, passive and obedient." I shook my head and drained my glass. "No, thanks. That's not my style."

"You are a cynical monster."

I nodded and stood. "Yeah. You want a drink?" I refilled my glass and turned to look at her.

She was watching me. After a moment she gave a nod. "Yes, please."

I found another glass and poured her a shot. I brought the bottle with me, sat and handed her her glass. She sipped it gingerly and made a face. Through it she asked, "What did you do tonight? Did you kill Pedro?"

I smiled and frowned at the same time. "I can't think of any reason why I would answer that question."

"He telephoned Jesus."

"What were you doing there?"

The question surprised me as much as it surprised her. "He is my brother! I was visiting and we were watching a movie. Pedro said there was a man who had shot him and was trying to kill him. He was in the kitchen of his house."

"Doesn't he have body guards at his house?" It was a question I'd been asking myself all the way home.

"Usually, yes. But they were scared of retaliation from the *Iluminados*, Pedro begged Jesus to go with him to his house, with the bodyguards…"

"But Jesus refused to leave his house, and kept the bodyguards with him."

"Pedro thought he would be safe out there, in the suburbs."

"Apparently he was wrong. So what happened?"

"You know what happened."

"Do I?"

"Pedro's girl came to Jesus' house. She said she saw the man. He was not an *Iluminado*, not a Mexican. He was a *gringo*, tall, dressed in black, like you, with goggles to see in the dark. She said he had a strange gun, like something from a science fiction movie." She pointed at the Maxim on the table in front of me, with its chunky suppressor system under the barrel. "Like that one."

I smiled and raised an eyebrow. "You wearing a wire?"

"You know I'm not. I'm not here to make you confess to anything, just to ask you to stop. Don't perpetuate this bloodbath. Let the police do their job, please."

"And what if the police are not doing their job, Luz?"

She shook her head. "Conspiracy theories? Excuses for people who don't want to take responsibility and do the right thing!"

I decided in that moment that I liked her a lot. I gave a small laugh and scratched my eyebrow. "I called Detective Mike Shannon. I told him there would be reprisals from the *Santos* gang against the *Iluminados*, because Jesus believed they had hit Eulogio's boys and Pablo. I told him there could be innocent victims. I called from Pablo's bodyguard's phone, as an anonymous caller. Now you tell me, Luz. If you had been Shannon, what would you have done?"

"I don't know…"

"Really? You don't know? Let me tell you. You would have done something. You would have acted on that tip off, wouldn't you?"

"Yes, I suppose so. Of course."

"Well, I watched Jesus' house all day. I saw the cars drive off to hit the *Iluminados*, I saw Pedro and Jesus argue, I saw Pedro drive home. And in all that time I didn't see a single surveillance cop, not a thing. And when the hit went down, there was nobody there to stop it or take them in. Conspiracy theory?" I shook my head. "Bent cop."

Her face flushed and she sat forward, gesturing at me, my bag and the gun. "But this is not a solution!"

"I disagree. Until somebody comes up with something better, it's the only solution."

"Murdering? Murdering is the only solution? Then God help us!"

I put down my glass and leaned forward, suddenly getting mad. "He won't! He never has and He never will! You show me a better solution! You're very keen on telling me what not to do, Luz! How about you tell me what I *should* do? What's your brilliant, peaceful solution? Pray? Sit back and let the bastards murder innocent people, enslave young girls for their prostitution rackets, destroy vulnerable lives? And hope that sooner or later they will see the light? Or should we trust in the likes of Detective Mike Shannon?"

"Stop shouting at me!"

"Answer my question! Stop telling me what we shouldn't do and tell me what *should* we do!"

"We should *resist* them! But *not* with violence! Gandhi did it! Why can't we?"

An unreasonable flash of anger welled up inside me. "*Grow up, Luz!*" I stared at her and she stared back at me. "Gandhi was up against the British Empire! They were governed by the rule of law, international law and public opinion after the war against Hitler's Germany! Of course passive resistance was going to work! We are up against the Sinaloa Cartel! You know what they do to people who resist them! They dismember them alive and leave their corpses in the street as a message! You think they give a damn about public opinion?"

She stood, speaking quietly. "Don't tell me to grow up. Believe me, I have done plenty of growing up!"

I stood too. We were just a few inches away from each other. "Maybe so, but your attitude to the gangs is naïve. If you go up against them with passive resistance and prayer, they will destroy you, just like they destroyed Celeste."

"But not you! You are the indestructible *gringo*! You can go up against them and they will back away in fear..."

Her breathing was heavy and shaky. I could hear my own heavy too. I snarled, and my voice was thick. "I seem to be doing OK so far. You know what they'll do to you if they know you've been visiting me?"

"He's my brother..."

"That won't save you, any more than passive resistance will. You need to get out of town. Go away somewhere for a few days..."

There were tears in her eyes. She gripped my shirt in her fingers. "Please don't kill my brother. He is all I have left..."

I gripped her arms and pulled her close to me. Her body was warm, supple and hot. "Then make him give himself up, turn state's evidence, do whatever he has to do!"

"He won't! He won't listen to me!"

"Then leave! Get out of town! Go somewhere safe..."

My mouth closed on hers. She didn't fight me. Her arms went around my neck and we stumbled toward the bed as she tore off my T-shirt and I stripped her sleeves from her smooth, tanned shoulders.

THE SKY WAS TURNING pale gray through the window. I was somewhere between sleep and waking, feeling the slight weight of her head on my shoulder, her hand on my chest, her leg across mine.

She stirred, shifted, moved and sat up. I opened my eyes and saw the curve of her tanned back, her black hair tussled and uncombed.

"I have to go."

"Where? What are you going to do?"

She didn't answer for a bit, looking down at her feet. "There was a note under your door when I got here. I forgot to tell you. It wasn't signed. It just said he, or she, would get the four AM flight back home, not to worry about booking a ticket."

So Kenny had gone. That was a relief. I said again, "What are you going to do? It's not safe for you here."

"You care?"

"Don't be childish, Luz."

"What's your name?" She looked at me and smiled. "I surrendered my virtue to a man, and I don't even know his name."

"Lacklan."

"Lacklan? That's a weird name."

"Luz, stop playing games. What are you going to do? There is no point in putting your life at risk."

She stood and went to the bathroom. After a moment, I heard the shower. I got up, pulled on my pants and my boots and started to think. Pedro's girlfriend had obviously not bought my FBI line. That meant that Jesus would now be looking for a *gringo*. I didn't know how far Shannon was in Jesus' pocket. He might just be turning a blind eye when told to do so, but I had to assume the worst—that Jesus controlled him completely. If that was the case, it would not be long before Jesus came looking for me. It was time for me to disappear.

I pulled on my shirt and made a pot of coffee, and Luz came out of the bathroom toweling her hair. When she was done, she pulled on her blue dress.

"I'll talk to Jesus. I'll beg him to stop what he is doing. I'll talk to him about Celeste and ask him to use the money he has made to take up her cause."

"Don't."

She frowned at me. "What?"

"Don't do it, Luz. He'll laugh in your face, and if you persist, he'll kill you. I know men like Jesus. He is psychotic, paranoid, a sociopath. If he feels you have betrayed him, he'll kill you. And if he doesn't, Carlitos will."

Her face looked mad as she pulled on her pumps. "And you? What about you, Lacklan? Will you kill me? Who else is going to kill me for doing the right thing?"

There was a bitter twist to my voice when I answered. "You're a Christian. You should know the answer to that one."

She stood and faced me. "He came to teach us the right way. That is why He died on the cross."

"Yeah? I thought he died on the cross because he challenged the Romans. But you know what? Personally I always favored the version where Arnold Schwarzenegger played Jesus. He blows away the Romans with a General Electric Minigun, steps onto a flying saucer in the Garden of Gethsemane and says, 'I'll be back.'"

"Not funny."

"You getting killed isn't funny either, Luz. Celeste already paid the price for being naïve about these guys. If you want to win this war, be smart. Let me take you to Phoenix for a couple of days, or put you on a bus to L.A. I'll put you up in a hotel, come and get you when it's over."

"You mean after you've killed my brother."

I sighed. "OK, you win. I won't kill him. I'll bring him in, hand him over to the Feds, with Shannon. Just get out of town, Luz. Be safe."

She smiled, but there was a touch of irony in it. She spoke with an affected accent. "Boy, Latinas really be white boy's kryptonite, huh?"

"Cut it out. I'm serious."

She sat on the edge of the bed and sighed. "You'd do that?"

"Yes. Of course I would. Your life is obviously worth more than his death."

She reached out and took my hand, looking up into my face. "Let me talk to him, Lacklan. He's my brother. We both know he'll tell me to get lost. When he does, I'll call you. Then you can drive me to Ellesmere Island if you want to, and do what you have to do…" She hesitated a moment. "But if last night meant anything to you, you'll hand him over to the FBI instead of murdering him. I want that for him, Lacklan, but I also want it for you. Because I don't want you to be like him."

I nodded. She stood and took her purse. I said, "Give me your number."

She recited it and I entered it into my phone. Then I called her. It rang once and I hung up and smiled. "Save it as Paquita."

She saved it, then opened the door and stepped out into the early dawn. I watched her walk across the parking lot toward her white Ford truck, her hips swinging and her shoulders back. It made me smile. Then I noticed the slight shudder of a red Toyota truck a hundred yards down. Alarms bordering on panic went off inside me. A fraction of a second of indecision paralyzed me. The Maxim was back on the dresser. The car was moving, sliding out of its bay. Luz was walking, watching her feet, unaware.

I started to run as the Toyota accelerated. Luz raised her head to look. I screamed, "*Run!*" The passenger's window was open. An Uzi 9mm spat at me. His aim was all over the place. I fell to the ground. Showers of asphalt leapt around me. Brakes squealed.

Luz screamed, "*Dejenme! Dejenme! Leave me alone!*"

I was on my feet again. She was on the far side of the truck. Through the window I could see them dragging her in. The truck took off, its tires spinning, smoking. I sprinted, reaching for the tailgate, missed it by an inch and the truck roared out of the lot and onto the East Benson Highway.

Rage and frustration welled up inside me, but turned me cold. The guy with the Uzi had not been one of Jesus' boys. I had seen him once before, at Carlitos' place. This was their reprisal against the *Santos del Diablo*. I turned toward my room; my only weapons were the Maxim and my Sig. My mind was racing, but not coming up with any solutions, and the more I thought about it, the more I felt panic at what they would do to her as Jesus' sister. Death, when it came, would be a liberation.

I ran.

TEN

I snatched up the Maxim and slipped it into my waistband. Then I ran to the Focus and took my Sig from the glove compartment. I had no idea what I was going to do. My plan was simply go to Carlitos' place and get Luz back. I climbed behind the wheel, getting the wild panic under control, turning it to work for me, to force me to focus my mind. I headed for the exit to the parking lot, realizing that if I went to Carlitos' place, all I would achieve would be to get both of us tortured and killed. In my mind I could see Sergeant Bradley scowling at me: "Never pick a fight you cannot win, and *always* choose your battles."

How?

I drove fast down to Fairgrounds, down South Park Avenue, past the cop shop and Cora's Golden Café onto Freemont. At the end of Freemont I stopped and climbed out of the car, staring at the house where I had spoken to Carlitos. My idea, such as it was, was to offer myself in exchange for Luz. It was a stupid idea, but it was the only one I had.

The house was empty.

I looked at my watch. It was almost seven. I went up and hammered on the door, kicked it and leaned on the bell. There was nobody there, there were no trucks or bikes in the yard. The place was empty.

Then, slowly, faced with the inevitable, my brain started to work. I began to think, and realize what I had to do. I climbed back in the Ford and drove north to East Fair Street, and from there to the railway lines and the abandoned Sinaloa Club. Then I drove down to Jesus' house, parked in front of his gate and walked up to his door. Here there were trucks in his yard, and bikes. Nobody was up, but they were in there. I hammered on the door, kicked it and leaned on the bell, yelling at the top of my voice, "*Jesus! You son of a bitch! Get up, you lousy piece of shit! Get up!*"

I heard a door inside, then bare feet slapping on a tiled floor. The lock on the door rattled and it opened. There were two guys there in jeans with no shirt and no shoes, but they both had guns: a Glock and a Taurus. One of them was big and bald, the other was younger, and scrawny. I said, "Where is Jesus?"

The big, bald one said, "Fock you."

I broke his nose with the heel of my hand, then smashed his big, bald head into his pal's face. His pal went down. I hammered my fist twice into his big gut and threw him back on the floor. Then I yelled again.

"*Jesus! You piece of shit! Carlitos has your sister, Luz! He is going to rape her and torture her! You are on the clock! Now get your ass out here and talk to me, you son of a bitch!*"

The place was small, and it was a mess. I could see three threadbare couches that seemed to have been positioned anywhere by accident. There was a coffee table in front of one of them. It had a mirror on it, and even in the dim light that was filtering through the open door and the drapes, I could see traces of powder. Beside the mirror there was an ornate silver box. There was a bottle of Scotch single malt a third full, an empty bottle of vodka, another of rum. The floor was littered with empty two-liter Coke bottles, beer bottles and pizza cartons. There were also pieces of clothing, jeans, women's panties, a bra.

A door opened and the man I knew was Jesus stepped out. He ran his fingers through his hair. His eyes were puffy. He looked pallid and sick. I was struck again by how young he was, and now, close up, I could see that unlike his sister and his cousins, his eyes were a very pale blue. They made him look psychotic. He squinted in the light from the door. "What the fuck, man?"

I shook my head, feeling I had somehow slipped into a nightmare version of Alice in Wonderland. "You didn't think the *Iluminados* would retaliate? You all just got stoned and went to bed? You hit them twice in one week, both your cousins have been killed..."

"Who the *fuck* are you?"

I exploded. "I'm the man who killed your cousins, you fucking asshole!"

His mouth sagged and he frowned at the two guys on the floor. The small one was slowly getting to his feet. Then he looked at me. "You? You come to my house...?"

"You better get your head out of your ass, Jesus, and start listening. We are wasting time..."

His expression was turning from incredulity to rage. "You come to *my fockin' house?*"

I shouted at him, "*Your sister! Jesus! Listen to me! Carlitos has your sister!*" His face flushed. I pointed out the door. "I've been to his house. He's not there."

He put his fingertips to his brow, shaking his head. "Am I going crazy? Somebody tell me. Am I going out of my *fockin' mind?*" He looked at the young guy, who was mopping blood from his nose. "Joselito, am I...? Do I look insane to you?"

"No, Jefe."

I sighed. "Jesus, cut it out, will you? I'm talking about your sister, for crying out loud!"

He was still looking at Joselito, but gestured at me with both hands. "This... this *motherfocker*, comes to *my house*, and tells me he *killed my fockin' cousins!* And now he is..." His face flushed red with rage and he bellowed, "*Tellin' me I godda fockin' listen to him?*" He took a step toward me. "*Are you out of your fockin' mind?*"

I spoke quietly. "Yes." That made him pause. I went on. "Your sister came to plead with me not to kill you. When she left, two of Carlitos' boys were waiting. They snatched her and took her away in a red Toyota truck. I went to his house. There was nobody there. I need your help to find her. If we don't get to them in time, they will rape her and torture her before they kill her."

He pointed at me. "You killed Pablo, you killed Ernesto and Javi, you killed Eulogio's boys and you gave my coke to the cops. All of this, all of this fucking mess is your fault."

"Yes, and when it's over you can exact whatever punishment you feel you're entitled to. But right now we are *running out of time*. Where would Carlitos take Luz?"

The big, bald guy was levering himself into a kneeling position. Jesus took another step toward me and snarled, "What you got with my sister, you piece of shit?"

"Nothing. It was Celeste I cared about. Now quit stalling! Your sister's life is on the line, for Christ's sake! *Where would they take her?*"

His eyes had gone to pinpoints. He danced his head from side to side for a moment. "You figure you need our help to get her back. But answer me this, *gringo de mierda*, what the fuck do I need you for?"

I didn't hesitate. "Because you and your gang are incompetent. Look around you, Jesus. These two schmucks opened the door to me. I killed Pablo, Ernesto, Javi, Eulogio's two boys—you keeping count? I didn't kill these two bozos because I need them. Last night I killed Pedro and eight more of your boys in a Jeep and a Dodge RAM. You're fucking amateurs. If what's left of your fucking gang goes storming in, you'll get Luz killed, like you killed Celeste. Let me do it and she has a chance of coming out alive."

He winced, seeming to be unsteady on his feet. "You killed eight of my boys last night?"

"For crying out loud, Jesus! They could be raping her or cutting off her fingers right now while we stand here arguing! Do what the fuck you like to me, but first let's get Luz out of that place! I am your best chance of saving your sister! React, for fuck's sake!"

He stared at me, blinking, then suddenly nodded. "Yeah. Yes, you're right. I will do what the fuck I like to you. I will punish you and make you sob like a little girl, you motherfucking piece of shit." Then he was screaming, thrusting a Desert Eagle in my face. "*You come to my house, telling me you killed eight of my boys? You fockin' piece of shit! I will destroy you! Rómpanle la cabeza!*"

The pain was indescribable. My head seemed to split in half. But it was blissfully short, because an instant later, darkness enfolded me.

———

I WAS awoken by the shock of cold water. As I came around and blinked the drops from my eyes, the pain seeped back into my head. The door was still open and I registered that it was not much brighter outside than it had been when I had arrived. I wasn't surprised to discover that I was duct taped to a chair. Each ankle was taped to a leg, and my arms were taped to the back.

Jesus was standing, smiling down at me. He sniffed a couple of times and I knew he had just snorted, and felt like the king of the world. The big, bald dude and his small friend were standing on either side of him and their faces said they were keen to exact their revenge. A wave of nausea washed over me and I bit back the reflex to vomit. Instead I said, "While you're standing there leering at me, your sister is getting raped and tortured. What kind of a sick animal are you?"

He nodded. "No, you're right. We have to go and get Luz. And I was thinking about everything you said, dude, and you are right again. You are one *bad ass* motherfocker. You like a fockin' killing machine, man. But then I got to thinking some more, like, what if there was more to this crazy situation than you were telling me, huh? I mean, you gotta admit, right? It's kinda fucked up. You kill Pablo, you kill Pedro, you kill *ten of my boys!* He staggered back, staring up at the ceiling, opening his arms like he was calling on God to explain this thing to him. "*Ten of my fockin' boys!*"

A noise over by the coffee table made me look. There were four girls half dressed. They looked sleepy. One ran her fingers through her hair and said something about coffee. Another sat on the couch and looked at Jesus. She pointed at the silver box. "Can I...?"

He waved his gun at them. "Get the fuck outta here!" Then he waved his gun at me. "So I'm thinkin' what if?" He paused, studying my face. "What if Luz ain't been taken by Carlitos at all? What if you and Luz are lovers? What if Luz is your fuckin' bitch? And you know what? It makes sense. Why else would you be so crazy to save her, right?" He sat on the corner of the coffee table, a couple of feet from me. "You know, you turn up just a couple of months after I get Shannon in my pocket, six months after I get Kirkpatrick at the border patrol on my payroll, and you just happen to be there when we hit Carlitos' boys and take over the supply to their clubs. That is one hell of a coincidence. And Shannon, he didn't like you one bit, you know that? He said there was more to you than met the eye. What are you, a Fed? You told Cheryl you were a Fed. Is that true? Are you a Fed? Were you working with Celeste and Luz all along?"

"I'm not a Fed, Jesus. I am..." I sighed, wondering where to begin. I decided to make it simple. "I'm a rich playboy. I used to be in British special forces. I was in the Special Air Service for ten years. I made captain. You can check my ID in my wallet. I inherited a lot of money from my father a couple of years back. If you let me go, I can make it worth your while. I was drifting, traveling. It was pure chance that I was there when Celeste was killed."

"You're so full of shit."

"For Christ's sake, Jesus! Your sister has been taken by the *Iluminados!* What if I am telling the truth? Can you risk it?"

He leaned forward, so his face was just a few inches from mine. "Let's find out, motherfocker."

He picked up a pack of Marlboros from the coffee table and lit one with a blue plastic disposable lighter. He inhaled deep, blew out the smoke and reached over with the cigarette, passing the burning tip close to my eye and my cheek. Then I felt two powerful arms grab my head like a vise. Jesus started to laugh. The skinny guy behind him started to laugh. I saw the burning tip of the cigarette close in on my left eye. I squeezed it shut and felt the searing tip rest on my cheek. I smelled the burning flesh and heard it sizzle and crackle. I clenched my teeth, swearing to myself I would not scream. But then the searing pain tore into my head, and there was a horrible, tortured, twisted noise filling my brain and I knew it was me screaming through my clenched teeth.

He withdrew the cigarette and the big, bald dude let go of my head. I sagged forward. Jesus laughed. "You know what is worse than that pain?"

"Jesus, for God's sake, you have to go and get your sister."

"You think I am stupid? You think I don't realize you got an ambush waiting for me?" He laughed again. "*Pendejo hijo de puta!* I was telling you, you know what is worse? If I melt some plastic onto your face, and then set fire to the plastic. I'm telling you, man, that will take you to new heights!" He turned to the skinny runt. "Eh, Joselito, go to the kitchen. Get me one of those plastic cups. We gonna melt some plastic onto this *cabrón*'s face." Joselito left and Jesus leaned toward me. "And now I'm gonna tell you about my fockin' sister, *cabrón*. When I get my hands on that pig fockin', saintly little bitch sister of mine, I'm gonna wrap her in plastic bags, melt the bags and set fire to them. Maybe that will teach that stupid bitch to stop preachin' the *fockin'* Bible at me! Maybe that will teach her not to fuck with fockin' pigs!"

It was one of the few times in my life when I felt real, genuine terror. Joselito came back from the kitchen with a plastic mug and gave it to Jesus. He grinned at me and spoke to Joselito and the bald one. "OK, get this motherfocker on his back. Let's burn his fockin' face off and see if Luz still wants to fock her little pig."

ELEVEN

He played the flame from his blue, plastic lighter over the rim of the cup, and after a moment it caught and began to burn, releasing a thin column of acrid, black smoke. The plastic began to bubble and twist and melt into globules. The big, bald guy seized my chair and pulled it back while Joselito grabbed my face and held it so I couldn't turn away. Flaming droplets of burning plastic began to drip from the cup onto the floor. Jesus leered at me.

"Where should we begin, *gringo*? On the lips you used to kiss my sister? Then we can move up, over your cheeks, so your face starts to burn?" He laughed. "Then my sister can call you a real hot lover!"

They all thought that was hilarious and stared at each other, shouting laughter.

Sometimes what kills you is dumb luck. That was what killed Celeste: bad dumb luck. And sometimes dumb luck is what saves you. The cup was burning, releasing flaming gobbets of searing, molten plastic. Jesus was reaching out to drip it over my mouth and face, where it would cling and burn off my skin. I was telling myself I would not scream, though I knew I would. And in that moment, his cell rang.

He sighed, hesitated, looked at the screen and frowned. His eyes shifted to me. "Luz..."

He jerked his head at the bald guy, put his phone to his ear and answered.

"Yeah..."

Bald guy put the chair upright and for a while I was grateful for the duct tape, because they couldn't see how my hands were shaking. I could hear the voice on the phone. It wasn't Luz's, it was a man's voice. Jesus' face seemed to tighten and he turned, walked away toward the door where he stood silhouetted against the bright day. After a moment he said, "You hurt my sister, *hijo de puta,* and I will gut you right here on my floor. I will burn you..."

He listened a little longer, then hung up and turned to look at me. "They got Luz..."

I narrowed my eyes and shook my head at him. "You are one fucked up son of a bitch. What is wrong with you, Jesus? *I told you they had her!* Ten minutes ago you were going to wrap her in plastic and set fire to her!"

He took three strides and thrust his face into mine. "*My* sister! I can do what I like to *my* sister! But that *cabrón* Carlitos? He can't touch *my* sister!"

He backed up a step and gave me two backhanders that made my lip bleed and my ears ring, but at least it wasn't molten, burning plastic. I swallowed the blood, waited for the room to settle and asked, "What does he want?"

"Fock you..."

"Be smart for just once in your stupid, fucking life, Jesus.

Do you know how much government agencies and private industry pay for a guy like me?" That caught his interest and he frowned. I pressed on. "You've got me for free, you stupid fuck. Use me."

"...How much?"

I studied him a moment before answering. "It depends on the target, but a political target, or private sector industry?" I shrugged. "A sergeant I used to work with went private and he was getting one fifty to two hundred and fifty K a hit, into a numbered account in Belize. He was doing two or three hits a year. I'm a captain."

He smiled. "You the business, huh? Like Jason Bourne, or that Mechanic guy. You got the skills."

"I'm good at what I do. I've been doing it a long time. What does he want?"

"The *cabrón* knows you wiped out my gang. I should kill you."

"Yeah, you should. On the other hand, you could be smart. Use me to even up the odds. I can do the same to his gang as I did to yours, only more." The three of them looked at each other. I insisted, "What does he want?"

"What the fuck do you care what he wants? What difference does it make to you?"

I sighed. "Jesus Christ!"

"You being funny?"

I spoke slow and deliberate, like I was talking to an idiot child. "What he wants, Jesus, is what makes him weak. If we know what he wants, we can lead him to where we want him, and then kill him. Use your fucking brain!"

He came back to the coffee table, sat on the edge and studied my face. "He wants me out. He wants me to leave town. He wants my territory. He wants my supplier and my buyers. He wants my stash."

"How did you leave it?"

"He wants me to go to Swan Lane tonight, half past eleven."

"Where's that?"

"East of Summit, in the desert, there're a few houses out there."

"They'll kill you."

"I know that. I ain't gonna go."

I sighed again, playing up how stupid he was. "No, Jesus, listen to me. You call him back. Not now, later on, and you tell him you agree to his terms…"

"Bull shit!"

"Shut up and listen. You call him back, you tell him you agree." He drew breath and I cut him short. "Just shut up and listen. You tell him you agree but you don't trust him. You want to meet on safer ground. You propose the place. The Rancho Grande Road."

His eyes narrowed. He was suspicious. "Why there?"

"You tell him that's where your supplies are delivered. You have a shipment coming in tonight."

"How'd you know that?"

"Pablo told me. Tell him you have, I don't know, fifteen K of coke, and ten K of H coming in. That's a street value of over two and a half million bucks. He's going to want that. He knows you're down to a couple of boys and he can out gun you. He might complain, but he'll bite in the end. You tell him he brings Luz, you give him the dope and you leave town. He can have your clubs and your supplier. You just want your sister back."

"So when does this become a good thing for me?"

I didn't answer. I glanced at the bald guy and Joselito. "This it? Have you got anybody else you can call on?"

They all looked at each other. Joselito shrugged. "Nelson will come if you tell him. And El Ninja."

Jesus nodded. "I can get maybe two more."

"OK, you meet Carlitos and his boys on the Rancho Grande Road. I'll tell you how you position yourself. You're with Nelson and El Ninja. I take Joselito and..."

I looked at the bald guy and he said, "El Calvo."

I nodded. "Of course, El Calvo. So I go with Joselito and El Calvo up into the hills. I have a stash of weapons there. We ambush them and wipe them out."

He creased his face into incredulity. "You have a stash of *weapons* there?"

I gave him the dead eye. "Yeah, I was going to kill you, remember?"

He laughed. "And I'm supposed to set you loose with a stash of guns and two of my boys? You out of your fockin' mind, *gringo*!"

I nodded. "Yeah."

He started nodding, shaking his head and shrugging, like he had a whole internal dialogue going, asking himself questions he couldn't answer. "Would you like to explain to me exactly why I should do something so goddamn stupid? Why I shouldn't just shoot you in the fockin' head right now?"

"First, because your sister made me promise I would not kill you the way I killed your cousins..."

"I'm supposed to believe that shit?"

"Yeah, you're supposed to believe that shit. I was doing

this for Celeste, remember? But Luz made me see that murder and revenge were the last things Celeste would have wanted. I told you I am a very rich man. Celeste wanted to set up a foundation to help kids who were the victims of violence and drugs—the victims of bastards like you—your sister made me realize I had to start by changing my own ways. Instead of seeking revenge for Celeste, I had to let you live and help fund the foundation."

He looked at Joselito and El Calvo. "Jesus Christ, I think I'm gonna be sick."

I said, "That's one reason. The other reason is, you can't do this alone. To pull this off, you need a pro."

"So you gonna let *me* live, but you gonna kill Carlitos and his boys?"

"Killing Carlitos and his boys is not revenge. That's to save Luz's life."

He scratched his cheek, then grinned. "You like Luz, huh? You like her a lot." He pointed at me. "I think you're fockin' in love with my sister, *cabrón*."

I let a shadow of a smile cross my face, then started speaking fast. "Cut me loose, put these two on me. They can watch everything I do. Maybe they'll even learn something. If I step out of line, they can cut my throat. We set up the ambush before Sandra's delivery comes into the ranch, on the Rancho Grande Road. We prepare some parcels of talc and brown sugar, swap them for Luz, take Carlitos by surprise and hit them during the switch, from front and back. You get their vehicles. If you're smart, you get their cash and their stash too, plus you take control of the whole south of Tucson. You'll need to recruit more men afterwards, but that should be easy. You'll be the boss." I saw him hesitate a moment and went for the kill. "But you have to promise me one thing. When we get Luz back, you will respect her and you will not hurt her. You hurt her and I'll cut you open from your balls to your chin. You understand that?"

It was a simple trick in persuasion and he was too damn stupid to spot it: information overload and end up on the assumption that we have an agreement. Then demand a concession from him so *he* has to persuade *me* to go along with my own plan. He swallowed the hook, the line and the sinker whole.

"If I find she has betrayed me, *gringo*, I'll kill her. But if, like you say, she was just beggin' for her brother's life, she's OK." He shrugged. "I love my sister. She's my sister, for Chrissakes!" He looked at El Calvo and jerked his head at me. "*Déjenlo libre*."

The big guy came over and cut the tape around my ankles and my wrists. There have been few times in my life when I felt that much relief. I didn't show it. I stood and held out my hand. "I need my Maxim and my Sig."

He gave Joselito the nod. Joselito went to a dresser, opened a drawer and took out my guns. He handed me the Sig, then held up the Maxim and screwed up his face. "What *is* that thing, man? Looks like Judge Dredd's gun!" He pointed it at my head. "I am the Law, punk!"

If you don't hesitate, and you practice a lot, you can disarm a man pointing a gun at your head in .25 of a second. You make like you're clapping, but you smash the blade of your right hand into his wrist, and with your left you grip the barrel of the weapon and lever it in toward his face. It takes an instant then to seize the grip and the trigger. It's a fast, violent action and it had Joselito staggering back, gripping his bruised wrist and fingers. I could have killed all three of them in the next two seconds. Instead I kept Joselito lined up and spoke quietly.

"Next time you point a gun at me, I'll kill you. This is not a game." I slipped the weapon into my waistband behind my back and put the Sig at the front. As I did it, I said, "It's a suppressed gun. It has built in silencers, but there is no loss of power."

He was watching me. He didn't know whether to be interested or resentful. I glanced at him and gave him a way out. "Killing people is a serious matter, Joselito. You destroy a life, you devastate the lives of that person's family, you cause a lot of pain. It's a serious business, and if you do it well you can make a lot of money, a real career, and earn a lot of respect. Clown around and you end up dead, or worse, spending the rest of your life as somebody's bitch in prison. If you're going to do it, do it properly."

I had made captain in the best special operations regiment in the world. You don't do that without learning how to gain the respect of hard men. I had gained the respect of the toughest of the tough, the best of the best, and I knew that within the next couple of hours, I would be Joselito's sensei and he would be my devoted disciple.

Jesus was watching me through narrowed eyes. He hadn't missed the fact that I could have killed them all and didn't. El Calvo had listened to what I'd said and now he was nodding. "That was…" He nodded some more. "That was pretty good."

"You put in the hours, you get the results."

Jesus snarled, "So what now?"

"You contact Nelson and El Ninja. If there's anybody else you can call on, do it. We need as many guys out there as we can get. When you're sure of your numbers, call Carlitos. Tell him you agree to his terms, but you have conditions of your own: you demand to talk to Luz. Stress that is an absolute priority. You need to know she's alive and well. You understand?"

"Of course I understand. I ain't stupid."

"He has to believe you are sick with worry about your sister. Second, you want assurances he isn't just going to kill you. Let him know you're worried about that too, because later you are going to call him back to change the meeting place. That won't surprise him too much if you already told him you're worried. Understand?"

"Stop askin' me if I fucking understand, man."

"Third, ask him to let you keep some of the dope so you can set up wherever it is you're going. He won't let you, but that's the concession you're going to make to him. Don't give in too easy. Play hard ball. That's the sticking point *he* is going to focus on. Don't settle anything on this call. You agree when you call back. Got it?"

"I got it, *gringo*."

"OK." I sat on the sofa and cleared a space on the coffee table. "Get me some paper and a pencil." Joselito went away to get them. I continued talking. "A mile into the Rancho Grande Road there is a turn to the left. Just past that there is a track that goes into the undergrowth, right?"

El Calvo was nodding. Jesus said nothing but looked like he really wanted to kill me. Joselito came back with paper and a pencil and I set about drawing a map of the area.

"The track is just a footpath that climbs toward a stream

that comes down this narrow canyon." I drew it in and circled a fictitious spot on the river. "Here I have stashed a couple of automatic rifles with grenade launchers, a dozen hand grenades, a sniper rifle with a night scope and some night vision goggles." I looked Jesus in the eye. "My plan was to stop the delivery tonight…"

I left the rest unsaid, but they all knew my plan was to kill them and their suppliers. After a moment I went on.

"You'll tell Carlitos and his boys to come down the Rancho Grande Road. You tell them you'll meet them five hundred yards in, just after the barn, here on the right, and the lay by on the left, here." I marked the spot. "They'll like that, because they can send men up the canyon on the right, here, and behind the barn on the left, here, to catch you in a pincer movement." I drew a couple of arrows in from either side.

Jesus looked at me like I was crazy. "Why the fuck would I let them do that?"

"You won't, Jesus. You only tell him that so he'll be willing to agree. Actually, when they arrive, you'll be waiting for them two hundred yards closer, before the barn, here." I made an 'X' on the road. "Meanwhile, earlier in the afternoon, Joselito, Calvo and I will have collected the weapons from the stash and we'll be waiting, up on the hill. There are a couple of water holes and a copse of trees, just about here," I drew them in. "We'll be waiting in among the trees, behind them. As soon as they release Luz, you get her to cover and we open fire. When we open fire, you open fire and mow them down. They won't stand a chance."

Calvo had his bottom lip stuck out and he was nodding again. "Is a good plan, Jefe."

"Shut the fuck up, Calvo. I can see that. I'm still not happy about you running around the hills with assault rifles and grenade launchers." His voice was heavy with sarcasm. "I figure that's a small problem in the plan."

I sighed. "Answer me a question, Jesus. Forget whether you can get Luz back and wipe out Carlitos' gang without me. Forget that. Ask yourself, can I get Luz back without you? It's the very reason I came to you in the first place. I risked my life to save her, because I need you. So it would be pretty damned stupid of me to kill you just as she is about to be set free, wouldn't it?"

He grunted.

I shrugged. "I want to honor Celeste, Jesus, and I want to save Luz. Once the operation is over, we can talk about my making it worth your while, financially, to head up a foundation in Celeste's name, to get kids off the streets and stop the drugs trade. You and the boys could get respectability, a lot of money and be free of the fear of death and prison." I noticed Joselito and El Calvo glance at each other. Jesus was frowning hard. I ignored him. "It's what your sister wants, and it makes a lot of sense. But that's for tomorrow. Right now, this is the plan and this is the strategy. It'll work."

He took a deep breath and sighed. "OK, we do it."

TWELVE

We took their Jeep and El Calvo drove, west along Ajo Way. It was late afternoon and hot under a blue-white sky. I sat up front in the passenger seat and Joselito sat behind me. I knew he had his Glock trained on the small of my back, and if I went for El Calvo, he'd plug me without thinking twice. We drove in silence till we were past Wakefield and the JFK Park, then Joselito started to ask questions:

"So you was in Iraq and Afghanistan?"

"Yeah. A few times. Other places too, Africa, South America..."

"So you train in kung fu an' all that ninja stuff."

I looked at him in the mirror. "The Regiment trains us in basic self defense, based on Major Fairbairn's techniques, and a lot of experience, but most of us do some form of martial arts on top of that. A lot of the guys like Krav Maga."

"How about you? I know you do something."

I nodded, looking out at the passing desert, the heat and

the white-blue sky. After a moment I said, "Jeet Kune Do for the techniques. Whatever they say about Bruce Lee, he was the best. I also practice old style Tae Kwon Do, coupled with Zen Buddhist meditation, for the discipline."

They were both very quiet then for a while. Eventually Joselito said: "You do Zen meditation?"

"Yeah."

"What… like… what is that? Like mind control?"

"It helps you control your own thoughts and your emotions. It helps you focus, concentrate your attention, and see things as they really are."

"As they really are…?"

El Calvo said suddenly, "You know, I always think about that—meditation and shit. Maybe… you know, maybe you can help me. I read that the Samurai, or maybe I saw it on a documentary. I like to watch National Geographic, and the History Channel, know what I'm sayin'? So, it might have been a documentary. Anyway, it said that the Samurai, after a life of violence and fighting and killing, they would often become Buddhist monks. I thought that was cool. I'd like to do that, you feel me? Maybe you can help me, man."

"It takes a lot of devotion and dedication. The simplest thing becomes the hardest. Do you understand what I mean by that?"

Joselito nodded. "Yeah, I get that."

El Calvo shook his head. "No, that don't make no sense to me."

I smiled. "OK, what could be more simple than focusing your attention on the breath coming in and out through the tip of your nose? Pretty simple, right?"

El Calvo glanced at me, frowning, and nodded. I looked in the mirror. Joselito was watching, frowning too.

"Yet, it is the most difficult thing to do in the world. Because within one second your mind has started to wander. It is impossible to hold the mind on a single thing for more than a tenth of a second. So a Buddhist master who can concentrate his attention for twenty or thirty minutes can achieve extraordinary things, because the concentrated mind is a very powerful thing. When you practice, if you stay with it, not only can you achieve huge speed and strength, but you also begin to find a deep, inner peace." I looked at El Calvo. "There, in that peace, is true redemption."

On our right, we passed the turn off for the abandoned barn where I had killed Pablo. I glanced at the mirror again and spoke to Joselito. "The usefulness of a net is in the empty spaces. The value of a window, is the emptiness inside. That is Zen: focusing on the emptiness."

He was shaking his head. "Man! That is deep. That is too deep for me, dude."

I shrugged and smiled. "You make your choices."

"You get that, Calvo?"

"I think so." He gave his slow nod. "The usefulness of a *net*... is in the *empty* spaces... Yeah, I mean, that *is* true, and it's kinda weird. And the value of a window—it's like the net—the value *is* in the emptiness inside. I get that. It's not the wall all around it. It's the emptiness. Because it's only the emptiness that allows you to *see*, right? So we have to focus our mind on..."

He trailed off. He'd sensed it, but lost the thread.

"We are all empty inside, Calvo. Everything we think of as us, as our identity, who we are..." I shook my head. "It's an illusion. When you strip away everything that is not you, what are you left with?" They were both frowning hard now. "I'm not my head, I'm not my body, I am not my hands or feet, I am not my thoughts—all these things belong to me, but they are not *me!* Right? I am not my emotions, I am not even my brain or my spirit, because these things *belong* to me. So, what am I?"

El Calvo puffed out his cheeks and blew. "Man, that is heavy shit..."

I laughed. "I am the one watching, observing, I am the one asking the question! I *am* the emptiness. It's hard to get your head around, but that is the heart of Zen Buddhism. And if you can master that meditation, it gives your fighting skills a real edge. No hesitation, no doubt, no inner conflict."

If I had been a hundred and fifty pound accountant, they would have jeered at me. But because I'd beaten them both to the ground, almost broken El Calvo's fingers, and killed two of their three bosses, they were awed into silence. I was the master.

We came to Three Points and turned south toward the border. We drove on and began to draw level with the Keystone Peak on our left. El Calvo suddenly put his right hand on his chest.

"You think a man like me...?" He turned to look at me. "I have no education. I can read. But I never got what you could call an education. I left school when I was nine or ten, got in with a gang. Back then we called ourselves *Los Sicarios*, the Assassins, you know? You think a man like that, like me, can become a Buddhist monk? Like, you know, when I am older and I have made my money and I retire?"

I held his eye. "There is no future, there is no past,

Calvo. There is only now. Now is the moment where you do it, whatever 'it' is: killing somebody, saving somebody, changing your life. Whatever it is, now is when you do it. But there is one, fundamentally important lesson, that is more important than all the others. Are you ready for it?"

"What's that?"

"Compassion. You need to learn compassion."

He made a face which said that wasn't a thing he was all that interested in learning.

"All the most important lessons will be hidden from you, unless you learn compassion."

"Huh." He didn't sound convinced.

When we reached the Arivaca intersection, he said, "Would you, like, help me?"

I nodded once. "Yeah."

Joselito spoke up from the back. "I mean, maybe you could teach us, like, your style and your philosophy and stuff. Dude!" He laughed. "I mean, we could be like real ninjas!"

El Calvo sighed and shook his head. "It ain't about that, man. You ain't listening. You know what I'm sayin'? We didn't choose this fuckin' life. We are born, and before we know what's happenin' we got all this bad shit coming at us. We gotta fight to survive. The spoils go to the worst badass, feel me? And by the time you got enough sense to be askin' questions, it's too late. You already fucked up too bad." He pointed at me. "You said the word, dude. You said 'redemption'. I can go a thousand times to the church and ask for forgiveness and redemption, but I don't believe in that shit. If I go out and kill another dude, or a chick, I don't believe that any god is gonna keep on forgiving me. You hear what

I'm sayin'? I don't think redemption comes that way. I think it's like you said. You gotta find that empty place inside of you, where peace is, where forgiveness is. And maybe that's why you need to learn compassion to be able to get there." He nodded a few times and pointed at me. "I think y'all is a natural teacher, dude. You made me think today."

Joselito sighed too. "Yeah, I know, man. I'm just sayin'. You ain't the only one who had it tough as a kid, Calvo. You know how old I was when I first kill a guy."

"Yeah, you told me, Joselito. You told everyone."

"You wanna know?"

I nodded. "Sure."

"I was nine years old."

Calvo nodded and shrugged. "Is true. His mom was a whore."

"I never met my dad. Never mind who he was, my mom didn't even remember who he *might* have been. You know? There were so many, she didn't remember one day from the next. She was just hustling to get enough money for the next fix."

El Calvo took over. "So his mom is servicing a client, right? They bangin' in the bedroom, and he starts to get rough. He don't just want to fuck her, he wants to fuck her *up!* So she screams for Joselito…"

Joselito interrupted, "'Go get a knife! Go get a knife!' She's screamin' at me, in Spanish. '*Ve a por un cuchillo! Ve a por un cuchillo!*' like that, and this guy, a big motherfucker, is on top of her beating her with his fockin' fist, man. So I run to the kitchen and I get the big knife for cutting the vegetables. I take it to the bedroom and I wanna give it to her, you know? I'm only a kid, right? I don't know what to do with the fockin' knife! But she's covering her face with her arms and this big, fockin' Irish *gringo* is beating shit out of her. And now she's screaming, '*Clávaselo! Clávaselo al hijo de puta!*' Stick him! Stick the son of a bitch! An' he don't speak Spanish so he don't know what's comin'!"

El Calvo started to laugh. "That's fucked up, dude."

Joselito was laughing too, a high-pitched giggle, covering his face with his hands. "So I don't know what the fuck to do, but I'm thinking if I don't do what I'm told, I'm gonna get into trouble, right? And believe me, when you was in trouble with my mom, you was in *trouble!* So I took the knife in both hands, I run at this dude and I just *hammered* that knife into his back. *Bam!* It went in all the way, man. All the way up to the handle. He screamed like a... I don't what he screamed like. It was crazy loud, and like a girl, real high, kinda, aaaaah! Real high, and squeaky."

El Calvo said, "Yeah, we get the idea."

"But now I'm terrified, because I'm thinkin', if he ain't dead, I am in *real* deep shit, right? I mean, I'm only eight."

"You said you was nine."

"OK, nine, but still. You don't go around stabbing big fuckin' Irish *gringos* when you're nine. This guy is gonna be so fuckin' pissed if he ain't dead. So I pull out the knife and *wham!* I stab him again. The motherfucker won't go down. He's on his feet now, butt naked, with his legs bent like the fuckin' hulk, and he's walking around the room, boom, boom, boom, that's his footsteps, and I'm thinkin', this bastard ain't *never* gonna die! So I pull the knife out again, and this time I hold it like a lance, and I run and *bam!* I stick it in what now I know is his kidneys. Back then it was just where I could reach, 'cause I was only small. And he just falls flat on his face, dead. That was the first time I ever killed anybody. I'll never forget it. I was nine."

"You told us."

"I never told Lacklan, though. That's something, huh, Lacklan? At nine years old?"

I nodded. "That's something, Joselito."

We'd reached Rancho Grande Road and turned right into it. We moved fast, raising a big cloud of dust trailing behind us. As we approached the small turn off where Kenny and I had hidden the Zombie, I pointed. "Slow down and turn in here."

El Calvo gave a small frown as he slowed. "This ain't the place you said on the map."

"I know. I left a few stashes here and there, in case I was chased. Standard practice. I like to have fall back positions."

He stuck out his lip in an expression of approval and nodded. "OK."

He slowed and turned in, and we bumped and jolted our way slowly toward where I had hidden the Zombie. I could see him squinting. I said, "Keep going till you get to the canyon there. Then stop. I'll show you what I have here and we can work out our exact tactics."

He drew level with my car, stopped and they both stared. Then El Calvo grinned and started to laugh. "You gotta be kidding me. Is that a '68 Mustang?"

I laughed too. "It is and it isn't. Get out and I'll show you."

We climbed out and as they approached the Zombie, I leaned my ass against the Jeep and started to talk. "The chassis is a '68 Mustang fastback, but she's got twin electric engines and twin lithium ion batteries. She's got eight hundred horsepower, and almost two thousand pounds of torque. Acceleration is almost instant. From a standing start, she'll hit sixty in one and a half seconds."

El Calvo's jaw literally sagged. "Holy shit! Are you serious?"

"Two hundred miles an hour top speed."

Joselito was doing his weird giggle. "How much a car like that cost you, dude?"

"Two hundred and fifty grand. It's not expensive for what it is. Have a look in the trunk, see what I have there."

I threw him the keys. He caught them one-handed and pulled the branches I'd used to camouflage it off the back of the car. He fitted the key and unlocked it. I pulled the Maxim 9 from behind my belt and stepped toward them. El Calvo looked at me and then at the gun. I was saying, "I wanted to show you guys what the Maxim can do."

It was a strange moment. A deep sadness crept into El Calvo's face and he looked me in the eye. Joselito was staring into the trunk expostulating, "Woah! Dude! This is a fuckin' arsenal!"

He sensed the change in the mood and looked up at me. He said, "What...?" then looked at El Calvo. He frowned when he saw El Calvo's expression and looked back at me.

I said, "The emptiness inside," and shot El Calvo first, a single round through his head. Joselito backed away a step, with both hands up. He was moving so I double-tapped him in the chest. Both rounds went through his heart and he died instantly.

I put the Maxim back in my belt and rolled their bodies down into the canyon. They crashed through the undergrowth and I heard a splash when they hit the bottom. Then

I went back to the Zombie and selected my weapons. I strapped on a double holster for the Sig and for the Maxim. It gets cold in the desert at night, so I pulled on a warm jacket with plenty of big pockets and slipped in a spare magazine for each. I was going to need the DI MKII, with the night vision scope. I figured one magazine would do the job, but I put a spare in along with the other two, just to be safe. I had my knife in my boot and I figured that would do, at least for now.

 I dumped everything else Kenny had brought me into the kit bag, slung it over my shoulder and started making my way east and slightly south, across country, toward the Rancho Grande. The shadows were growing long and the sun was slipping fast down to the western horizon. I had some preparation to do once it was dark, before the gang arrived.

THIRTEEN

I made the preparations I needed to make on the slopes to the north of the road, and as the sun slipped behind the Baboquivari mountains in the west and darkness closed in, I slipped across the road to the Rancho Grande and snooped around for an hour or two. There was a modern-looking house surrounded by barns and a large stable, which I explored. I found there was a lot of hay but no horses; there was also an interesting trap door.

I made some more small preparations, left myself a stash hidden in the hay, and slipped back to the north side of the road. By that time it was after eight. I made a call to my hotel, lay down, covered myself with a few small branches and slept for a couple of hours.

At ten I awoke, drank some water, crawled into position and waited. At ten thirty two sets of headlamps appeared on the Sasabe Road and turned in to the Rancho Grande Road. They approached slowly, with the whine of heavy diesel engines carrying on the cold night air. They came to a halt where I had told Jesus to wait, then maneuvered themselves facing back, toward Sasabe, so they could blind Carlitos with their headlamps. They killed their lights and settled to wait.

I tucked the butt of the MKII into my shoulder and lined up the two trucks. In the nearest one, a Toyota, I could see a guy at the passenger window, and through the windshield I could see the chest of the driver. The second truck was a Jeep Cherokee, and I could see the two guys in the front. Jesus was in the passenger seat, but I couldn't see into the back. There might be four, five or six of them. I'd find out when Carlitos arrived.

Carlitos arrived fifteen minutes later, fifteen minutes early. He was in a convoy of three trucks. The front truck looked like a Land Rover and had its lamps on high beam. As they approached Jesus' two cars they slowed, and the Cherokee and the Toyota put their lights on high beam too. Then Jesus and four other guys climbed out, went behind their trucks and trained handguns and rifles on Carlitos' caravan.

Men began to climb out of Carlitos' trucks, twelve in all. They seemed to be carrying mainly shotguns, but I saw a couple of assault rifles too. They looked like AK-47s. I didn't see Luz. I found Carlitos and lined him up. He was standing behind the Land Rover. He was about fifty paces away and I had a good, clean shot. I heard him shout, but I couldn't make out the words. There was a little more shouting back and forth and all the headlamps were dimmed.

A moment later, one of Jesus' guys walked half the distance between the two sets of trucks and placed a couple of large packages on the ground. That was the talc and the brown sugar. Then he backed up to the Toyota. I held my breath. The next moments were crucial.

One of Carlitos' guys reached into the Land Rover and pulled out a woman I recognized as Luz. He walked her past the front of the Land Rover as far as the packages, then gave her a small shove. She took a couple of paces and ran the rest of the way. I saw Jesus grab her, and I squeezed the trigger and blew the top of Carlitos' head off.

There was a second of stunned silence as the eleven remaining guys just stood and stared at his body sliding down the Land Rover into the dirt. It was all the time I needed to readjust my aim. I opened up, small bursts of five rounds hammering into the back and sides of the trucks, shattering glass, tearing at the tires, and shredding the bodies of the guys standing there, dithering, not knowing where the fire was coming from.

Then the Cherokee's and the Toyota's headlamps came on high beam again, and Jesus and his boys opened up, catching Carlitos and his gang in a killing zone between two fields of fire. For a few, desperate seconds they returned fire, kicking up spouts of dirt further down the hill, shattering the windshield of the Totota, but it was wild and ineffectual. I counted them go down. It didn't take long. I took three in a single burst as they tried to run for the cover of the trees on the far side of the road. Two more had gone down just after Carlitos. Two sought refuge in one of the rear trucks and tried to drive away. Their windshield imploded under a hail of lead and their truck rolled back into the ditch. Two more tried to run back along the road. Two short bursts tore them to shreds. When I turned back to take the remaining two, they were dead, killed by the barrage from Jesus' men.

For a moment, there was stillness and silence in the night.

I pulled my cell from my pocket and called Jesus. I saw him pick up. He looked incredulous.

"What the hell? You callin' me on the phone? You're right here. Where are you?"

"I have you lined up with a telescopic sight. You also happen to be parked on a landmine of my design. It explodes if I press the letter 'J' on my phone."

"What the fuck...?"

"This is just a small precaution, Jesus. Don't take it personally. Put Luz in the Jeep and give her the keys. I want you all to stand well back. Understood?"

"What the fuck do you think..."

"I'm counting to three. One's already gone. Two..."

"OK! Fuckin' *pendejo!*"

I saw him hand Luz something, she climbed in the Jeep and he handed her his cell. As she took it I said, "Are you OK? Single word answers."

"Yes."

"Start the engine."

There was a small pause. I heard the engine start. "OK."

"Drive downtown. Dump the Jeep and get a taxi to my hotel. The receptionist knows you're coming. He'll give you a key. Go to my room and don't come out until I come and get you, or I call you."

"OK."

"Now, give your brother his cell back, and go."

I watched her hand Jesus his phone, then the Cherokee pulled away and accelerated down the road. I kept Jesus lined up until the red taillights had disappeared onto Sasabe

Road. Then I heard Jesus' voice in my phone. He sounded pissed.

"OK, she's gone. Now what?"

"I'm coming down."

I buried the MKII, along with the night vision goggles, and made my descent.

They looked like something from a sci-fi movie: long, black shapes, vaguely humanoid, backlit by the headlights that were still on long beam. I didn't go to them. I went to Carlitos' trucks and turned off the lights. Then I confirmed the kills. A couple of the guys were still alive, barely, and I shot them in the back of the head with the Sig.

After that I walked toward the Toyota. "Turn the damn lights off. You want to attract every damn federal agent in the area?"

I saw Jesus' warped silhouette lean forward and heard him clear his throat and spit. The lamps died and the stars seemed to leap out of the sky. Jesus said:

"I own every damn federal agent in the district, Special Ops."

"Sure, keep dreaming, Dr. Pangloss." I stopped in front of him and looked down into his insane, pugnacious face and his pale blue eyes. "What's your annual budget, Jesus?"

He screwed up his face. His boys were watching. "*What?*"

"It's a simple question. What's your annual budget?"

He stepped away from me, waving his hand in the air. "Leave me alone, man! You talking fucking shit! Fockin' budget!"

"The DEA is just short of three billion, the Bureau of Alcohol, Tobacco, Firearms and Explosives is just short of two billion, and the FBI is just short of nine billion. That's a total in the region of fourteen billion dollars, destined to stop you. And you think you've bought every federal agent in the district. You're full of shit, Jesus. Wake up."

His eyes were wide and his face had gone tight. "I should have killed you back at the house."

"Yeah, maybe you should have at that, then we could all have gone to hell together. Because Carlitos, who is now lying over there dead, with the top of his head missing, would have killed you and your boys before the day was out, after raping, torturing and killing your sister. But that didn't happen, did it, Jesus? Instead you now control the whole of south Tucson. Think it through, genius. Just exactly how did you get here?"

He had no answer, so instead he glanced around. "Where are El Calvo and Joselito?"

"They didn't make it. Now tell your Sinaloa pals they can come on out. We can go to the ranch now."

His eyes were like slits. He stepped toward me. "What...?"

"Isn't that what happens next, genius? Your Sinaloa pals from the ranch come out and we all go to wait for the delivery?" I pointed at Carlitos' trucks. "You need to get those trucks out of here, and the bodies and the blood cleaned up. However much you think you control the federal agents, believe me, you don't control shit. You don't control the bureaus, and that's what counts. They are watching you." I paused and smiled. "They are watching you, and they are watching Shannon, too."

I walked to the Toyota, leaned against the hood and pulled a pack of Camels from my pocket. I lit up and inhaled deep. He watched me do it, made a brief, one word call on his phone, then turned to his boys and told them to go clean up the mess. At the same time, I heard several trucks fire up to the south side of the road. Four sets of lights came on and started to snake along an invisible road out of the ranch toward us.

Jesus came and stood in front of me. "You're too smart, *gringo*. I don't like it."

"Then wise up. I'm no danger to you, Jesus. Look around you. I just made you a very rich, powerful man. I'll tell you what your big danger is, your damned arrogance and the coke you snort. They've got you believing you're indestructible, but you're not. You don't plan, you don't think things through. You think things are going to work out for you just because you snort some damned powder. You're in a fool's paradise."

The trucks had reached the Rancho Grande Road. Three of them rolled by and went to help Nelson, El Ninja and the others, and the fourth, a Range Rover, drew up next to us. The doors opened and four guys got out. They all looked Mexican, but the guy who got out of the front passenger seat was wearing a cream Stetson and cowboy boots. He didn't look much older than Jesus. He was clean-shaven and slim. The other three who got out with him were older and tougher, and had the look of experience about them.

He ignored me and I watched him and Jesus embrace and talk in Spanish for a while. Finally he turned and looked at me. His eyes were direct. He looked wide awake.

"Captain Lacklan Walker." His accent was Mexican, but

not strong, and what he said was a statement, not a question, so I didn't answer. "What are you doing?"

I raised an eyebrow at him. "I'm not going to insult your intelligence by telling you I'm smoking. But if you want any other kind of answer, you'll have to be more precise. Also, who are you?"

"I'm Joaquin Dorado Beltran. I want to know why you are helping Jesus."

"Your mother is the Queen of the Sea?" He didn't answer; he waited. I sighed. "It's a long story. How about you offer me a whiskey and something to eat, and I tell you the story."

He didn't wait. He turned to one of his guys and said, "*Encárguese de la limpieza. Ustedes conmigo.*" To me he said, "OK, let's go," and to Jesus, "You come in the Toyota."

Jesus looked alarmed. I was riding with the big cheese and he was riding behind in a shot up truck, but he wasn't about to argue. I climbed in the front of the Range Rover, Joaquin got behind the wheel and two of his boys got in the back. He turned the truck around and we headed back, toward the Ranch.

As we wound and bumped down the track he held out his right hand, palm up. "You got a Camel?" I shook one out of the box and handed it to him. "Give me a light. I have to do everything myself?"

He grinned. I smiled and lit the cigarette. "You spooked Jesus. He thinks he's being relegated."

"Jesus is an asshole. I still don't know if I'm gonna kill him tonight." He gave a small laugh. "You know Camel in Spanish is the same as Mule in English? He's the guy who carries the drugs from one country to another." He gave a teenage laugh. "Everybody thinks Mexico is full of *burros*, but really it's full of *camellos*."

The guys in the back thought it was hilarious. So did Joaquin. I smiled and sighed and looked at the cold black glass of the window. "How long have you been using him?"

He shrugged. "Few months."

"Did his cousins keep him in line?"

"Pedro was smart. He kept things together."

"You got a shipment coming in tonight."

"Why all the questions, Lacklan?"

"Because I'm curious. I'm getting involved in this thing and I never intended to. So I want information. Preparation is the key to success, and for preparation you need information. So I want to know. I want to know what I'm getting involved in."

We had wound around the back of the ranch complex. It was hard to make out detail through the black windows, but I recognized the barns and the stables, and at the center the sprawling, modern house on several floors. Light was glowing yellow from the front door and from plate glass windows that overlooked a cactus garden. We came to a halt and he smiled at me with his youthful face.

"That's cool, I like that. But try to remember, curiosity will get you killed in this game. You don't need to know what I know. You only need to know what I want, and what I expect of you. And if you get nosy, I have my boys dismember you while you're still alive. As Voltaire would have said, *pour encourager les autres*."

"Droll. Noted."

We climbed out and he strode ahead on short, rapid legs. Behind me I heard the Range Rover doors slam as his two boys got out. I dropped my butt in the sand and trod on it. As he reached the front steps to the door, five or six paces away, I said, "Is it coming from the tunnel? What time do you think it will arrive?"

He stopped dead on the first step and turned to face me. I was smiling at him. His face said he was reassessing me and maybe he should kill both me and Jesus. The red Toyota came into the yard in front of the house, playing its beams over the barns and stables, until it came to a halt beside the Range Rover. The lights died and Jesus and one of his boys climbed out. I ignored them and stepped up to Joaquin. I paused beside him and said quietly, close to his ear, so all Jesus could see was me whispering to his head honcho.

"I don't scare easy. Let's play nice, and maybe we can do something useful."

I went past him, opened the door and stepped inside.

FOURTEEN

THERE WAS A STACK OF LARGE LOGS BURNING IN A fireplace the size of a small room. The room we were in was not small either, it was big. It was the size of a small apartment. The ceiling was high, the walls were cream and hung with modern paintings that looked like originals and probably were. There were four plate glass, floor to ceiling windows. The drapes were open and the glass looked black, populated with ghostly reflections of the room and the people in it, and the dancing flames of the fire.

The floor was hard, high-polished wood, strewn with bull skins. The sofas, the chairs and the occasional tables were modern, comfortable and expensive. The light came from lamps, each one an original work of art.

A servant had served us with drinks and retired. Now Joaquin stood by the fire, occasionally going up on his toes. I figured when he wasn't on his toes he was probably five ten, but he looked shorter. I was sitting in a large, leather armchair and Jesus was on a sofa. He looked worried.

Joaquin made a kind of sweeping gesture with his right hand, which was holding a gin and tonic, and shook his head. He might have been a young executive at an informal board meeting.

"There is almost nothing about this situation that I understand, and that makes me nervous, kind of mad, Jesus. We trusted you, but you seem to have lost your grip on the situation, and you have to understand that we, as a family and as a business, are worried by that."

Jesus drew breath, sat forward and said, "I…"

Joaquin shifted the position of his glass, so that it meant shut up, gave a small nod and said, "Don't speak yet. I'll give you a chance to explain in a minute. Right now, be silent."

He turned to me and smiled. It was more a smile of interest than pleasure. There was a tap at the door. It opened and his three bodyguards came in. One stood on either side of the door and the third went across the room and sat by one of the windows.

Joaquin pointed at me. "Retired Captain Lacklan Walker. You are a billionaire. You have been called a playboy from time to time, but that ain't true. Fact is you are a recluse. The FBI have a file on you, but it is sealed. You got friends in Congress. You got strings you can pull. You were honorably discharged from the British SAS. Your mother is British, your father, a leading financier in his day, is dead."

"So you hired a private eye, am I supposed to be impressed?"

He shook his head. "I doubt you are easy to impress, with a background like that. But, with a background like that, what the hell are you doing here? Why the hell are you involved in this and, above all, why were you trying to hurt

Jesus, and then, at the last minute...?" He stuck out his arm and gestured in the general direction of the road where I had just massacred Carlitos' gang.

I sighed, took a sip of my whiskey and set it on the table while I pulled my Camels from my pocket. "I was passing through Tucson. I've been drifting, for personal reasons that don't concern you and have nothing to do with what happened." I pulled a cigarette from the carton, poked it in my mouth and lit up with my old, battered, brass Zippo. I took my time inhaling and letting out the smoke.

"Jesus ordered a hit on some of Carlitos' boys. I witnessed the hit in the parking lot of a café. A girl was killed, Celeste Martinez. She was a sweet kid, just nineteen, beautiful, inside and out. I gave a statement to the cops, and the detective in charge made me understand that the crime would go unpunished. That made me mad. So I decided to administer justice myself and kill Jesus and his two cousins."

He grinned, gave a small laugh followed by a longer laugh, and turned to look at Jesus. "*Que par de cojones tiene el amigo!*" Jesus looked sick. Joaquin turned back to me. "So you just went right ahead and took on the gang."

I shook my head. "I didn't take them on. I wiped them out. When I killed Pedro, I killed eight of the *Santos* with him. Carlitos got to hear about it. He knew who I was because I had asked him for help to kill Jesus. When he realized there was only Jesus and two of his boys left, he moved in. He snatched Luz, Jesus' sister, and tried to lure Jesus into a trap."

"But you wanted to save Luz."

I nodded. "Luz was a close friend of Celeste's. Together they planned to set up a foundation to encourage poor kids away from the gangs and help them make a life without drugs. It seemed to me that saving her was more important than killing Jesus—for now at least."

"So you teamed up?"

"Something like that."

He walked slowly across the room, looking at his feet as he went. Then he stood staring down at his bodyguard, who met his eye. Joaquin said, "*Que le parece? Los huevos del güey!*"

The bodyguard gave a small shrug, like he wasn't impressed. "*Tiene valor, Jefe, pero esta loco, y es muy peligroso. Mátelo ya.*"

I understood enough to know they were discussing my balls, and the opinion of the bodyguard was that I was brave, but I was crazy and dangerous too, and his boss should kill me. He was probably the smartest guy in the room, apart from me.

Joaquin turned and walked back to the fireplace, still looking at his feet. "Nestor, my chief of security, thinks I should kill you."

"That's the same advice I'd give you if I were your chief of security."

"He thinks you are crazy."

"I'm not crazy. I'll tell you something else. However crazy I may be, and however dangerous, that guy right there," I pointed at Jesus, "is the one who is going to cause you real problems. Your head of security is a smart man, Jesus is an idiot. Kill Jesus and install Nestor to run things here. Then my work will be done and I can be on my way and leave you in peace."

He laughed out loud, for a long time. I looked at Jesus

and his boy. They both looked pale and sick. Joaquin pulled a handkerchief from his back pocket and wiped his eyes. "You," he pointed at me. "You have destroyed the two gangs I had available, that I could use for distribution. And now you give me this advice, you are..."

"There are plenty more desperados where those came from, Joaquin. You'll have no shortage of stupid kids to distribute your dope. But Jesus is not just a psychopath, he's a stupid psychopath..."

"Come on!" It was Jesus. He sat forward in his chair. "You said you'd give me a chance! This guy is talking me down, trying to manipulate you, calling *me* a psychopath... He killed my fucking cousins! What about *hermandad*? I should have the right to kill him, man! Instead of this..." He gestured wildly at me with his open hand. "This crazy shit!"

Joaquin turned to Jesus and placed his index finger over his lips, signaling him to be quiet. Then he turned to me. "So you are not interested in getting involved in the business?"

"No."

"That's a shame."

"But I am interested in a proposition that could benefit both of us."

"What's that?"

I took a last drag on my cigarette and crushed it out in a brass ashtray. "I want to set up a foundation in honor of Celeste. The foundation would set up a school and various projects to encourage, and help, kids to get out of the ghettos, out of the gangs and out of the drug culture. It would bear her name, the Celeste Martinez Foundation. I want you to provide a yearly sum of money, something substantial, couple of million bucks at least, and whoever runs your operation here in Arizona heads up the foundation as chief executive. He'd need to have some kind of legitimate business too."

He was frowning at me in fascination. "It's brilliant."

"He gets instant respectability. Choose the right guy, somebody outgoing who's going to get involved in the community. He could even run for public office of some kind, mayor, governor, whatever. You get to launder a lot of money, through the foundation and through the business, my foundation thrives and a lot of kids get a second chance in life. You don't care because they are the kids who were probably never going to buy your drugs in the first place, but the hard core will still join your gangs and take your drugs."

He paced up and down for a bit, smiling at the floor. "It is fantastic, truly superb. I cannot wait to tell my mother about this. She will like you." He laughed and pointed at me. "Which is maybe not such a good thing! Because most of the men my mother likes wind up dead!" He stopped, faced me and sighed. "But we both know that sooner or later you are going to turn on us and attack us."

I stuck out my lower lip and shook my head. "We know no such thing. As far as I am concerned, it is a symbiotic relationship. I left the Regiment two years ago because I was sick of killing and fighting. I don't give a rat's ass whether you go for my suggestion or not. I just want to go home to Boston and get on with my life. You and your cartels are a necessary evil. If you go down, somebody else will rise up in your place, like weeds feeding on shit. If I can balance that with the foundation, and honor Celeste's memory in the process, I'll be happy. But him…"

I pointed at Jesus. "Him I want to kill, for personal reasons."

Jesus was shifting this way and that in his chair. He'd turned a nasty gray color and had started sweating. Now he burst out, "*Hijo de puta, pendejo, cabrón!*"

Joaquin started to laugh again. He was a happy kind of guy.

Jesus stood up, gesturing at me with both hands. "He killed twelve of my men! He destroyed my operation! He is the enemy, Joaquin! Please, stop playin' this crazy game! Let's kill him. Let me kill him, *por favor!*"

Joaquin grinned, from Jesus to me, "*A la muerte*! To the death. A fight to the death! What do you say?"

Jesus' eyes went wide with alarm.

I shrugged. "It'll be short and boring. If you're looking for entertainment, think of something else."

It didn't discourage him. He laughed, clapped his hands and rubbed them together. "*Venga, Jesus!* Here is your chance. I was going to kill you, but prove to me you can solve this problem and maybe I'll give you a second chance."

He was still on his feet. I knew he had a piece under his arm and I was sure he had a knife in one of his pockets. I didn't wait to find out. Joaquin hadn't finished talking and I stood up. I didn't rush. I didn't run. I might have been going to the can. I took two steps toward Jesus. He was frowning. His right hand was twitching. He took half a step back, away from me. My third step brought me up close and I reached behind the back of his neck and gripped the back of his head. He made a kind of, "A-a-ah!" noise and I smashed the heel of my hand into the tip of his chin.

As he went down, I stepped behind him and encircled

his neck with my right arm, tucked tight under his jaw. I squeezed, lifted and twisted, felt the snap of his vertebrae and dropped him on the floor. Less than five seconds.

"I told you, short and boring. Can we get down to business now?"

I returned to my seat. The room was very quiet. I could see Nestor, the chief of security, watching Joaquin. I pulled another Camel from the pack, flipped the Zippo and leaned into the flame. Joaquin was now staring at Nestor, in some kind of silent communication. He blinked, took a deep breath and turned to the guys by the door, pointing at Jesus' slumped, staring body.

"*Llévenselo, con los demás.*"

They picked him up between them and carried him out. When the door closed I said, "So that narrows your options."

He was looking at Nestor again, like he was evaluating him, or what he thought. "It does. You know? You're a very smart guy, Lacklan. What you've done?" He shook his head. "Fantastic. You are the best of the best of the best. No doubt. But..." Now he nodded. "Maybe, maybe you are too smart. Is that possible? Is it possible you are too smart?"

"I'm pretty sure you're about to tell me it is, and I am."

"You're a billionaire. You know the biggest criminal racket in Mexico, apart from dope?"

I nodded. "Kidnapping."

"And yet, here you are. Alone." He laughed. "What do you think I am going to do now?"

"I think you're going to introduce me to your mother."

"What?"

I stood. I saw Nestor flinch, but ignored him and made

my way to the sideboard, where I poured myself another whiskey. I turned to face him, rested my ass against the credenza and took a drag from my cigarette. As I let out the smoke, I said:

"General Francisco Ochoa." He went very still. I went on, "Raul Ochoa, Minister for Mines and Energy in Brazil, Narciso Terry, Minister for Scientific Development in Argentina, Felipe Gonzalez, the governor of the Free and Sovereign State of Sinaloa, Samuel Zapata, nicknamed '*El Vampiro*' because he is said to drink human blood, and of course, as I said to begin with, General Francisco Ochoa. All five murdered within a few days of each other, end of June, early July. Gonzalez, Zapata and Ochoa, all at Zapata's place, up in the hills above Cosalá."[1]

"How can you know about that?"

I shrugged. "Maybe I'm too smart. Or maybe I killed them."

"You are bluffing."

"Somebody had to do it. And you said yourself, I am the best of the best of the best. It was a massacre. The whole place was blown to hell. Zapata and Gonzalez were killed in the dining room. Ochoa was killed outside, stabbed in the heart with his own knife, with his windpipe broken. All his men were around him, some shot, some run down by a truck. And I am one of the few people alive who knows what was in that lab. I'm figuring your mother knew the lab existed, but she wasn't one of the club. So she doesn't know what they were doing in that lab." I smiled. "But she'd sure like to."

---

1. See *The Omicron Kill*

I looked at Nestor. Joaquin followed my gaze. Nestor gave his head a small shake. "*Mátelo, Jefe. Mátelo ya.*"

He was telling him to kill me. He was wise, but he was also too late. Joaquin was suddenly out of his depth. Nestor could not guide him—or at least that was what Joaquin thought. The only person who knew the waters where I had taken him was me. I flicked ash into an ashtray while he stared at the floor and bit his lip. I said, "You need to call Sandra. You need to tell her what you've just heard. She needs to know about this."

He pointed at Nestor. "Give him your weapons, and your cell."

I shook my head. "No. I told you, we play nice. I'm cooperating with you as a friend. Don't set yourself up as my enemy." I gave a small laugh. "I helped Jesus. Instead of being grateful, he tried to kill me. For about half an hour, he controlled south Tucson. Now he's dead. I'm here to help you, Joaquin. Don't make the same mistake Jesus made. Call Sandra. See what she says."

He pulled out his phone, stared at me a moment, then dialed.

FIFTEEN

It had to go one of two ways, and Murphy's Law dictated that it would go the worst of those two ways. It did. He paced the room, talking too fast for me to follow. Halfway through his conversation, there was a tap at the door and his two goons came in. One of them mouthed to him that the shipment had arrived, then they took up their positions by the door again. After ten more minutes of talking, Joaquin said several times, "*Si, Mamita, si, claro que si, nos vemos ya, chao!*" and hung up.

He put his phone in his pocket and said, "You're coming to Mexico."

I gave a snort of a laugh. "My passport is at my hotel, and besides, I have my manicurist tomorrow at nine."

"I am not asking, Lacklan. You won't need your passport, and this is not a joke. You are coming to Mexico tonight. You are in deep shit."

"Am I supposed to be afraid now?"

"You should be."

"Did the shipment arrive?"

"Questions! Always the questions!"

"If you're taking me to Mexico to kill me, what difference does it make? And if you're not, what difference does it make?"

"Yeah, it arrived!"

"You've got a problem, then. You have a hundred kilos of dope and no distribution network. That is a hell of a big stash with nowhere to go. You're going to have to sit on it until you get a network set up. You'd better hide it in one of your barns, or the stables."

He was starting to get mad, but tried to control it. "I'm not expecting a visit from the DEA anytime soon. Thanks for your concern. Now, do me a favor, will you? Just shut up for a while. You hungry?"

"I could eat."

He turned to the two guys and rattled something at them. I caught the word hamburgers and stables. I figured he'd been told to go make some hamburgers, and to stash the dope in the stables. Joaquin dropped into his chair. I observed him from where I was standing. He looked rattled and an instinct told me he was scared of his mother. That didn't surprise me. Anyone in their right mind would be scared of his mother.

He ran his fingers through his hair, sighed and smiled like a snake. "Who do you work for?"

"Myself."

"That don't make any sense. Don't lie to me or things start to get ugly."

"Don't threaten me, Joaquin. I work for myself. I don't

need to work for anybody. When my father died, I made him a promise."

"What kind of promise?"

"That I would go after his enemies and kill them. Those five names I gave you were the last of his enemies. This place occupied all the time?"

He screwed up his face, like my explanation had a bad smell. He spoke irritably. "No, not all the time! Your father had enemies in the cartel? I never heard about your father till I checked up on you."

"Raul Ochoa and Narciso Terry were not part of the Cartel, were they? His enemies were part of a…" I thought about it for a moment, then shrugged. "Part of a syndicate. They were involved in international finance and business. He was a part of that syndicate too. Ever heard of the Bilderberg Group?"

"Sure."

"Well, it was a bit like that. He was a big shot in the syndicate, but he made enemies along the way, and that cost him his life. When he died, I made him that promise."

"It sounds like the worst kind of Mexican *telenovela*."

I snorted amusement. "And a female drugs lord called the Queen of the Ocean doesn't? But they both happen to be true."

"OK, so let's say I believe this story, what the hell are you doing in Tucson? You killed these guys in Mexico over a month ago, you live in Weston, Massachusetts, but you turn up in Tucson massacring my distribution network. What are you doing here?"

"I told you, I'm drifting."

He raised an eyebrow.

I sighed and made my way back to my chair. There I sat. "I was ten years in special ops, Iraq, Afghanistan, Colombia, Mexico, various parts of Africa. I quit because I was tired of killing and I wanted to settle. But I didn't like my father and I didn't like his billionaire way of life. So I went to Wyoming and set myself up in a small house with a mechanic's workshop. Then my father died, and I have spent the last two years honoring his dying wish. Mexico was the last job. I was done, but I didn't want to go home. So I was drifting, and while I was drifting I met Celeste, a few seconds before she died."

He puffed out his cheeks and blew, then shook his head. "It just sounds so much like bullshit, man."

I gave a small laugh. "I don't give a damn if you believe me or not, Joaquin. If I did, I'd come up with a more credible story."

He frowned, a little confused. "I like you, *güey*. If it were up to me, I'd like us to work together, do that crazy symbiotic project of yours. But my mother is going to want to torture you and kill you. You better start caring whether she believes you or not, man."

"I appreciate the sentiment. But it is what it is. That's what happened and that's why I'm here."

The door opened and the guard came in with a silver tray bearing two hamburgers in buns, a jar of mayonnaise and a bottle of ketchup. We ate in silence, then lit up and he poured us another shot of whiskey.

I was surprised when a half hour later I heard the drone of an approaching plane. I frowned at him, thinking. The plane had covered only about two hundred miles. I said, "Baja?"

He nodded. "San Felipe." He stood. "Come on, let's go."

It was a cold night. The desert nights can be very cold, even in summer in Arizona. We clambered back into the Range Rover, Nestor took the wheel and we followed a track through the dark, a quarter of a mile south, where they had a basic airfield covering maybe half a mile of desert. We sat in the truck and watched the lights approach from the west, winking as they grew closer. Then they banked and came head on, dropping ever closer to the ground as they approached. Next thing, a twin prop King Air 350 came into view and hit the tarmac amid a squeal of tires, slowing with a roar of engines and settling to taxi gently to where we were waiting.

We climbed down from the Range Rover and as we made our way across the sand toward the strip, Nestor turned the truck around and drove away, the rear red lights dwindling into the dark. The door opened in the fuselage and a big guy in a suit leaned out. He looked at me with hostile eyes but didn't say anything, then looked over at Joaquin and raised a hand.

I climbed aboard, with Joaquin behind me. The pilot exchanged some words with him and I gathered that if he needed them, they were just up front, and they were armed. I smiled as I took my seat across the highly polished mahogany table from him. "I'd have to be some kind of stupid to start a shoot out at thirty-five thousand feet. Tell him he can relax."

He didn't answer. We took off and within seconds we were over the border and into Mexican airspace. We turned west and began to climb, but nowhere near thirty-five thousand feet. We stayed comparatively low, and in little more than half an hour we were crossing the Gulf of California, coming in to land at the tiny *Aeropuerto Internacional de San Felipe*. At that time of night it was empty, like a weird, floodlit ghost airport.

We climbed down from the plane and crossed the tarmac on foot. The cop on duty at customs looked sleepy, but when he saw us he smiled, actually bowed to Joaquin and welcomed him home. Nobody checked our passports or our baggage.

Arrivals and departures was all one hall, and the only guy in it also bowed to Joaquin and told him he had the car waiting outside. We followed him out.

Outside, there was a tangy sea breeze blowing in off the Gulf. Over to the north I could see the glow of the town lights under the translucent turquoise sky. The guy who'd come to meet us led the way across the parking lot to a dark blue Audi A8. Joaquin, who'd hardly spoken since we'd had our burgers, said, "Ride up front, please."

When mobsters tell you to ride up front, it's a bad sign. It means they don't trust you, and they are probably taking you on a drive you don't want to take to a place you don't want to go. On this occasion, I didn't think they'd fly me all the way to Mexico just to kill me in the front seat of an Audi. I figured they'd want to get some information from me first. But still, the mood had changed since he told me I was a great *güey*.

I climbed in and we took off toward the coast and Sandra Dorado Beltran's house; the palace of the Queen of the Ocean. We followed the airport road down to the beach, though there was nothing to see in the darkness but the occasional winking light in the distance. After a couple of miles or so we turned left, and now, out the passenger's window, I could see the ocean, with the moon just rising in the east, casting fractured, liquid reflections over the bay. We continued north then, following the curve of the coast, past the port and finally after five or six miles, into the town of San Felipe. It looked like a nice, holiday resort town.

At this time of night there were still people out and about, there were small fish restaurants and cocktail bars, not East Coast style, but relaxed, with sand floors and thatched roofs. It was hard to tell from a passing car, but the people I saw didn't look as though they were afraid for their lives. I didn't see a lot of cops; neither did I see the tell-tail signs of drug lords, enforcers or protection rackets. It looked like a holiday town, having fun.

"Not what you expected?" It was Joaquin's voice from the back of the car.

"It hasn't got all the signs of fear and despair you usually find in towns controlled by your people. So no, not really."

His voice was even when he answered. "That's because we don't control it. She lives here, but very few people know that. She has her staff and her bodyguards, but little else. Her operations are north, at the border in Tijuana, Tecate and Mexicali, and San Luis on the Colorado. Also south, across the water in Sinaloa. There you will see fear and some desperation, mainly from the cops. This place is nice, it's a nice place to live."

We drove on, bearing east at the main roundabout, and into the suburbs for another couple of miles. We passed a small gas station on the right and then slowed to turn onto a road that seemed to be little more than the sand between two sets of fences. We followed this track out of town, away from the lights and the nightlife, and darkness closed in again. We were once more in the desert. Finally we came to a track on the left that led to a steel gate in a white wall, easily fifteen feet high. Above it I could make out the silhouettes of palm trees against the sky, growing lighter now with a rising moon. The driver pressed a button on his key ring and the big gate rolled back.

Inside, spotlights illuminated an asphalt road through elaborate lawns, orange orchards, palms and eucalyptus groves, to a Greco-Roman fountain showing Poseidon spewing water from his mouth among a pod of dolphins, all leaping around him. Just beyond the fountain, which should have been grotesque but somehow wasn't, stood a building that was more Renaissance palace than house. It was fronted by two narrow gardens of orange trees and jasmine bushes, through which polished granite steps rose to double oak doors that stood open onto an internal patio.

We climbed out of the car and Joaquin led the way up the steps and through the arch to where a second, smaller and less elaborate fountain, was playing among a plethora of potted plants and flowers. The patio itself was a mosaic, framed by a checkerboard walkway beneath a colonnade of oxblood and blue alternating marble columns.

An ornate wooden staircase rose from one side of the patio to a galleried landing above, which was also hung with potted flowers. Our driver disappeared and Joaquin led me across the patio and through a wooden door set with stained glass into a large drawing room. The furniture was eclectic, ranging from late sixteenth century to the early twentieth, though there seemed to be nothing later than the 1930s. The fireplace was massive and, like the house, seemed to be

Renaissance. Three huge logs were burning in the grate, and ranged around the fire there were two chesterfield armchairs and a sofa. There were Llaique lamps on the tables, and a credenza that looked like an authentic Spanish medieval piece. On it there was a silver tray with cut glass decanters and glasses. Joaquin went to it and poured two measures of whiskey, then rang a brass bell. He brought over the two drinks and handed me one.

"A nightcap."

"Thanks."

I took the glass and drank. Like the furniture, it was superb.

"My mother is in bed at this time. Celestino, our butler, will show you to your room. We'll all meet and talk over breakfast, in the back garden. Just ring the bell in your room and Celestino, or one of the maids, will show you where it is."

"This place... It's extraordinary. It looks authentic."

"It was a monastery, then converted to a convent when women started to come over. It's sixteenth century. Initially Franciscan, then Benedictine nuns. In the nineteenth century it fell into disuse, until my mother bought it, in 1999, and began to restore it. She is a remarkable woman, Lacklan. You will meet her tomorrow. I hope you will be friends."

There was an edge of menace to his voice, but he smiled. I nodded and drained my glass. There was a knock at the door and it opened to admit a man who looked old enough to have been around when the monastery was originally built. Joaquin addressed him in English.

"Show Captain Walker to the Mother Superior suite,

Celestino." Then he glanced at me. "Is eight thirty too early for breakfast?"

"Eight thirty will be fine."

"Call Captain Walker at eight, tomorrow, and show him to the breakfast garden."

Celestino bowed and answered in accented English. "Of course, Don Joaquin. Captain, will you follow me?"

He led me back to the patio with the fountain and the flowers, and up the ornate, wooden staircase to the galleried landing. I followed him around the dogleg, past three heavy oak doors to the far end, where he unlocked a fourth door and admitted me to a high-ceilinged room with heavy wooden rafters and a massive four-poster bed. A fire was burning in a marble fireplace, heavy burgundy drapes were drawn across a window and, to the right of the door, there was an en suite bathroom with a modern shower cubicle and a marble sink that was big enough to have a bath in.

"You will be requiring anything more, Captain?"

I shook my head, then pointed to the door. "Just the key, on the inside."

He gave a small bow and handed me the heavy, iron key.

"Thank you, Celestino, that will be all."

He left and I locked the door behind him. Then I crossed the room and pulled back the drapes. The moon was above the horizon now and casting its eerie, turquoise glow over the ragged peaks to the north of San Felipe, making the white sand glow as though with a light of its own. The walls, and the windowsill, were about three feet thick and I estimated my height above the ground at somewhere between twenty and thirty feet. I opened the window to let in the sea air and went to sit on the bed. There I checked my cell. The signal was good. I switched it off and pulled the second burner I'd bought out of my pocket. I called America's Best Value Inn in Tucson and asked to be put through to my room. The phone rang for a full minute before it cut out. I showered and tried the phone again but Luz wasn't answering. I went to bed.

SIXTEEN

I was up at six and spent an hour and a half training in my room. At seven thirty I showered and dressed and at eight I allowed Celestino to lead me down to the patio garden at the back of the house where a table had been set, near a cluster of palm trees, with a white damask linen tablecloth, a silver coffee pot, a butter dish and three different jam pots with three different kinds of jam. There were four men in suits, with wayfarer sunglasses, standing at a discreet distance from the table, with their hands clasped in front of their bellies, staring at nothing in particular a few inches in front of their noses. There were also a couple of pretty maids in pretty French maid uniforms standing by.

Sitting at the table was Joaquin, and across from him a woman who, in her mid forties, looked like a youthful thirty-five. To say she was beautiful would be to miss the point. Her features were good—better than good—and her figure was superb; but much more than that, she was fascinating.

There was a restrained passion about her, and a humor and intelligence in her eyes, that was magnetic.

Joaquin saw me approaching behind Celestino, wiped his mouth with his white damask napkin and stood, smiling. It must have been a signal, because Celestino stopped, stood aside, gave a small bow and left. The woman I assumed was Sandra watched me arrive as she sipped coffee. Joaquin reached for my hand and shook it. It was all very civilized.

"Good morning, Lacklan. I hope you slept comfortably. Please, allow me to introduce my mother, Sandra Dorado Beltran, and, Mama, this is Captain Lacklan Walker, whom I have told you about."

I stepped over to her and she reached out her hand, palm down, so I had to bow over it and kiss it. I was tempted to turn it around and shake it, but I'd had enough conditioning from my own mother to make me hold the fingertips and give a small bow.

"Mrs. Dorado…"

When she spoke, her accent startled me. It was more French than Spanish.

"Please, call me Sandra, I intend to call you Lacklan." She snapped her fingers and one of the maids approached. "What will you have? Bacon and eggs? Pancakes? How do you breakfast?"

"Just some rye toast and coffee." The girl poured my coffee and withdrew to get the toast. I smiled at Joaquin. "This is a pleasant surprise, Joaquin. I was expecting to be tortured, but this is very civilized. I feel almost like James Bond."

His smile was thin and said he wasn't amused, but Sandra burst out laughing, a high-pitched laugh that sounded almost like a parrot. She clasped her hands in front of her chest, as though she were praying, and threw back her head. When she'd finished, she shook her head and offered me a mischievous smile. "We don't do that kind of thing here, Lacklan."

"Where do you do it, Sandra?"

"Further south."

"So if you decide to take me to Cosalá, I should be worried."

She smiled at her toast as she spread orange marmalade on it. "You are very provocative, and if you're scared, you hide it well. I like that. One meets so few real men these days." She bit into her toast with very white teeth and observed me while she chewed. "What I am hoping for, Lacklan, is that it will not be necessary to go to extreme measures, and we can reach some kind of working understanding."

"Your English is excellent."

She arched an extremely elegant eyebrow. "That is not an answer."

"I wasn't aware you had asked me a question, Sandra."

She leaned forward and there was hunger in her eyes. "It was more an invitation to concur with me."

"How could I possibly resist an invitation to concur with you?" She giggled and Joaquin cleared his throat. I ignored him and asked, "What kind of working understanding are we looking at?"

She sat back and sipped her coffee. As she set down the cup, she licked her lips. "Joaquin tells me you want to set up a foundation in honor of Celeste Martinez. I have to say, looking at you, I am a little skeptical. It seems almost contradictory in a man like you. You don't strike me as the sentimental type."

I smiled and leaned toward her. "The past and present wilt, I have filled them, emptied them, and proceed to fill my next fold of the future. Listener up there! what have you to confide to me? Look in my face while I snuff the sidle of evening, Talk honestly, no one else hears you, and I stay only a minute longer. Do I contradict myself? Very well then I contradict myself, I am large, I contain multitudes."

She raised her eyebrows high. "My, a skilled killer and erudite too, Walt Whitman, no less. I didn't think anybody quoted him anymore."

The girl came with my toast and I set about buttering it and spooning marmalade on my plate as though she had not spoken. After a moment, she said:

"Let us assume that I agreed to fund your foundation…"

"It would be a cooperative venture. I would put half the money."

"All right, I put the other half. What do I get in return?"

I bit into the toast and chewed, studying her face. It was classically beautiful: oval, with perfect, olive skin, arched eyebrows and long, oval eyes. The lashes were long too, thick and black, the iris was dark, chestnut brown. Her lips were full and well-formed. Her hair, dense and black, was pulled back in a bun.

"It seems to me," I said, "that you get three distinct advantages in return, especially if you set up whoever runs the organization in a private business of his own. You get two legal, functioning entities through which you can launder very substantial amounts of money, you acquire the cloak of respectability within Arizona society, and, if you are smart, which I have no doubt you are, you get the opportunity to get one of your own—whoever heads up the foundation—elected into public office. That right there is a passport to a great deal of power."

"What is to stop me from doing this anyway? Why do I need you?"

I shrugged. In the eucalyptus tree, a house finch had started to sing. "You don't," I said, looking for the finch. "You could go right ahead." I turned and smiled at her.

Joaquin broke in then. "But, Mamita, what he is thinking and not saying, is that if you or I approach the state authorities, or the federal government, for permission to set up a charitable foundation, our names will bring up red flags. They will also want to know what interest we have in Celeste Martinez. Once they start looking, it won't take them long to connect Celeste to Jesus and Jesus to the Rancho Grande, and a little more digging will show that the Rancho Grande belongs to us."

I turned my smile on him and nodded.

He went on: "But Captain Lacklan Walker, an unsung hero of Iraq and Afghanistan, who held Celeste's hand while she died, whose father was a pillar of Boston society, would have no such difficulties."

She nodded. "Good, so there is an advantage for me in helping to set up your foundation and installing one of my men as the director. The advantage to you is in having the foundation set up and the satisfaction of knowing that drug money is being used to strike against the drugs trade. You also assume, presumably, that if we set this thing up with you, we won't kill you."

"That would seem reasonable."

"But…" She sat back in her chair, screwed up her napkin and dumped it on the table. "I have to say, it still seems to me that you get the better deal. You are, after all, asking me to commit slow suicide. If the foundation is successful, I lose my grass roots support, witnesses start to inform, protection rackets start to collapse, clubs get raided… I eventually get forced out of Tucson. And worse still, if it is *not* successful, you are still alive, a powerful, influential man who can be invaluable to the FBI in hunting us down and eliminating us. You might even do it yourself. It seems to me that long term, I lose both ways."

"There is always the middle way, Sandra. Not too successful, not too much of a failure, but something in between. Bumbling along like that, we could go on forever, a bit like Jehovah and Satan, I save a few souls, you sell your coke and your heroin to a few of the damned."

She narrowed her eyes. "You are playing me, Lacklan. You are not even trying to hide it. What do you really want?"

I shook my head. "That is not the issue here, Sandra. You're asking me that because you're curious." I turned and gestured at Joaquin. "Your son wants to know the same thing, not because he is curious, but because he is worried. He can't work out whether I am lying, telling the truth, bluffing or extremely dangerous." I smiled at him. "He is inclined to believe the latter, but…" I pointed at the four men surrounding us. "*You* hold all the aces. You have let me keep my weapon as a courtesy, while we negotiate, but you both know that you have me entirely at your mercy. So the real question is, what do *you* want? You tell me what you want, and then I'll tell you what I want in exchange. If it's acceptable, we have a deal. If it isn't, you'll have to torture and kill me."

It was Joaquin who answered. "I'll tell you what I want. I want to work with you. I think you would be a superb asset, but I don't know that I could ever trust you."

I shook my head. "If I joined your organization, I would take over." I turned to Sandra and took my time giving her a smile. "Perhaps we should marry, like the kings and queens in the middle ages."

She laughed. "Maybe we should, at that. But let me tell you what I want."

I didn't let her. "No. I'll tell you. You want to know what *El Vampiro* was doing with Ochoa and Gonzales at the lab they had set up at the *Castillo* in Cosalá[1]."

Her face became serious. Even her voice changed. It became flat and stopped being flirtatious and playful.

"All right, yes, that is what I want. But I want more than that. I want to know the real reason you killed them. I want to know why you killed Raul Rocha and Narciso Terry. And I want to know why you are here."

"I explained that to your son."

"You told him a lot of *connerie!* I do not buy this Sir Lancelot image that you are trying to project. The dying promise to your father, the dying promise to Celeste Martinez. *Mais bon sang!* Are you always promising things to the dead?"

The question shook me. Was I? Was that my search for redemption? Eternally making promises to the dead, while neglecting the living? It dawned on me that I was more

---

1. See *The Omicron Kill*

committed to my dead father and Celeste than I was to Marni, the woman I professed to be in love with, and Abi, the woman I had married. Sandra's eyes narrowed. I had kept my face a mask of indifference, but her intuition told her she had struck a nerve.

I gave my head a small twist to the side. "Perhaps you're right."

"Rocha and Terry were friends of Ochoa and Gonzalez. Ochoa and Gonzalez were friends of Zapata, *El Vampiro*, what did they have going on?"

"If I told you, you wouldn't believe me."

"You told Joaquin they were part of some kind of secret group, like..." She frowned.

I said, "The Bilderberg Group."

"What is that? I Googled it, it was like some kind of crazy conspiracy theory."

"The history of the world is the history of successful conspiracies, from the kidnapping of Helen by Paris, through the murder of Julius Caesar to the dividing up of Europe by Roosevelt, Churchill and Stalin. When they are secret, they are crazy conspiracy theories, when they are successful, they become history."

She made a face.

I said, "Tell me something, how many U.S. judges, DAs and Congressmen have you got on your payroll?" She smiled. I smiled back. "Crazy conspiracy theory. Let me ask you something else. If you were a multibillionaire, so rich that where you put your money affected the world stock markets, would you get together with your equally rich pals and discuss how to manipulate world markets to your mutual benefit?"

"Of course."

"And if one of your pals happened to be a U.S. President, and you both owned shares in the military industrial complex, do you think an unusually high number of wars might occur in the Middle East...?"

"OK, you made your point, Lacklan. So these associates of your father were also associates of Rocha, Terry, Ochoa and Gonzalez?"

"And Zapata."

"But he was a cartel boss, not a politician or an international financier!"

I sighed. "There were twenty-four members of this group. They were a varied bunch. In Europe they were mainly politicians. In the U.S.A. they were mainly billionaires in finance, IT and the film industry. In Latin America, there were a couple of politicians, but predominantly they were in the Sinaloa drugs trade."

She looked momentarily irritated. "There is more to Latin America than drugs, Lacklan."

"You're preaching to the choir, sister. But the real power here is in heroin and cocaine. You know that as well as I do. That's why we're here having this conversation."

"So why did you want them dead? Also, what was *El Vampiro* making in Cosalá?"

I reached over and picked up the coffee pot. I offered her and Joaquin more coffee. They both shook their heads, watching me with hostile eyes. I refilled my cup and sighed. "You're hoping I'm going to tell you that it was something that is going to boost your drugs sales, or improve your smuggling techniques, or that it is some kind of dope that is a hundred percent more addictive that heroin. But it is none of those things, and when I tell you what it was, you won't believe me. I didn't believe it myself when I broke in and saw it." I took a deep breath. "As to why I killed them…" I shrugged. "My father was a ruthless son of a bitch. You would have liked him. He was your kind of man. But later in life, he began to hate what he had become. He came to hate the organization and started looking for ways to hurt them and bring them down. That got him shot, and while he was in hospital, dying, I promised him I would finish the job. What I told you is true. I am not a Sir Lancelot, but I hated the organization and everything it stood for as much as he did, or more."

Joaquin said, "You're talking in the past tense."

"The organization is finished. The American branch had been destroyed. The European branch had been destroyed. The South American branch was pretty much all that was left of it. When I killed Ochoa, Gonzalez and Zapata, I killed Omega."

I watched her face for a flicker of recognition when I mentioned the name. There was none. I looked at Joaquin. He was watching his mother.

She ran her finger slowly along the edge of the table. I noticed she had very long, red fingernails. Her voice was strained, as though she were fighting to keep it under control. Joaquin was watching her carefully. "What do I have to do, Lacklan, to make you tell me what *El Vampiro* was doing in Cosalá?"

I was quiet for a long moment, looking at her hand, her finger with its red nail resting on the white cloth. I wondered how many people she had killed, how many with her own hands. Finally I looked up at her face and smiled and said, "Probably marry me."

SEVENTEEN

"I'm running out of patience, Lacklan,"

I saw her eyes flick at the guy in the suit who was standing opposite her. I saw his chin rise slightly and his back straighten.

"I wouldn't do that, Sandra. If it goes down here this morning, you'll be the first to die, then Joaquin, then, maybe, me."

"Are you threatening me, Lacklan?" Her voice was dangerous.

I held her eye and answered her with no inflection at all. "Yes."

Joaquin stood and walked away from the table, stood staring at the tall, jagged hills that lay between the house and the sea. He turned and walked back. "Why are you playing this game? What do you hope to achieve?"

I watched him till he'd finished speaking, then turned to Sandra as though he wasn't there. "Why is it such a crazy idea? What are you worth, financially? A couple of billion?

More? I don't know what I'm worth right now, but it has to be that at least. My affairs are all legitimate, but the people my father employed to run his affairs were all crooks. They are experts in laundering. Can you imagine the kind of power we would wield between us? We would control the biggest crime syndicate in human history, plus a vast swath of the financial markets and private enterprises. There isn't a judge, a senator, a president on the planet we could not buy, blackmail or assassinate."

She was frowning at me like her brain hurt. "You're serious..."

I turned to Joaquin. "Why am I playing this game? What do I hope to achieve? I'll tell you. I'm *bored!* I've been to the limit, I've gone past it. I've been to hell and back again. I've seen the worst that human beings are capable of, I've inherited a fortune most people wouldn't even dream about, and I'm still only in my thirties. What's left?" I turned back to Sandra. "I fell in love with a genius who wanted to save the world. She didn't satisfy. I married Mother Earth. She made the best apple pie this side of the Elysian Fields, but she didn't satisfy. Maybe I was looking in the wrong place. You're bad, you're cruel, you're a different kind of genius. You're also the most beautiful, fascinating woman I have ever met. And you are also frustrated, because you have never met a man who could match you. Until now."

Her mouth had actually sagged. She stared at her son. She was smiling, but the smile was hard to read. She said, "*Est-il sérieux?*"

He shrugged and shook his head. She turned to me. "What about this..." She looked back at her son and snapped her fingers a few times.

He said, "Luz, Luz Santos. The girl you were prepared to die for."

"What about her? She got away. She's safe now."

Sandra was leaning forward, frowning, squinting, shaking her head. "Are you crazy or just desperate? What about your feelings for that girl?"

I laughed. I was genuinely amused. "I have no feelings for Luz! She's a sweet kid, but outside the bedroom she has nothing to offer me. She still believes that salvation lies in devotion to God."

Her voice was close to frantic. It reminded me of something a Zen teacher once told me, that the absolute imperative for the human mind is to find meaning. If our minds cannot find meaning, they spiral into despair and ultimately we seek our own destruction. She half-shouted at me, "Then *why?* Why would you do everything you did...?"

I smiled. "You still need to ask?"

"*Enough games!*"

"You asked me at the beginning what I want. I asked you the same question. OK, then here it is: you want the secret of what *El Vampiro* was doing at Cosalá. I want you."

Her voice was a whisper. "*Dios...*"

Joaquin snapped, "Fine!" She looked at him, startled. He shrugged and spread his hands. "Let's see if it's true."

Alarm bells went off in my head. After a moment she smiled, holding her son's eye. "And if it is?"

"That's up to you, Mami. *Si dice la verdad, lo cierto, es un buen partido.*"

"What's that in English, guys?"

She was still smiling when she turned to me with hooded

eyes. "He says that if you're telling the truth, you're a good match."

"What do you think?"

"I think you're a crazy *fils de pute*, but if you're telling the truth, I think you're a good match."

Joaquin raised an eyebrow at me. "Excuse my mother's French, they shipped her off to the *Institut Villa Pierrefeu* in Switzerland when she was sixteen, to learn to be a lady."

"Did it work?"

She stood. "Let's find out."

She began to walk. She was in a light, turquoise summer dress that swung nicely with her hips. I followed her around the side of the house, where a kitchen garden and a walled orchard stood a short distance from the main building, and opposite, against the wall, a flight of stone steps led down to a cellar. My feelings of misgiving increased. Somehow I was guessing there was more than just wine down there.

Joaquin was just behind us and with him was the guy in the suit who had been standing opposite Sandra at breakfast. She now stopped and watched him approach, trot down the stairs and unlock the old, wooden door. He pushed it open, reached inside and flipped on the light. Then he stood aside.

Sandra went ahead, Joaquin was just behind her and I followed. The big, silent goon followed me. I was aware that I still had the Maxim 9, my Sig and my knife. Nobody had made the slightest attempt to remove them. I was as confused about that as Sandra and Joaquin were confused about what I was doing. All I could think was that they half-bought my story about the foundation, were impressed by my wealth and wanted to keep me on side in case I could be useful. But even if that was true, I was walking a perilously fine line: they must still have some kind of ace up their sleeve to allow me to remain armed, knowing what I had done so far.

We descended a second flight of gray, granite steps to a short, flagged passageway. Sandra spoke over her shoulder as she walked. "They used to make wine here at the monastery, and it was stored and matured in this cellar."

Another door, not locked, led into a vast chamber that was cool and quiet, and had the feel and resonance of a small cathedral. It was a honeycomb of high arches and tall columns that supported the floor above, and created echoing caverns below, dimly lit by low wattage bulbs suspended from the ceiling. By their limpid light, among the great arches, I saw pyramids of old barrels, ten and twelve feet high, many of them blackened, rotting and decaying. Her voice reverberated among the shadowy arches: "It is on my bucket list to buy a vineyard and fill this place with new, Californian oak barrels to mature the wine. *Bodegas Reina del Mar*. It has a good ring, hasn't it?"

"Sounds like a worthy project."

She slowed and linked her arm through mine as we walked. Joaquin was laughing softly. She said, "Do you like wine? Are you knowledgeable? Perhaps we could do it together."

"That would be fun, if you don't have me tortured and dismembered first."

"Well." She smiled as we turned a corner. "Let's get this little doubt out of the way, and maybe we can discuss things in more detail over dinner."

We came to a wooden door in the stone wall. There was

no lock, only a deadbolt. She slid it back and pushed open the door.

I didn't flinch because I was half expecting it. Instead I sighed and shook my head. Luz was sitting on a bare mattress on the floor. She had bruises on her arms and wrists and her dress, the one she had been wearing the night before, had been torn. Beside her there was a plastic pitcher of water and a dirty, pink plastic plate and spoon. Her jaw had dropped and her eyes, eloquent of horror and betrayal, were wide. Her expression was one of the most appalling things I had ever had to look at. I forced anger into my own face and snapped.

"What the hell are you doing here, Luz?"

"*You?* You are *with* them?"

I turned to Joaquin. "Why the hell is she here? She has nothing to do with this. I am not happy about this at all. I sent her home. What the fuck are you playing at?"

Sandra let go my arm and stepped back. "You look upset."

I turned on her, allowed the hot anger in my belly to twist my face, and shouted, "*Of course I'm upset! I'm furious! This girl was supposed to live! I need her for the foundation! Don't you ever fucking listen?*"

The bodyguard stepped forward, squaring his shoulders, reaching for his piece. I ignored him and went on shouting at Sandra. "*She was essential for the foundation! She was Celeste's friend! It was a perfectly integrated plan! You stupid, incompetent fucking idiots! Now she will have to die! It ruins the whole damned plan! She was supposed to live!*"

I turned to Luz. She was fighting back the tears, shaking her head. "I trusted you. How can you do this...?"

"*I gave you precise instructions! What did you do?*"

"They came to your room! They took me! I think they followed me. Please don't kill me..."

Joaquin spoke; his voice was even, cool: "Jesus told us you were obsessed with her. When you sent her away, we had a car waiting and followed where she went, then I had her brought here."

I stared at him a moment, then at Sandra with contempt all over my face. "This ruins everything. *Everything!*" I sighed noisily. "I'm sorry. You weren't to know." I pointed at the bodyguard. "But you do not touch her. *No tocar!* She is mine, you understand? *Comprende?*"

He looked from me to Sandra. I turned to her. "I do not want this girl touched. She is mine. *I* will deal with her tonight, or tomorrow. I need to think this through." I allowed irritation to edge my voice with anger. "It's not your fault, but your trying to be smart has completely fucked up my plan. You don't *think!*" I put my fingertips to my forehead. "You are so focused on those two little things you know how to do, traffic dope and kill people! You can't see anything else. Use your fucking imagination from time to time!"

I turned and stood in front of Sandra, close, so we were almost touching, leaning in toward her. "Can you imagine the weight they would carry in public opinion if your guy heading the foundation had Luz by his side? Are you aware of the doors she could have opened as Celeste's best friend, carrying on her cause?" I shook my head. "Get her out of here. I want her locked in a room with a guard. But I want her comfortable and I want her fed." I turned to her. "I'm sorry, Luz. I'll see what I can do..."

I turned, walked back through the cellar and climbed the steps out into the late morning sunshine. There I stopped, with my hands on my hips, biting my lip and staring at the wall of the kitchen orchard. Sandra and Joaquin followed in silence with the bodyguard. He stayed by the steps and they joined me. I stared at her, and then at Joaquin.

"That was a really stupid thing you did. I guess you thought you were being smart, and you'd test me, but you had quicker and easier methods at your disposal. She's a poor, sweet kid who could have been *really* useful heading the foundation. Now she'll have to die."

Sandra raised a hand, staring down at the ground, thinking. After a moment she said, "We can bribe her, blackmail her. We can still use her."

It was a trap and not a very subtle one. I made like I was thinking about it, then shook my head. "No, she has too much integrity. It's too risky. She has to die. It's OK, we can find another way around it. But I don't want her suffering. Make her comfortable. We'll take her out tomorrow, pretend we're sending her back to Tucson. I'll do it. In the desert. I'll make it quick. You can come along to confirm the kill."

She glanced at Joaquin and suppressed a smile. I raised an eyebrow at her and smiled. "You like that idea?"

She turned to the big guy by the steps and told him to take the girl up to one of the rooms with an en suite bathroom, and lock her in.

I added, "I want a guard on the door at all times."

She translated. He nodded and went back down the steps. Then she placed a hand on my chest. I noticed it was trembling, but didn't know how to interpret that. She had her confirmation that Luz meant nothing to me emotionally, but this was something more, like a repressed excitement. She said:

"Joaquin has to fly to Culiacán. I am going with him to the airport."

I nodded. "You have to discuss my proposal with the *Patron*."

"That's the way it is, *amor*, but I leave you here, *mi casa es tuya*. I just ask you two things: do not leave the grounds of the house, and do not try to see the girl until I come back. If you do, they will kill you. Do this for me and tonight we will discus your plans... our plans."

I managed a smile and nodded. "OK, good. That sounds like a plan."

A noise behind me made me turn. The big bodyguard was climbing the steps, holding Luz by her arm. Her eyes were wild as she stared at me. I gave my head a small shake.

"It's going to be OK, Luz. We'll sort something out."

He led her away toward the back of the house and Joaquin went to follow. He hesitated, looking at his mother. "*Te veo dentro.*"

She nodded. "I'll see you inside."

He left and she came close to me, placed her hands on my shoulders, flicking her eyes over my face, like she was trying to read it, hoping to find something there. When she spoke, her voice was thick, husky.

"If you betray me, I will have them do things to you you cannot imagine. They'll make you sob like a child. I will destroy you, physically, emotionally, spiritually. You won't be even human anymore, but you will still be alive."

I smiled on the right side of my face, where it looks more amused.

"I love it when you talk dirty."

She gave a small snort and went to turn away. I snatched her wrist savagely and yanked her back, crushing her against me with my left arm so it hurt and she could barely breathe. I snarled, an inch from her face.

"How many men have you gutted with a knife, Sandra? How many have you burned with a torch? How many men have you strangled? How many necks have you snapped? How many men have you killed with your own bare hands, baby? It seems to me you do all your hurting and killing second hand. It's different, you know, when you do it yourself." I let go her wrist and took a fistful of her hair in my right hand, pulling her head savagely back, and let my eyes run over her throat. "Be careful with me, Sandra. You come after me, you're liable to get burned."

The knot in her hair came loose in my grip and I let it slip through my fingers until her lips were brushing mine, then I gripped it tight and she whimpered.

"And never, never threaten me again."

Her breath was trembling, her whisper was a rasp in her throat. "Or what?"

I crushed her harder with my left arm and circled her neck with my right hand, pressing my thumb gently against her throat. "There will be consequences."

She swallowed. I let her go and shoved her gently away. She stumbled and I smiled, allowing just enough contempt into my voice. "Get the hell out of here."

She turned away and hurried, with her hair and her dignity in disarray, after her son. I watched her disappear around the back of the house, pulled my pack of Camels from my pocket, shook one loose and poked it in my mouth.

Then I stood a while thinking before I flipped my Zippo and lit up.

I strolled along the path back to the table where we had been having breakfast and found Celestino there with the maids, clearing away the plates and cups. I approached him, flicking ash onto the dusty path.

"Celestino, what is the lady's favorite dish?"

He looked vaguely surprised. "Lobster Thermidor, *señor*, preceded by oysters with Tabasco sauce, and iced Dom Perignon. She is a lover of the sea food."

"Prepare that for her for tonight. I'll have a T-bone steak. Red wine for me, you chose the vintage, Spanish or Chile, I don't mind."

He raised his eyebrows high on his forehead and sighed. "Yes, sir, as you say."

As he turned to go, I said, "And, Celestino? Don't feed the girl tonight. You know the one?"

He looked at me curiously, then nodded. "Yes, sir, I know the one."

I grinned. "I want her hungry tomorrow."

EIGHTEEN

I took a walk around the gardens and found a swimming pool. So I had Celestino send one of the maids up to my bedroom. I told her to go into town and buy me a pair of swimming trunks. While she was at it, I had her measure me for a shirt, a jacket, and a pair of chinos. We had some fun with that and I told her to get me two of everything, plus six pairs of socks and some sensible shoes.

Meantime, I tore the legs off my jeans above the knee and spent the rest of the morning in the pool, taking runs around the grounds of the house and drinking freshly squeezed orange juice in between bouts of training. Around eleven thirty, I noticed a couple of the bodyguards watching, and called them over to the poolside. They didn't know whether to be hostile or not, so they shuffled over and tried to look serious. I smiled at them, like I was really a nice guy.

"You want to train? *Entrenar?* You and me?"

They did a lot of Latin shrugging for a bit, then stripped

off their jackets and took off their shoes and socks and we spent a couple of hours sparring and training. By the end of it, I was Lacklan and they were Emilio and Chavez, and we were pals. When they eventually went off to lunch, tired, hungry and thirsty, they had me down as a nice guy, good, but not *that* good.

I had a light lunch in the shade of the palms by the pool and at one thirty I went into the house and sprinted lightly up the stairs to the galleried landing, then down the passage to the room where Luz had been put. Emilio, one of the guys I'd been sparring with, was sitting by the door, as I had guessed he would be. He was reading a book about lost civilizations. He put it down and stood as I approached, holding up a hand, looking friendly but serious. "You no come here, *Señor Lacklan*."

I shook my head, smiling, but didn't stop. "No, no, I just want to know, *quiere saber*, what time..." I pointed at my watch. "What time you finish. *Que hora tu termina?*"

He smiled. "One tonight... *doce horas...*"

I frowned and puffed out my cheeks, like that was a long shift. He never knew I'd hit him. The first punch was a pile driver to the solar plexus which momentarily paralyzed his heart. The next two, in rapid succession, cracked his sternum and sent him into cardiac arrest. I caught him as he fell, lowered him gently to the floor, face down, and stamped on the back of his neck for good measure.

I found the key to the door in his pocket, opened it and went into the room. Luz was sitting up on her bed. She looked startled.

"What's happening...?"

I put my finger to my lips, grabbed Emilio's ankles and dragged him in. When she saw what I was doing, she scrambled off the bed, onto the far side, and looked in horror at Emilio's body. "What have you done?"

"Shut up. Pull the bedcovers back."

She hesitated a moment, but did as I asked, and, with great difficulty and no help, I bundled the body up onto the bed and covered it. Then I grabbed her wrist. "Come with me, be fast and do not make a noise."

We stepped out of the room and I locked it. I put the key in my pocket and we ran down the passage to the galleried landing over the patio with the fountain. I paused and listened. The only sound was the unsteady splashing of the water. I jerked my head and we ran down the stairs and out the front door. From there we sprinted through the gardens and down the side of the house, back to the stone steps that led to the cellar. I unlocked and opened the door.

"Get in there!"

"*What?*"

"I'll be back for you before midnight."

She clawed at my chest and shoulders. There was sheer panic in her eyes.

"Please don't leave me!"

"Get a grip, Luz, or you'll get us both killed."

"Tell me what's going on, please, Lacklan!"

I took her face in my hands, kissed her mouth and said, "Shut up. Find somewhere to hide. Be silent," and then added with a smile, "I'll be back."

I closed the door, locked it, and returned to the pool. I figured the whole thing had taken five minutes. I sat on the deck chair and closed my eyes, and prayed nobody would go to her room until tonight.

A little later on, the pretty maid in the French uniform came to tell me she had left my new clothes in my room, but she had brought my swimming trunks to the pool, if I would like her to help me try them on.

After that it was a sleepy, drowsy afternoon until five fifteen, when Celestino came and informed me that *La Señora* would be back at eight, but that Don Joaquin would not return until the following day. Would eight fifteen be a suitable time to dine? I told him eight thirty, and we would have cocktails in the drawing room before that, as soon as *La Señora* arrived.

"What is her favorite cocktail, Celestino?"

"She especially like the champagne cocktail. Very cold."

"Then as soon as she arrives, you have one ready for her. I'll have a vodka martini, and Celestino? Make sure it's shaken, not stirred."

He raised an eyebrow, bowed and withdrew. After he had gone, I lay a while, comparing him with Kenny. I decided he wasn't in the same league as Kenny, not at all, but some pretty maids with French maid uniforms might be a definite asset at Weston...

I shelved the thought and went for another swim.

At seven thirty I went upstairs, had a shower and a shave and dressed in my new clothes. I strapped on my holster under my linen jacket and slipped in the Sig. The Maxim I left under the stack of white, fluffy towels in my bathroom, and the Fairbairn & Sykes fighting knife I strapped to my calf, underneath my new pants. Then I went downstairs to the drawing room and rang the bell. Celestino appeared shortly afterwards, looking like he wasn't trying very hard to hide his irritation.

"*Señor?*"

"I'll have a martini, Celestino, while I wait for *La Señora*. Vodka, and shaken."

"Yes, *señor*, no stir, as you say."

He mixed me the drink and I sat in one of the chesterfields, beside the fire, thinking things through.

At five past eight, the door opened and Sandra came in. She paused, holding the door and looking down at me. She'd done more than simply go to the airport. She'd had her hair done and was wearing a violet, satin dress that hugged her body and looked like it never wanted to let go. On her feet she had violet satin shoes with little straps that should have been a criminal offense. I sipped my martini and said, "I just died and went to Mexico."

Then I stood, crossed the room and kissed her. There was a tap at the door and Celestino cleared his throat. I smiled into her eyes and said, "Come in, Celestino."

He crossed the room as she threw her coat and purse on the sofa. He set a silver tray on the credenza, poured her champagne cocktail and brought it to her.

"*Su cóctel de champán, Señora.*"

She took it and gave me that look that said I'd got it right. Celestino gave a small bow.

"Dinner will be served in twenty minutes, *Señora*."

He left and she sipped her drink. "What's for dinner, Captain Walker?"

"For you, oysters and lobster Thermidor, accompanied by extra cold Dom Perignon. For me, oysters and T-bone steak. I trusted Celestino to choose a wine. I figured if he's your butler, he knows something about wine, and rare meat."

She sat by the fire and watched me light a Camel. "Are you trying to seduce me, Lacklan?"

I inhaled and spoke as I released the smoke. "Yes."

"I know you're rich, so it can't be for the money. You know I am dangerous and my husbands die like flies, so it's certainly not for security. So what are you after, tell me?"

"You know our regimental motto: Who Dares Wins. You're the most exciting woman I have ever met. I was serious about what I said before. I want you. Together we could build a real empire."

"You like power..."

"No." I shook my head. "I love power. I also love excitement, and I am running out of things that turn me on."

"So it would turn you on to marry me?"

"A lot."

"Couldn't we just do business together?"

I took a deep breath and yawned elaborately. "Why don't I just give you my business administrator's card and you talk to him?"

"You're a bastard."

"And you're a five star bitch."

I smiled and she smiled back, then threw back her head and laughed. "You are crazy, Lacklan."

"We covered that."

"I never met a man like you."

"That's a little better." I hesitated. "And the feeling is mutual. There is only one of you. No other woman has ever done what you have done. Any other woman would bore me. I mean to have you, and create something unique together."

Her face said she liked what she was hearing, but she arched one of her perfect eyebrows and asked, "Do I get to have you?"

"I don't do sentimental very well, Sandra. But if I let any woman have me, it would be a woman like you." I made a lopsided smile. "And I already said there is no other woman like you..."

"Careful, tough guy, I might think you're weak."

I shook my head. "No, you won't."

There was a tap at the door, it opened and Celestino stepped in. "Dinner is served, *señora*."

The dining room was through a set of tall, walnut doors at the far end of the drawing room. The table was a twelve-seater, oval and dark mahogany. Two places had been set at the end, with a silver candelabra and place mats instead of a table cloth. The lights were low and here also there was a fire burning in a vast fireplace. The drapes were closed and the ceiling was lower than the drawing room, with exposed, heavy oak rafters. The effect was that of a baronial hall.

Celestino drew back the chair at the head of the table and Sandra sat. I sat on her right. She shook out her napkin with her left hand and draped it across her lap.

"*Madame,* at the *Institut,* always said that it was *nouveu riche* and vulgar to use a table cloth."

"It means you are concerned about damaging the wood, and it is unforgivably middle class to worry about such things. I know. My mother was the same. So how does the daughter of a Mexican drugs baron wind up in the last surviving Swiss finishing school?"

The pretty maid who'd helped me put on my bathing trunks brought in the oysters and set them before us. We ignored each other and Celestino brought in the champagne and poured. Then they both discreetly withdrew.

"My father was born in a *chabola*. You know what that is?"

"A shanty, a shack..."

"He was actually born there. His mother died giving birth to him. His father was a *cabrón*, son of a bitch who had died or disappeared as soon as he discovered that my grandmother was pregnant. So my father was raised by the women in the *barriada*, the shanty town. He had no name. He was never baptized, but they called him *El Loco*, the Crazy One, or *El Diablo*, the Devil. Because from the time he could walk he was always creating trouble. Nobody ever taught him to respect rules, laws, or authority. He was his own law. There are not many men like that in the world. In the old days, these were the men who became kings, heroes and even gods."

She took an oyster, put a drop of Tabasco on it and slipped it into her mouth. She swallowed it without chewing and smiled at me as she sipped her champagne.

"He was not smart. He was very, very intelligent. He made the women teach him how to read. When he was seven years old, he was already going downtown in Mexico City, begging and stealing. He learnt fast that when you have things, people want to steal them from you..."

She paused, reading my face. I raised an eyebrow at her. "Unless they already have more than you."

"Maybe." She took another oyster and sipped. "Anyway, so he learned to hide his stuff, especially his money, and he learned to fight. He said the secret to winning a fight is not how big or strong you are, or how fast. It is, and these are his words, not mine, 'how fuckin' crazy you are'. Do you agree?"

"He was right."

"And he was a crazy devil. He used to tell me he was not a psychopath, he was a nice normal kid who needed a mom and a dad, but to survive, he taught himself to become psychopathic when he needed to. Do you understand that?"

"Yes. Why are you asking me these questions? You make it sound like a test."

"Maybe it is." She took another oyster, clamped her teeth on it, smiled and swallowed. "By the time he was twenty, he had killed ten men, and he was the head of his gang. He also had a lot of money saved. But you know what he did? He moved to the Sinaloa area and started investing his money in small business, and he joined Pedro Aviles Perez's organization. He learned a lot from him, and all the while he was building up his legitimate business interests, and educating himself. He studied everything. He learned to play chess, became a master, he studied psychology, law, Japanese Budo, he was always learning. He joined Mensa, and to join he had to do an IQ test. He had an IQ of one hundred and fifty-five."

"A genius."

"He was not evil. He never took pleasure in causing pain, always looked for the opportunity to avoid it."

She finished her oysters in silence, methodically, systematically, leaving the fattest one till last. Then she drained her glass.

I refilled it and my own.

"But he was a practical man. He used to tell me that reality was always changing, but the one thing you can never change, is reality. A paradox. All you can do is accept it, and adapt with it as it changes. And a necessary part of reality is that sometimes, to survive and to triumph, we must cause suffering, because the ability to make others suffer, and to destroy them, is the source of all power. Do you agree with that?"

"It is a reality that is not likely to change for a very long time."

"So a wise man, or a wise woman, will educate himself to learn two things." She held up two fingers in the victory symbol. "All the sources of pleasure, and all the sources of suffering, and he will teach himself to apply both dispassionately."

"And did he do that?"

"He did. He was a great man."

Celestino came in, removed our plates and took them away. The pretty maid came in and placed Sandra's lobster before her, and a T-bone steak before me. Then Celestino returned with a bottle of 2009 Viñedo Chadwick from the Maipo Valley. I had never tried it. He poured me some to taste. I swirled it around, looked at the mantle, took in the bouquet and tasted it. It was a good wine. I let him give me some more.

When Celestino was gone, she started talking again.

"He made a fortune from trafficking drugs, and he made a parallel fortune in legitimate business, which he used to hide and disguise his illegal income." She paused, fingering her champagne glass. "So you can see that when you brought me your proposition, and Joaquin told me that you had killed Ochoa and the others, I was very interested in you. You are the only man I have known since my father who had this kind of anarchic power."

I nodded, cut into the steak and watched the blood ooze into the oil. "How did he die?"

"Of cancer. The only time I ever cried since I was five years old."

"Was he ever arrested?"

"Never. He was investigated a few times, but they were never able to pin anything on him."

"What happened when you were five?"

"My father made me watch him kill somebody."

I spoke through a mouthful of tender steak. "That's harsh."

"It was good for me. The next time I didn't cry. I got a powerful thrill. After the third time, I used to ask to go with him if I knew he was going to punish or execute somebody."

"You got addicted to the adrenaline."

"Like you."

I smiled. "It's the most powerful addiction there is. And it's totally natural and healthy."

"Do you take drugs?"

"That's for losers and fools."

"Not even a little snort to make you feel powerful?"

I ate in silence, looking at my plate. Then I looked at my glass as I picked it up and drained it. As I set it down, I looked at her under my brows. "I already feel powerful. I said, it's for losers and fools, and if you have that habit, you better start thinking about losing it."

"Relax, Captain Walker, I was testing. I never touch it. Neither did my father."

"I don't care what your father did. I do care what you do."

She seemed not to hear me. "When I was sixteen he sent me to Switzerland, to learn to be a lady, and when I was nineteen he sent me to university in California. He made me study history. I developed a passion for the middle ages and the Renaissance. But all the time I was separated from him I felt lost, a little frightened, as though the world might collapse around me. I think it was a premonition, because when I finally came home, I learnt that he had cancer, and only a very short time to live."

"You have brothers?"

"You know I had."

"You killed them?"

She shook her head. "I had them killed."

I made a question with my face while I chewed. She ate for a while, as before, methodically, systematically, as though she was demolishing the food, eradicating it from her plate. When she had finished, she sat back and drained her glass. I refilled it and she picked it up.

"He wanted me to inherit the business. His sons reminded him of his father—what he imagined his father to be like. They were wasters, drunkards, lazy, always snorting coke, stoned on marijuana. But when he died, they made a power grab. They wanted to run the empire between them, and Mexico being what it is, all his directors and lieutenants wanted a man to run the show."

Her cheeks were flushed and her eyes were bright. Her chest rose and fell under the satin dress, slipping over her breasts. She was breathtakingly beautiful in that moment.

"I had both my brothers killed. Not quickly. I wanted

them to die slowly, painfully. I took my father's lessons to heart, you see. I had their bodies found in the street, dismembered. When that happened, my position was secure as the CEO of his legitimate corporate interests, but also as the head of the cartel. However, I was not satisfied by that, Lacklan. There were five directors on the board who had vociferously supported my brothers' claims against me. I had each one of them crucified."

I gave my head a small, sideways twist. "I get it, you're a badass."

"That's not the point. You knew that already."

"What's the point then, Sandra?"

"I want you to know me. These are the things I don't discuss. I have never let anybody this close. But there seems to be a chemistry with us." She gave an odd, shy smile that was almost demure. "They say that two people know, within seven seconds of meeting, whether they want to have sex with each other. I think it was less than that with me. Have you ever killed a member of your own family?"

"I threw my brother off a balcony." She giggled and I felt a pellet of anger in my gut. "I grabbed him by his hair and the seat of his Armani pants and I threw him off the roof. I did it in front of my father. That was the day he died, and the day I made him my promise."

Her breath had started trembling softly. She reached her hand out toward me and laid it on the table top. "Lacklan, I want you to take me upstairs, to the bedroom. I am feeling very strange."

I raised an eyebrow. "Strange?"

"But before you do, you must answer my one final question."

"Yes…"

"What was *El Vampiro* doing in Cosalá?"

I stood and she stood with me. I pulled her to me and she leaned against me, pressing her body against mine. I put my lips to her ear.

"I'll whisper it to you in bed."

She seemed not to hear me. She said, "I feel so guilty, I have been so bad, so wicked. I feel you should punish me…"

NINETEEN

I TOOK HER BY THE HAND AND LED HER THROUGH the mosaic patio, past the splashing fountain and up the stairs. All the way she kept grabbing me, clawing my back and biting at my neck and shoulders. I felt a strange craziness overtaking me and fought to keep a grip. I played the part, bit her back on her throat and shoulders, then picked her up in my arms and carried her to my room. There I threw her on the bed and snarled, "Take off your clothes."

I stepped into the bathroom. When I came out again, I had stripped off my jacket and had my shirt untucked, but I was still wearing my shoulder-holster, with the Sig in it. She was standing, stripped down to a violet, lace bra and panties. She was the most desirable thing I had ever seen. My belly was on fire. I reached down and took my knife from its sheath, strapped to my calf. I held the blade and handed her the hilt.

"Before we make love, there's something I want you to do."

She was trembling. She had caused the deaths of hundreds, possibly thousands of men, women and children. But she had never taken a life with her own hands. She knew what I was going to tell her to do. I said, "Luz. I want you to do it."

It was her father all over again, but going one step further. She stared at me with shining eyes. She smiled. Her breath was hot and unsteady. I said, "I told Emilio to leave the room unguarded." I reached in my pocket and gave her the key. "I want to watch you do it."

If she had wanted proof that I was sincere, here she had it. She walked out of my room and I followed her along the gallery and down the passage to where Luz had been imprisoned. She stopped and looked back at me. Her beautiful face was radiant. "You will take me there, beside her, after it's done…"

I nodded.

She said, "We will be so powerful, you and me…"

I smiled. "Do it."

She unlocked the door and went in on quiet, naked feet. The light was off, but the moon, shining through the open window, lay warped across the bed, and the bulk of the body inside it. I stayed a few paces behind her as she crept forward. Now the moon glow laid across her exquisite back and hips as she came to a halt beside the bed, and raised the knife in both hands.

That was when I shot her with the Maxim 9. I shot her twice: once through the heart and once through the back of her neck.

I recovered my knife, left, and locked the door behind me. Then I went quickly to my room, tucked in my shirt and put on my jacket. I collected her dress and her shoes, along with my big jacket and my cell phone, and trotted down the stairs to the drawing room. There I took a stiff shot of whiskey and rang the bell.

A couple of minutes later, Celestino came in. I smiled at him. "Dinner was superb, please thank Cook. We are going out for a drive along the coast. We'll be back late, don't wait up. Listen, I sent Emilio to bed. He looked sick. Tell Chavez to go up and stay on Luz's door until tomorrow. Nobody goes in, nobody comes out. Tell him I said so. And give me the keys to the Audi, will you?"

"As you say, *señor*, the keys are in the bowl, by the door. The car is outside the front. You want a driver?"

I winked at him. "No, Celestino, we want to be alone. But you might tell the staff to expect a surprise announcement tomorrow."

He made an effort to look pleased, bowed and left the room. I grabbed her coat and her purse and walked out the front door. The air was cool. I could hear frogs or possibly crickets. Above my head there was an insane number of stars, and a fat moon, turning from orange to silver, was rising in the east. It was the same moon, I told myself, by which I had seen her exquisite back and her violet, lace panties, just before I had shot her.

I put the thought out of my mind, lit a cigarette and walked past the gardens and down the side of the house. I moved quietly down the stairs and unlocked the cellar door. I pushed it open, then slipped in and closed and locked it behind me. I switched on the dull, dusty light and rasped, "*Luz, it's Lacklan! Come! Fast!*"

There was no reply and I moved further in, calling to her, "*Luz! Come on! Where are you?*"

I found her in the cell where she had been held before. She was sitting, hugging her knees on the mattress, trembling and fighting back her tears and her sobs. I felt a twist of pity, but threw the clothes on the mattress and knelt beside her, gripping her shoulders.

"Listen to me. Give in to your fear and panic and we *will* die. There is no time for this. Put on the dress and the shoes, and breathe!" She stared at me wide-eyed. I held her eye and said, "Do it now."

She didn't move. I grabbed her under her armpits and dragged her to her feet, spun her around and pulled down the zip on her dress. She gave a small cry and struggled to hold it. I wrenched it from her hands and threw it on the floor.

I bent, picked up Sandra's dress and handed it to her. "Put it on, now, or I'll carry you naked to the car."

She backed away from me a step, but pulled on the dress. It fit OK. I went behind her and zipped it up, then handed her the shoes. "Let's go, Luz, put them on."

She slipped them on and I searched in Sandra's purse. Her cell was there, about twelve hundred pesos and a comb. I pulled out the cell and put it in my pocket, then handed her the purse and the comb. "Sort out your hair, fast!"

She straightened her hair and I put Sandra's coat over her shoulders, then took her elbow and led her up the steps to the door. I pulled it open and stepped outside. There I stopped and listened. There was only the sound of the frogs on the chill air, nothing else. "Let's go."

We walked the length of the house and came to the corner where the gardens were that flanked the front door. I glanced over and saw a puff of smoke. I put my arms around Luz and whispered in her ear, "*Kiss me, you are Sandra, understand?*"

She went rigid. "*What?*"

I drew her a few steps so we were in sight of the door, stopped, took hold of her face and kissed her, long and deep, then put my arm around her shoulders and guided her toward the car, laughing comfortably. "I'll do you a deal, baby," I said, loud enough to be heard. "You lead me to the best whiskey in town, and I'll go dancing with you, deal? Giggle for daddy…"

She forced a strangled cross between a laugh and a sob, which I covered by raising my free hand to the guy at the door and calling "*Buenas noches!*"

He watched me a moment, then raised his hand, with the cigarette held between his fingers, and said, "*Buenas noches.*"

The car bleeped and I bundled Luz into the front passenger seat. The guy at the door called, "*No quiere que les lleve, señor?*"

Did I want him to drive? I smiled and winked. "*No, gracias, solos esta noche.*"

He smiled and nodded. Unlike Celestino, this guy liked the idea of his mistress having a guy in her life. Clearly Celestino was the wiser man.

I fired up the engine, turned around the fountain and headed for the big gate. I slowed as we approached and pressed the button on the key ring, and the big gate began to roll back. It was slow. It moved a couple of feet, three, four. My stomach was burning and my heart was pounding hard, high up in my chest. All the while I kept my eyes on the mirror. The guy who'd been smoking at the door was now on his cell. I told myself it could be anyone, his girlfriend, his mother.

Then the gate clunked and came to a halt. I heard a whimper from Luz. "What's happening? Have they...?"

"No!" I cut her short. "Stay cool."

In the mirror, I could see the guy at the door trot down the steps and start walking toward us up the drive. He was maybe a hundred or a hundred and fifty yards behind us. I got out of the car and walked toward the exit. As I approached, I noticed for the first time a hut in the shelter of some palms fifteen or twenty feet from the gate. There was a guy approaching me from the hut. He was wearing a suit, but he had an assault rifle slung over his shoulder. As he approached, I recognized him as the bodyguard who'd stood opposite Sandra at breakfast and let us into the cellar.

I smiled at him. "What's the problem with the gate? We were just going dancing."

"I stop the gate."

"You did? Why?"

"I need to ask, where is Emilio?"

"How the hell should I know? Now open the gate, the *Señora* and I are going dancing."

He was a couple of feet from me now, watching me with narrowed eyes. "The *Señora* is in the car?"

I looked at him like I was going to smack him. "Yeah! The *Señora* is in the damned car. She wants to go dancing. Now open the damned gate!"

"Let me see the *Señora*."

"Jesus Christ! Fine!" I turned and walked toward the

passenger door of the car. As I did it I could see the guy who'd been smoking on the steps. He was now about a third of the way up the drive. I yanked open the door and the big guy came around to look in. As he did it, I pulled the Maxim from behind my back and pressed it into his side.

"You and I know that death from a bullet wound in your belly is one of the most painful ways to go. So salute, back up, and go back to your hut."

He took a step back. He looked scared. He raised his hand like he was saying goodnight. I laughed like somebody had made a joke, and said to Luz, "Look in the mirror, what's the guy behind us doing?"

She leaned over and looked. "He's standing, watching."

I laughed and leaned on the roof of the Audi, looking at the gorilla, and said, "Laugh or I'll shoot you."

He made a real effort, then gave the 'thumbs up' to his pal down the drive and Luz said, "He's turning 'round, going back toward the house."

I jerked my head at the big goon. "Back to your hut."

"*Por favor, no me mate!*"

"No problem, back to the hut."

He backed up another couple of paces and when I figured he was out of sight of the house I double tapped him in the chest. The only sound was the *phut! phut!* of the Maxim's baffles, and the muted thump as his body hit the ground.

I got back behind the wheel, pressed the button on the key ring again and the gate started to roll back. I waited till it was open all the way and cruised out at a modest speed, then pressed the button to close it again behind me.

We followed the long, sandy track back to the main road and there turned right toward Mexicali.

As I started to accelerate toward the border, I said, "OK, one problem at a time, you have no passport, and you look Mexican. That is going to be a problem at the border. So what we are going to do is, fifteen minutes before we get there, I'm going to put you in the trunk. You don't make a sound. You just lie there and try to go to sleep."

She stared and swallowed. "I have claustrophobia."

"Superb. Can you control it for half an hour while we drive across?"

"You don't understand. I lose control. I get hysterical. Even if I just feel trapped under a sheet, I go crazy. Can't we just go to an American consulate?"

I smiled. "How long do you think it would be before they discovered you were Jesus Santos' sister? 'Have you any family we can contact, Miss Santos?' 'Well, there's my brother, only…'"

"OK, I get it."

I reached in my pocket then and pulled out Sandra's cell phone. I scrolled through the address book and found Joaquin's number. I pressed call.

It rang a couple of times and he answered.

"*Hola, Mami!*"

I laughed. "Hey, son-in-law, how's it hangin'? Listen…"

He interrupted me. "What are you doing with Sandra's telephone? Where is she?"

"Relax, take it easy! She's in the shower. We've had a superb evening and a great talk. I had Celestino arrange oysters and lobster Thermidor for her. She loved it. She's an amazing woman. Listen, she asked me to call you. We need to meet up at the Ranch. We have a hundred kilo problem there that needs taking care of. How soon can you be there?"

"I can be there in the morning, but let me talk to my mother."

"I told you, junior, she's in the shower. Relax, I'll get her to call you when she gets out, OK?"

"Do that."

"How are things going at your end?"

"There is a lot of talking going on. Some people are saying she's crazy…"

"Yeah, well, that's to be expected. We'll figure it out. Basically they get on board or we take over their operation. It's that simple."

He grunted. "I hope you're right."

"I am. OK, listen, take it easy. I'll get your mom to call you in a while."

I hung up, then handed Luz the phone. "Give it fifteen minutes, then send him a Whatsapp in Spanish saying you're exhausted and you're going to bed, but you'll see him tomorrow morning at the Rancho Grande."

She was quiet for a while, then looked at me and shook her head. "It's got to be a thousand miles from here to the Rancho Grande. Even if you went at a hundred miles an hour all the way, it would still take you ten hours minimum. You can't do it. Plus we still have the problem of how we get across the border."

"I know."

"Besides, we just escaped from them, Lacklan, why the hell do you want to meet up with them again at the ranch?"

"Not them, him."

"You want to kill him. You haven't done enough killing. You have to kill him too…"

"Yes. I have to."

"Why?"

"Because he is now the head of the operation, and he is one of the people ultimately responsible for killing Celeste."

"Come on, man! What the hell is this really about, Lacklan? You didn't even know her!"

I glanced at her. "I can't explain it, and I don't know if you would understand even if I did, but I did know her. It was less than a minute, but it was like, for those few seconds we were outside time and we…" I paused, searching the black road ahead for the right words. "We connected! It is hopelessly inadequate, Luz, but that is the word. We connected. I knew her in that moment, it was kind of timeless. Like we had always known each other." I smiled at the memory. "Last thing she said to me—the only thing she said to me—just before she died: 'Nice to meet you.'"

"Those were her last words? Nice to meet you?"

"Yeah. I had just told her I was Lacklan, and she was going to be all right. She kind of smiled, said, 'Celeste, nice to meet you,' and that was it. But in that short time, we knew each other."

She sighed. "She got to you, I can see that. But you have to stop killing, Lacklan."

"I will."

"Did you kill Sandra?"

I nodded. After a moment, she typed out a Whatsapp and sent it. A moment later the phone rang. It was Joaquin. She didn't hesitate. She answered it in a sleepy, groggy voice, in English with just a hint of a French inflection. It was very good.

"We talk about it tomorrow, *amorcito*, let *Mamita* sleep now. OK?" She listened a moment and sighed. "*Mañanita, cielo, besito, chao chao.*"

I looked at her, curious. "Little tomorrow, little heaven?"

"We love our diminutives."

"That was very good."

"Yay, I'm learning to be an assassin."

"No, you're not. You're learning to save your ass. After this, you have nothing more to do with this."

"Did you have sex with her?"

I scowled. "No. I shot her. You don't want to know about this, Luz. It's for people like me, not you."

She looked at me resentfully. "Are we that different?"

"Yes. You're a good person. I'm a son of a bitch."

"So what happened, with us, in your room…?"

I sighed. "This is not the time or the place, Luz." I smiled. "*Mañanita, amorcito.*"

"It sounds awful when you say it."

"Yeah, well, it sounds nice when you say it, which is another big difference between us, see?"

"Asshole."

I pulled out my cell, switched it on and scrolled through the numbers till I found Senator Cyndi McFarlane[1]. She wouldn't appreciate my calling at this time of night, but we'd become close enough as friends, and I figured the situation warranted it. I pressed call. It rang half a dozen times and finally a sleepy voice said, "Lacklan? What the hell?"

---

1. See *To Rule in Hell*

"Sorry to wake you, Cyndi, I need a favor."

"What a surprise. Maybe one day you'll call when you want to do me a favor."

"I promise. Listen, I'm two hours out of Mexicali, on the Mexican side. I have my driving license, but my passenger, who is a U.S. citizen, has no identification with her."

"Lacklan..." Her tone was a warning.

"I'm telling the truth, Cyndi. I wouldn't get you involved in anything illegal. You know that."

"The hell I do!"

"She's a U.S. citizen, Cyndi! She was kidnapped by a cartel and I'm trying to get her back home. So I need to be waved through at the border, and on the other side I need a chopper waiting to take me to Tucson."

"What the hell, Lacklan! Do you know what time it is?"

"Yes. I'll make it up to you, Cyndi. Do this for me. I just took out Sandra Dorado Beltran, I have her gang on my trail, I'm driving one of their cars and I need to take out her son tomorrow morning. Don't give me a hard time, babe."

"Wh... *what?* Look, send me the details of your car. I'll make a call. I'm going to hang up."

I sent her the details of the car and five minutes later, Luz looked at me and said, "Babe? You called Senator McFarlane 'babe'?"

I snorted. "What should I have called her, *amorcito?*"

She crossed her arms and looked away, at the black window where our reflections were suspended like ghosts, and said, "*Dios*, he called Senator McFarlane 'babe'..."

TWENTY

By the time we got to the border, it was past two in the morning. Cyndi had called half an hour earlier to say we were to cross at the Calexico East Port of Entry, over the All American Canal, and head for the Route 7 '*Exportación*' lane.

Technically, at that time of night, the crossing was closed. It wouldn't open for another forty minutes, but Cyndi had done her stuff and there was a single border guard on the Mexican side, standing in the desolate, spot-lit complex, who waved us through. We crossed the bridge and another guard on the U.S. side raised a hand to halt us. As we pulled over, he leaned in the driver's window and asked to see some ID. I showed him my driver's license and he pointed at the check point that stood open.

"Drive through, you'll see a parking lot on your right. There's a chopper waiting for you there. Leave the car with the keys in it."

I thanked him and drove through the checkpoint. As

he'd said, the road forked, and the right branch opened up into a large parking lot with a square building at the center. In the middle of the lot there was a black, unmarked Sikorsky UH-60 Black Hawk. I pulled over, killed the engine and the lights and left the key on the seat. Luz was staring at me with an expression that was hard to read.

"Who are you?"

I shrugged. "A friend." Then I smiled. "Come with me if you want to live."

"The Terminator? Really? That's not funny."

"Come on, we're on the clock."

We climbed out. The doors echoed across the empty lot as we slammed them, and the chopper's turbines began to whine. We ran the few yards to the Hawk and the side door slid open. A guy in jeans and a sweatshirt with a balaclava over his head reached down to help Luz climb in. He shouted to me over the rising thud of the blades, "Any problems? Anything I need to know?"

I shook my head as I jumped in. "No!"

"Let me see some ID!"

I showed him my driver's license and he nodded. "Welcome aboard, Captain! Take a seat and strap in, please." He slid the door closed, Luz and I sat on the bench of seats and strapped in, he shouted, "*OK! Let's go!*" and we started our climb.

Choppers are never silent, but there are some Black Hawks that have modified rotors to reduce the 'thud' effect, and this one was quiet compared to others I had flown in.

The guy in the balaclava stood with a hand on the ceiling to steady himself and asked, "Where are we going, sir?"

It was a good question and one I had been asking myself since I'd called Cyndi.

"You got a rope?"

"Yes, sir!"

"Then drop me one mile northwest of the Sasabe border crossing, on the north side of the Rancho Grande. I don't think there's anybody at home, but just in case, try to keep north of the ranch."

"Ten-four, sir, and the lady?"

I looked at her. "Trust me."

"Right..."

I looked at him. "Do me a favor and I'll owe you. Make sure she's on the next flight to Boston."

"I'll take care of that personally, Captain."

Luz turned in her seat to face me. "*Boston?* What the hell am I going to do in Boston?"

"I'll have somebody meet you at the airport. You'll be my guest for a few days. You'll be safe. When I get back, we'll talk about what we do next."

"Do I get a say in this?"

I shook my head. "Not right now. We don't know who Joaquin has in Tucson or what he's liable to do. We got this far, let's keep you safe."

She sighed.

Balaclava said, "Joaquin, Captain? Joaquin Dorado Beltran?"

"You know him?"

"Sandra Dorado Beltran's son. We're aware of them..."

He left the words hanging, inviting me to share. I smiled. "I wouldn't know, my girlfriend and I were simply on holiday in Mexico, and she was abducted, but rumor has it that Sandra Dorado Beltran was killed last night at her villa in San Felipe, following the virtual extermination of the two gangs she supplied with coke and heroin in Tucson."

"That's a hell of a rumor."

"Bar talk, you know. The same rumor, which I wouldn't know anything about, says that Joaquin will be at the Rancho Grande tonight to shift a hundred Ks of coke and heroin…"

"Because they have nobody left to distribute it."

"I guess that's the reason. Apparently there is a tunnel a mile west of the Sasabe border crossing, where the merchandise was brought across. According to this bar talk, the entrance to the tunnel on the Arizona side is marked by a mesquite tree, seven yards east of a broad track that runs to the borderline, and fourteen yards from the border itself. The reason it has never been found, according to the rumor, is down to a border patrol officer, name of Kirkpatrick." I shrugged. "If information like that ever got into the hands of an enterprising sergeant from, say, Delta Force, seems to me he'd find it easy enough to mine it, or something."

"Save an old SAS captain having to do it, right?"

"I have no idea what you're talking about, but if he was otherwise engaged, I guess this captain of yours might be grateful of the help."

He was quiet for a moment, then excused himself and went to join the pilot. Luz was looking unhappy. "Is this how our country is run, Lacklan?"

I shook my head. "No. If it were, Celeste might be alive today, and there would be no need for her foundation."

Forty-five minutes later, we were hovering seventy-five feet over the Rancho Grande Road, the door was open and the rope was dangling, dancing in the downdraft. As I grabbed it and made ready to drop, Luz unfastened her belt and stood, staggering unsteadily. Balaclava moved toward her, shouting, "*Ma'am! Sit down! Sit down now, please!*"

But she grabbed hold of me, kissed me on the mouth and said, "Please come back. I will be waiting for you."

I kissed her back and said, "Sit down! I'll see you in a couple of days!"

Then I was out, in the cold night air, sliding down toward the dirt, with the dust kicking up in clouds around me and the bushes and small trees bowing and dancing in the turmoil of air. I hit the ground and ran for the slopes, heading up the hill to where I had been lying when I'd shot Carlitos and his men. The chopper rose and banked and I watched it disappear north, making very little noise.

The moon was past its zenith and declining in the west, casting weird shadows from the rocks and trees over the translucent sand. I scrambled up the last few yards and found the place where I had buried the MKII and the night vision goggles. I scraped away the sand and pulled out the weapon, the spare magazine and the goggles. Then I scrambled down the hill again and set off at a jog for the Ranch.

As I moved down the pitted path toward the complex of barns and the main building, I could see that there were no lights. Aside from the odd sound of an owl, or some small animal scurrying through the undergrowth, there was only stillness and silence.

I had little doubt in my mind that Joaquin had not bought my story. Besides, Luz's mimicking of Sandra had been good enough, but I was certain that by now they would have found the body by the gate, and Sandra and Emilio's bodies in the room. But I was equally certain that he would come to the ranch, even knowing I'd be waiting for him. He had two compelling reasons. First, he would need to avenge his mother, for his own satisfaction, but also for his reputation within the cartel; and second, because he had a hundred kilos of dope sitting there with no one to distribute it and me closing in.

I headed first for the side of the house, crouch-ran to the corner where I had a view of the yard, and dropped. I pulled on the goggles and lay still for three minutes, listening and watching for any kind of movement. There was nothing, just the translucent green light of the moon making inky shadows.

The stables, where they had stashed the dope, was fifty or sixty paces across the yard to the left of the house, and my path to it was overlooked by the plate glass windows in the living room and the bedrooms above.

Hugging the wall, in the shadows cast by the moon and in the cover of the gardens that flanked the wall, I crawled on my belly across the front of the house. On the far side, I got to my feet and crouch-ran again to the stables. There I dropped and waited. There was still nothing. I was almost certain that there was nobody at the ranch yet, but certainty has been the death of many a man. So I waited and listened.

Finally, after another five minutes, I went and opened the padlock on the big, rolling door. I opened it a couple of feet, squeezed in and rolled it closed again. As before, there were no horses there, just the stalls. I figured the place was rarely used, and when it was, it was not as a ranch, but simply as a distribution point for the dope. Joaquin had said as much.

Despite there being no livestock, there were huge stacks of hay bales. They were useful for giving the illusion that the place was used as a farm, but also as a way of hiding things. And along with the bales, the place was stashed with everything from sacks of fertilizer and old bikes to drums of fuel, propane canisters and wheelbarrows. The possibilities were intriguing, but right then there was just one thing on my mind that I needed to do, and that was confirm that the stash was there. It was barely forty-eight hours since they had brought it in, and without Jesus or Carlitos to take it off their hands, it was unlikely it had been moved yet, but it was not impossible.

In my earlier inspection of the ranch, after I had dropped off the Zombie, I'd found a trap door in the stable floor, under a stack of hay bales, and I had assumed that was the place where any dope would be hidden, but I had not had the chance to confirm it. Now I crossed the floor, moved the bales and pulled up the trap. There was a short ladder down into a cellar, twenty feet across and seven or eight feet high. I descended the steps three at a time and there, across the floor, stacked against the far wall, was the stash. Fifty kilos of cocaine with a street value of around six million dollars and fifty kilos of heroin, with a final street value of possibly as much as thirty million, once cut and packaged.

I didn't hang around. I moved back up the steps and found my own stash that I had left there during my first visit. There was a Heckler and Koch, some more ammunition and a couple of other bits and pieces I had planted, buried under the hay bales, in case I needed them. It was looking as though I was going to.

After a few minutes' work, I closed the trap door,

replaced the bales and sprinted back across the yard to the house. There I picked the lock with my Swiss Army knife, closed the door behind me and, after inspecting the house room by room, went into the drawing room, poured myself a whiskey and settled in the dark to watch for Joaquin's plane.

It came in two hours later, after the moon had set, when the sky was at its blackest. It came as a winking light in the south, growing brighter, then splitting into red and green and white, growing larger until it seemed to hit the ground, a quarter of a mile away in the darkness, where the landing strip was.

A long time seemed to pass then, but eventually, gradually, through the predawn blackness, I began to see movement between the hulking shadows of the barns across the yard. It was men marching, like a small army, carrying rifles. It was hard to make out details at that distance, but as they drew closer it became clearer. There were fifteen of them all told. The King Air 350 will carry eight comfortably, plus the two pilots, so he must have crammed them in. Joaquin was at the front. His movements were rapid and jerky, eloquent of rage, and perhaps panic. Behind him, scattered about four deep and four across, were his men, and they were heading straight across the yard, for the house. It was not what I had anticipated. I had a fight on my hands.

When they were forty feet away, as I was about to smash the window and start shooting, he stopped. He was pointing at the house, then at the stable. One of his guys seemed to be arguing with him. I couldn't hear anything, but the rage on Joaquin's face was clear. He pointed back at the stable, then at a barn. He pushed the guy on the chest and started for the house again. The guy, and one other, headed for the barn; the remaining twelve guys made for the stables. I breathed. If my luck held, I might just take out Joaquin and get away alive.

Miracles do happen, sometimes.

I stood and walked to the drawing room door, then flattened myself against the wall. I heard the key in the lock, then the noises from outside crept in with the chill air: a barn door rolling back, the growl of a diesel. They were planning to shift the dope. I wondered if they planned to take it back to Mexico, or move it to a safer location in the States. It made little difference.

The light in the hall snapped on. The front door closed. Then the drawing room door opened and he stepped in, reaching for the light switch. The light snapped on and he saw the muzzle of the Maxim in his face.

"Breathe and I'll blow the top of your head off." He froze. I held his eye and counted one. "OK, now you can breathe. Go to the chair, sit and put your hands on your head, fingers laced."

He did as I said and sat slowly in the chair. "You killed my mother, you son of a bitch. She was in love with you. You should have heard the way she spoke about you..."

"Can it. You have a choice. Die now, or carry a message for me back to Culiacán."

"What message?"

"Make your choice. Messenger or dead?"

"I'll take your message."

"Good choice. Who did you go and see in Culiacán?"

"Ernesto Zapata."

"*El Vampiro's* son?"

"Yes."

"He's taken over from his father?" He nodded. I tossed him my pen and a piece of paper. "Write down the address."

He scrawled it on the paper and showed it to me. I nodded. "Get up." He stood and I stood with him. "Go and stand at the window."

He hesitated. "Why?"

"Because I told you to. Next time you hesitate or question me, I'll shoot you dead. Do it."

He went and stood, looking out at the yard, where a barn door stood open and a Jeep had pulled up outside the stables. The huge stable door stood open too, and light was flooding out across the yard. Inside, I could visualize them all moving the bales of hay to get at the trap door. I calculated that they must have it open by now and be climbing down to start shifting the merchandise. I said, "I'm going to dial now."

He turned to look at me. "Dial who?" he said.

I smiled. "The detonator."

The first blast was ten pounds of C4 in the basement. It destroyed the coke and the heroin and vaporized whoever was down there with it. It also shook the foundations of the stables. The second blast, less than a second later, was the other ten pounds, plus the propane cylinders it was attached to and the fuel drums ignited by the blast. It created a fireball that tore through the building, blowing out the wooden walls and igniting the hay, engulfing the entire building in flames. Within seconds, the structure had begun to collapse in on itself. Nobody could have survived.

"Turn and look at me."

He turned slowly. He was trembling. His face was sickly and pale.

"I told you I wanted you to carry a message for me to Zapata."

He swallowed. "Yes."

"But I decided to have Shannon deliver it."

I put two 9mm slugs through the center of his forehead and his brains, such as they were, splattered all over the plate glass window, through which I could see, a little less clearly now, his dope burning in the inferno which he had created, but which I had triggered.

Then I walked quietly, feeling strangely at peace with myself, back along Rancho Grande Road, to where I had the Zombie parked and waiting.

EPILOGUE

I sat across from Detective Mike Shannon at his desk in the Tucson PD Santa Cruz station. He looked slightly dyspeptic.

"What can I do for you, Captain Walker?"

I smiled amiably. "I have been hearing some rumors, and though I am not a man to put much store by rumors, these I feel you ought to be acquainted with."

"Yeah?"

"I heard, for example, that last night the drugs maiden known as the Queen of the Sea, Sandra Dorado Beltran, was shot to death in her mansion in San Felipe, Baja California."

"Why would that interest me?"

"Because I also heard that her son was murdered in the small hours of the morning at the Rancho Grande, where only a couple of days ago Carlitos and his *Iluminados*, and Jesus Santos, were both also killed."

"How could you know that?"

"I don't. I am just acquainting you with the rumors I've

heard. I also heard there was a great explosion, in which a hundred kilos of dope were burned, along with a dozen smugglers."

"What is your point, Captain?"

I ignored him and went on. "There are also rumors of a second explosion, just a mile to the west of Sasabe, in which a tunnel used by the Dorado Beltran family to smuggle dope into the U.S. was destroyed." He was staring at me fixedly. I held his eye a moment. I had stopped smiling. "I don't know if there is any truth in these rumors, Detective, but it seems to me that a wise man would distance himself from what is left of the Dorado Beltran gang, and their associates, because everyone connected with them seems to be dying off like flies."

He tried to say something several times, but never quite made it. After a moment I said, "You're a family man, aren't you? You have children. I have not been that fortunate, but I can imagine that a man like yourself, with a very distinguished *early* career in the force, would do just about anything to protect his family and his children."

"Yes..."

"Rumor has it that the threat is over, and that Ernesto Zapata, in Culiacán, will be receiving a package any time now, by UPS." I leaned forward, with my elbows on his desk. "Rumor has it that that package contains the head of young Joaquin Dorado Beltran, and a message reading, 'Arizona is closed for business.' What do you think about that, Detective Shannon?"

He took a slightly shaky breath. "I think it's high time."

I smiled and nodded. "Me too. And perhaps it's time

you yourself applied for a desk job. What do you say? It's a dangerous world out there for a family man."

"Perhaps I'll do that."

"For my part, I'll be moving on now. I hope we never meet again, Detective."

"Me too, Captain."

I made my way down to the parking lot with a light step. The Zombie was waiting there, matte black in the Arizona sun. I didn't climb in. I kept walking, crossed the intersection and through the parking lot of Cora's Golden Café, into Michigan Street. There I pushed through the gate to Estrella Martinez's house and knocked on the door. She looked surprised to see me.

"Mr. Lacklan, you still here? I think you gone home already."

"I'm leaving today. I came to say goodbye."

"Come in, you got time for coffee?"

"Sure."

She put the coffee on the stove and led me to the sofa, where we sat together. Her eyes were still puffy, but she smiled at me. "You hear the news?"

"What news, Estrella?"

"Jesus, his whole gang... And Carlitos too, all dead!"

"You don't say! How'd it happen?"

She arched an eyebrow. "Nobody knows, but I think the Lord send a warrior of God to kill them."

I patted her hand. "Let's hope so. Otherwise somebody's not getting through those pearly gates. I also heard that Sandra Dorado Beltran and her son were killed too. Must be an epidemic."

She wagged a finger at me. "You gonna get into trouble

one day. I am serious, Lacklan. You got to start lookin' for something else to do in life."

"Funny you should say that, Estrella, because I have some more news."

"Good news?"

"Very good. Celeste had a friend, she was with her when Celeste was killed. Her name was Luz."

"She told me about her."

"She wanted Luz to head up a project to help kids stay out of gangs and drugs, help to find a better way of life."

She shrugged. "She was a dreamer."

"Yeah, but it's the dreamers who change the world, Estrella. Me and Luz are going to set up the Celeste Martinez Foundation. She will run, I will keep an eye on it, and I would like you to be one of the trustees. You'll get a decent salary for life, pension, benefits, all that stuff. You'll have to work, spread the word, give interviews, do fund raising. All that stuff. What do you say?"

She didn't say much. She covered her mouth with her hands and tears spilled down her cheeks. I put my arm around her and held her, and we sat together while she wept, and I may have wept too, in silence, until the coffee began to gurgle in the kitchen. Then I gave her my handkerchief and went to set a tray with cups and sugar and milk.

An hour later, I walked back across the intersection to the Zombie, parked in the police parking lot. I rested my ass on the hood, pulled my Camels from my pocket and lit up, looking across the road at Cora's Golden Café. There was a family saloon parked now where Celeste had lain bleeding out, holding my hand. It seemed like a lifetime ago, but it was just a few days.

I took my cell from my pocket and called Kenny.

"Good morning, sir. Young Luz has just arrived. I have put her in the Primrose Room. She is eager to see you. Is everything all right?"

"Everything is fine, Kenny. How are things at home?"

"Not much to report. Young Miss Marni telephoned."

"Marni?"

"Yes, sir. Apparently she attempted to call you several times but your cell was either out of range or switched off. She would like to speak to you. She said it was not urgent."

"Oh." I suppressed a strange sense of discomfort and said, "All right, I'll get back to her, thanks. Listen, Kenny, do me a favor, will you? Tell Rosalia that I am in need of a steak and kidney pie, and you, old friend, you get yourself down to the cellar and find the best *Ribera del Duero* we have, and a bottle of our best champagne. I expect to be there in somewhat less than forty-eight hours. I am coming home."

Don't miss KILL: FOUR The riveting sequel in the Omega Thriller series.

Scan the QR code below to purchase KILL: FOUR.

Or go to: righthouse.com/kill-four

NOTE: flip to the very end to read an exclusive sneak peek...

DON'T MISS ANYTHING!

If you want to stay up to date on all new releases in this series, with this author, or with any of our new deals, you can do so by joining our newsletters below.

In addition, you will immediately gain access to our entire *Right House VIP Library*, which includes many riveting Mystery and Thriller novels for your enjoyment!

righthouse.com/email

(Easy to unsubscribe. No spam. Ever.)

ALSO BY BLAKE BANNER

Up to date books can be found at:
www.righthouse.com/blake-banner

ROGUE THRILLERS
Gates of Hell (Book 1)
Hell's Fury (Book 2)
Ice Burn (Book 3)
Judgement by Fire (Book 4)

ALEX MASON THRILLERS
Odin (Book 1)
Ice Cold Spy (Book 2)
Mason's Law (Book 3)
Assets and Liabilities (Book 4)
Russian Roulette (Book 5)
Executive Order (Book 6)
Dead Man Talking (Book 7)
All The King's Men (Book 8)
Flashpoint (Book 9)
Brotherhood of the Goat (Book 10)
Dead Hot (Book 11)
Blood on Megiddo (Book 12)
Son of Hell (Book 13)
Merchant of Death (Book 14)
Extinction C-14 (Book 15)

HARRY BAUER THRILLER SERIES

Dead of Night (Book 1)
Dying Breath (Book 2)
The Einstaat Brief (Book 3)
Quantum Kill (Book 4)
Immortal Hate (Book 5)
The Silent Blade (Book 6)
LA: Wild Justice (Book 7)
Breath of Hell (Book 8)
Invisible Evil (Book 9)
The Shadow of Ukupacha (Book 10)
Sweet Razor Cut (Book 11)
Blood of the Innocent (Book 12)
Blood on Balthazar (Book 13)
Simple Kill (Book 14)
Riding The Devil (Book 15)
The Unavenged (Book 16)
The Devil's Vengeance (Book 17)
Bloody Retribution (Book 18)
Rogue Kill (Book 19)
Blood for Blood (Book 20)
The Cell (Book 21)
Time to Die (Book 22)
The Reaper of Zion (Book 23)

DEAD COLD MYSTERY SERIES
An Ace and a Pair (Book 1)
Two Bare Arms (Book 2)
Garden of the Damned (Book 3)
Let Us Prey (Book 4)
The Sins of the Father (Book 5)
Strange and Sinister Path (Book 6)

The Heart to Kill (Book 7)
Unnatural Murder (Book 8)
Fire from Heaven (Book 9)
To Kill Upon A Kiss (Book 10)
Murder Most Scottish (Book 11)
The Butcher of Whitechapel (Book 12)
Little Dead Riding Hood (Book 13)
Trick or Treat (Book 14)
Blood Into Wine (Book 15)
Jack In The Box (Book 16)
The Fall Moon (Book 17)
Blood In Babylon (Book 18)
Death In Dexter (Book 19)
Mustang Sally (Book 20)
A Christmas Killing (Book 21)
Mommy's Little Killer (Book 22)
Bleed Out (Book 23)
Dead and Buried (Book 24)
In Hot Blood (Book 25)
Fallen Angels (Book 26)
Knife Edge (Book 27)
Along Came A Spider (Book 28)
Cold Blood (Book 29)
Curtain Call (Book 30)

THE OMEGA SERIES
Dawn of the Hunter (Book 1)
Double Edged Blade (Book 2)
The Storm (Book 3)
The Hand of War (Book 4)
A Harvest of Blood (Book 5)

To Rule in Hell (Book 6)
Kill: One (Book 7)
Powder Burn (Book 8)
Kill: Two (Book 9)
Unleashed (Book 10)
The Omicron Kill (Book 11)
9mm Justice (Book 12)
Kill: Four (Book 13)
Death In Freedom (Book 14)
Endgame (Book 15)

ABOUT US

Right House is an independent publisher created by authors for readers. We specialize in Action, Thriller, Mystery, and Crime novels.

If you enjoyed this novel, then there is a good chance you will like what else we have to offer! Please stay up to date by using any of the links below.

Join our mailing lists to stay up to date --> righthouse.com/email
Visit our website --> righthouse.com
Contact us --> contact@righthouse.com

facebook.com/righthousebooks
x.com/righthousebooks
instagram.com/righthousebooks

EXCLUSIVE SNEAK PEEK OF...

KILL: FOUR

CHAPTER 1

I lay still in bed, feeling an indefinable disquiet: the stillness of the small hours, hazy beams of moonlight leaning silent through the open window, lying in limpid, twisted oblongs across the foot of my bed, an owl calling for a mate, far off across the dark fields, the steady croaking of the frogs in the pond near the black woods outside.

I rose and went to the window. Everything was motionless. The almost turquoise glow of the full moon lay luminous over everything: the blacktop on the driveway, the softly glinting leaves on the trees, the rooftops and the chimneypots silhouetted against the translucent sky. There was nothing there—nothing visible.

I stood a while, not looking for objects but for movement, and eventually it came: a shifting of the dark among the trees that bordered Concord Road, then the muted cones of headlamps and the hum of an engine retreating toward Weston.

At breakfast the next morning, as Kenny set down my bacon and eggs and poured my coffee, I said, "Check the CCTV footage for last night, will you, Kenny? We had a prowler, somebody in a car parked on Concord Road. I want to know who it was."

His eyes searched my face for less than a second. "I'll do that right away, sir."

He withdrew and I sat alone, eating my eggs and bacon, more aware of the lawns and woodlands beyond the leaded windows, behind my back, than I was of the food and the coffee on the table in front of me.

At seven thirty I rose from the table, slipped my Sig Sauer p226 under my arm and stepped out for a walk along Concord Road. It was a fresh, bright morning. The early shadows were long, dense and cool among burnished light, but the sky was vibrant blue. Fall was just a few weeks away, and you could smell it in the air.

I walked slowly, scanning the blacktop and the verges of the roads. There wasn't much to see but grass, meadow flowers and an occasional fallen leaf. Above my head and deeper in the woodland there was sporadic birdsong, or the sudden flap of wings, but aside from these small, desultory bursts of activity, there was no movement. Nothing stirred.

I came to the spot where I had seen the headlamps, and hunkered down to examine the soil. There were impressions. I photographed them with my cell, but I was pretty sure I recognized the tread as belonging to a Range Rover.

I stood, moved in among the trees and made my way back to the house through the woods, exploring one by one all the spots where you could get a good, clear view of the house without being seen. My search was inconclusive. There might have been someone there, or not. But if there had been, they were good. They didn't leave tracks.

At nine thirty, Kenny knocked on my study door and came in, closing it behind him.

"Sir, we do indeed seem to have had a visitor last night. A dark blue Range Rover parked on Concord Road. It was captured by one of the cameras you had installed in the trees beside the road. In the footage, the driver does not exit the vehicle, so his face does not appear. Nor are his plates clear enough to make out in detail. It seems he was there for a couple of hours from two until four. Then he drove away."

I leaned back in my chair and sighed, gazing out at the luminous green lawn and the tree line thirty yards away at the back of the house.

"This was why I was reluctant to come home, Kenny. I didn't want to visit this on you and Rosalia. But I thought it was over. I thought we were done with this. I really thought we were done. I'm sorry, Kenny."

His expression was pained. "Sir, if I may speak freely, Rosalia and myself, we have known you all your life, and your father before you. It is no comfort for us to survive and live, if you are killed or hurt in some distant part of the world. This is your home, and ours, and we defend it together."

I smiled at the old guy who had been more of a father to me than my father ever had. "I know, Kenny. We're family. I'll see to it, don't worry. Stay on high alert, double check the security systems and see what you can hear on the grapevine about a dark blue or black Range Rover in the neighbourhood. I'm going to go into Weston."

I took the Kuga because it was inconspicuous, I opened all the windows and drove the mile and a bit to town, through dappled shade at a leisurely twenty-five miles per hour. On the way I scanned every front yard, every parking lot and every car that came my way. I didn't see a dark Range Rover.

I dropped the Kuga at Walgreens and took a stroll around the town, visiting every shop in turn and scanning the parking lots outside each of them. I even visited the Catholic church.

I eventually found the car at the dentist's. I guess even international hit men get trouble with their teeth. So I strolled up to the green beside the hot dog stand, where I had a good view of the dentist's parking lot, and sat myself down at one of the benches there to take the sun and wait for the driver to show.

He showed after half an hour, holding his cheek, and climbed into his car, where he sat without moving for five minutes before pulling out and driving slowly away. When he'd gone from view, I strolled down to the dentist's and pushed through the door. Peggy on the reception desk smiled up at me.

"Lacklan, we haven't seen you around here for a while. How are you?"

"All the better for seeing you, Peggy. How's Dave?"

"Can't complain. The practice is going well. Nothing much changes around here, does it?"

"Say, I must be wrong, but I am pretty certain I just saw an old colleague of mine come out of here and drive away in a dark blue Range Rover. I called out to him but he didn't hear me..."

Her eyes widened at the prospect of possible gossip. "This last guy who just left?"

"About five minutes ago."

She rattled at her computer. "From your time in the military?" I made an affirmative noise and she tapped a little more. "He had a kind of military air about him all right... He was not an American, I can tell you that. I think he was Australian or maybe British. Here we are, Mark Philips, just visiting the U.S. from South Africa. Broke his tooth last night eating a salted almond. Is that your friend?"

I frowned. "You know, I think it might be. It was a few years ago. I think I'll look him up. Where's he staying?"

"At the Arabian Horse, in Wayland."

I smiled. "Sure, where else?"

I stepped back out into the late morning sunshine and made my way slowly back toward my car. When I got there, I climbed in and sat for a while with the windows open, listening to the gentle sounds of late New England summer —and thinking. After ten years serving with the British SAS, there was no shortage of people in the world who might want me dead, but most of the ones I could think of were either from the Middle East or Latin America. I couldn't think of a single one from South Africa. And the name Mark Philips, apart from being the first husband of Prince Charles' sister, meant nothing to me.

Was I becoming paranoid? Probably, but that didn't mean they weren't after me, it just meant I knew about it.

I hit the ignition and pulled out of the parking lot, but instead of heading for home I turned east, as though I were going into Boston. At Conant Road I turned north and started cruising slowly through the woods. I figured the chances were better than good that if this guy was watching me, and had found my address, he also had my cell number and was tracking my GPS. So I followed Conant Road for about a mile through the forest until I came to Sunset Road on my left. There I turned west and followed that road for half a mile or so till I came to the grounds of Weston College. At the college, I turned left into Merriam Street and drove for a couple of minutes through the dense cover of the trees until I found a lay-by. There, I pulled off the road, left my phone in the car and sprinted back through the woods to the intersection, where I dropped on my belly among ferns and waited.

I waited five minutes, and was beginning to think I might have made a mistake and read too much into what was, after all, just a guy parking on a wooded road for a couple of hours, when his blue Range Rover nosed up to the crossroads. Then I felt a sinking feeling in my gut.

It wasn't over; not yet.

He waited a long time at the intersection, maybe a full minute and a half. Finally he slowly pulled onto Merriam Street and crawled at no more than four miles an hour along the black top until he caught sight of the Kuga. Then he stopped and backed up a bit.

There was no doubt in my mind now that he was tailing me. The question had become, what for? The fact that he was watching my house between two and four AM suggested he was planning either to break in and steal something, or break in and kill me, and anybody else he happened to find in there—the only purpose in watching a house at that time of the morning is to see what obstacles you're going to find when you force an entry.

I gave him another minute to see what he did. He didn't do anything, so I backed up in among the trees and took a circuitous route back toward my car. I allowed him to see me walk out of the forest, cross the road and climb into the Ford. Then I drove back to my house at a leisurely pace. He was professional enough to stay out of my rear-view mirror. But by that time I was pretty sure I knew who he was.

I got to my house, left the Kuga out front and crossed the hall to my study, where I stood a moment, looking around at the familiar room. Kenny had, as he had every morning since I had returned home, set and lit the fire and opened the French doors onto the lawn at the back. It was a quirk of mine, I enjoyed having a fire burning with the windows open.

I went to the sideboard and poured myself a Bushmills from the decanter, then lit a Camel and stood with my back to the flames, looking around the room. Throughout my childhood and my teens, it had been my father's study. I had been punished in this room more times than I could remember. It was in this room as much as any other that I had grown to hate him—long before I had learned about his membership of Omega.

It had been two years now since his death, and in that time I had spent very little time in the house I had inherited from him. I had not made my mark on it. I had not taken possession of it. I had spent all my time and all my energy destroying the organization he had been a part of.

And I had thought, after Mexico, that the job was done.

I took my drink and my cigarette to the desk, dropped into the large, leather chair and called Jim Redbeard in L.A.

"Lacklan, it's good to hear from you. It's been a long time. Sole asks after you. You know, Sole, my wife?"

"Hi, Jim. Would that be Sole, your ex-wife? Apart from discovering jealousy for the first time, how are you?"

"I am sensational, as always, and I am not jealous. I just hope your intentions are honorable. I'd hate her to meet another bastard like me."

"Right now I have no intentions, Jim. I just need to run something by you."

"Shoot."

"My house is being watched by a South African in a Range Rover. I get the impression he is a pro. He doesn't make sloppy mistakes, he's patient, he's meticulous and I am pretty sure he is here to assassinate me."

"Ah..."

"What do you mean, 'Ah...'?"

"South Africa has been popping up on the radar lately."

"Yeah? How?"

"Is your line secure?"

"As secure as any line on the planet at the moment."

"OK, I'll give it to you in general terms without buzzwords, but we should meet, soon, and discuss this."

"OK."

"I've received information about something, some kind of building, a structure, it's massive, that's being put up along the border with Namibia, on the South African side of the River Orange. I don't know what it is, and none of my informants knows what it is."

"What does it look like?"

"It's in its early stages, but it looks as though it's going to be a huge pyramid."

"A *pyramid?*"

"That's what I'm told. I haven't been able to get photographs, video—nothing. Just oral testimony. Which is in itself telling you something. It is being kept strictly under wraps. There is no official record of it, no licenses granted, no requests submitted. The thing does not exist officially, it is being built in one of the remotest parts of the globe, and it is vast. Estimates I have heard are in the region of the apex being up to a thousand feet high. That would give it a base in the region of two thousand feet across, or more."

"What the hell would they want to build something like that for? That's the size of a small city."

"I know. But there is more."

"What...?"

I asked him, but I knew what he was going to say, and he said it. "Your friends seem to have become active."

"Shit..."

"They seem to be organizing a reunion."

"Don't say any more. That's who my visitor is. A messenger."

"I'm afraid so."

"We need to meet. Soon. In the next day or so."

"What about your visitor?"

"I'll take care of him."

"Good. Let's meet in Seattle. I'll send you the details. I'll be in touch in the next twenty-four hours."

"Good."

I hung up and called Kenny. A couple of minutes later, he came in and closed the door behind him.

"Any development, sir?"

"Yes, I'm going to take a walk, cross country, to Plimpton. When I get back, I'll need to pack. I'm going away for a couple of days."

"Will you be back, sir?"

I stared at him, not sure for a moment what he meant. Then I smiled and relaxed. "Yes, Kenny. I will be back, for sure."

"Rosalia will be very relieved, sir."

"While I'm out, I want you on lock down, Kenny. Nobody comes in and nobody goes out. Anybody tries to force their way in, you shoot them."

"I understand, sir."

He closed the French windows and locked them. I cocked the Sig, slipped it into my waistband where it was less visible than under my arm, and stepped out into the front drive. Behind me, I heard Kenny lock the door, and knew that he was engaging all the house's security systems: the one my father had installed, and the ones I had added. Then I set off around the back of the house, through the old fence that separated our property from Marni's, and into the deep forest that stretched for over a mile between our small hamlet outside Weston and the village of Plimpton.

I walked like a man without a care in the world. The tall, ancient trees closed in about me, leaning in to form a translucent green cathedral over my head. Each footfall, rustling on the leaves or cracking on a dry branch, created a dull echo through the woodland, its sound bizarrely both muffled and amplified by the trees. I didn't follow a path. I meandered in a vaguely north-westerly direction, guiding myself by the familiar landmarks of the forest I knew so well. This had been my playground as a boy—mine and Marni's.

I knew, for example, that at the halfway point there was a steep slope, and at the bottom of that slope there was an ancient fallen tree, lying in a shallow trough, and that tree was what I was heading for.

I got there after about fifteen minutes of apparently aimless wandering and stood a moment in the diffuse green light, gazing down the slope, listening to all the sounds of the woodland. Then I took a step forward and screamed.

I hit the ground on my right shoulder and cried out again, rolling fast and out of control down toward the tree. At the bottom of the steep slope, I hit the tree. I had a million small aches, cuts and bruises all over my body, but I ignored them and crawled under the huge fallen trunk, over to the far side where there was a clump of tall ferns. I worked my way in among them, then pulled out my cell and tossed it over, under the tree, then lay and waited.

I didn't have to wait long. After no more than a minute, he appeared at the top of the slope. At first it was just his head peering over. He was cautious, but he saw my cell and concluded that I must be nearby, under the massive trunk. He stood and half-ran, half-scrambled down the slope to the tree. As he bent to peer under it, I stood and walked over to him, with my Sig held out in both hands. He sensed me before he saw or heard me, went very still and straightened up. I said, "Put your hands on your head. Turn to face me. Let me get a look at you."

He did as I said, speaking, as he turned, in a strong South African accent. "Look, friend, I don't know what this is about. I heard a scream and came to help…"

I studied his face and decided I'd never seen him before. "Cut the crap, Philips. Is that your real name?"

A flicker of surprise. "Yes, of course it is. But how did you...?"

"Turn around and get on your knees."

"Now look! This has gone far enough!"

"Right now you have two options, Philips. I shoot you in the face or you turn around and get on your knees so we can have a conversation."

The fear in his face was no act. He turned his back on me, but paused before getting on his knees. "Look here, mister. I don't know what idea you've got into your head, but I was just going for a walk when I heard a scream. I came to help, and find you brandishing a gun at me."

"What were you doing parked outside my house last night?"

"What?"

"I am not the most patient man in the world, Philips. Stop bullshitting me. You're not doing yourself any favors."

"You live on Concord Road?"

"Come on, Philips!"

He was swallowing hard and his skin had gone a pasty gray color. "I was shagging a hooker. I picked her up in Boston. It's impossible for a man to get laid out here! I phoned and picked her up. I couldn't take her back to the bed and breakfast, could I? So I shagged her in the Range Rover."

"What the hell are you doing out here anyway?"

He almost turned to face me. I snapped, "Stay put!" and he stopped, but he was craning his head over his shoulder.

"You fucking Americans! I'm sorry, but seriously! Where

else on the face of the planet is a foreigner held at gunpoint because he is a tourist in a place where you don't get many tourists? What fucking century are you in? This is one of the most beautiful places on the planet. I am here because I want to see it, try the seafood, wander in the woods! And what do I get for my troubles? Some gun-happy fucking Yank pulling a gun on me! And why? Because I am visiting a remote part of his country! You are a real piece of work, friend! I came here to help you because I thought you were hurt!"

"So you're not tracking my GPS?"

He half turned again. His face was creased with incredulity. "*What?*"

"So if we walk back to your truck now, we will not find a tracker locked onto my cell phone?"

"Friend, you seriously need help. I'm not being facetious. You are seriously paranoid. I mean it."

"Take your jacket off."

He went very still. "Why?"

"Because if you don't, I'll shoot you in the leg and take it off you myself."

"What is *wrong* with you?"

"I don't like people trying to kill me, Philips. Now take your jacket off before I run out of patience."

He was good. The movement was smooth and fluid. He didn't fluster and he didn't fumble. He took hold of his lapels, like he was about to take off his jacket, then his right hand slipped in under his arm and simultaneously his left leg slipped back and across to the right, so that as his Glock came out of his holster, he had already spun and was facing me. He was too good. He didn't give me a chance to wing him or wound him. I double tapped and both slugs went through his chest. He winced and coughed, his legs failed and he crumpled to the ground.

I knelt beside him and felt his pulse in his throat. He was dead. I searched his pockets for his ID and found a passport and a driver's license in the name of Mark Philips, but no other personal information. I kept his driving license, picked up my phone and left.

THE CALL CAME forty-five minutes later, as I was stepping out of the shower.

"Yeah, Walker." I wiped the water from my eyes with my fingers.

"Lacklan, it's Jim. I'm on a burner, but I don't want to stay on too long. How did you get on with your stalker? Any news?"

"We didn't get to talk."

"OK. Cape Coral. Book into an hotel. Day after tomorrow I'll call you. We'll meet and talk."

"Cape Coral. Florida?"

"Is there another?"

"You said Seattle?"

"And if anybody was listening in, that's what they are thinking right now."

"OK."

"Drive, and use something less conspicuous than that machine from hell you usually drive, will you?"

"See you in a couple of days, Jim."

I hung up and began to towel myself dry.

CHAPTER 2

I booked an apartment at the Westin, a holiday complex on the Glover Bight, and drove down in my Zombie, despite Jim's request that I leave it behind. The Zombie 222 is, as he described it, a beast from hell. The chassis is an original 1968 Mustang Fastback, in matte black, but under the hood it has twin lithium ion batteries that deliver eight hundred horsepower straight to the back wheels. It will accelerate from naught to sixty in about one and a half seconds with enough G-force to spread your face like a pancake across the rear windshield. It has a top speed of two hundred miles an hour, and because it runs on lithium ion batteries, it gets there almost instantly, and in absolute silence.

It was a twenty-two hour drive from Weston to Cape Coral, but I don't sleep much—I figure I'll have plenty of time to sleep when I'm dead—and with the help of the Zombie, I got there in just under eighteen hours, at five thirty PM on the following day, nineteen hours after I had spoken to Jim on the phone in my study.

I parked the car in the parking garage beneath the apartment block, checked in to my apartment at reception and rode the elevator to the fifteenth floor. There I threw open the terrace and stood a while under the Florida sun, taking in the view of the Glover Bight, Sanibel Island and, beyond it, the immense sweep of the Gulf of Mexico, wondering when Jim would show, what he would have to tell me, and where and when the Omega story would end.

If it would ever end.

After that, I dumped my case on the bed and stood under the shower for fifteen minutes, switching from scalding, steaming water to cold and back again, trying to wake myself up and wash away the long drive from the north. Then I toweled myself dry, called down for a Martini and dialed Jim's burner. He answered as I dropped into a chair on the terrace. He didn't waste time on preliminaries.

"You're there already?"

"I just checked in. I'm at the Westin, Cape Coral."

"You either flew or you drove down in that machine from hell."

"Where are you?"

"I'm on my way. I'll be there in the morning. I'll pick you up from Pier Two at nine AM. Forgive me for asking the obvious, but were you followed?"

"I'm pretty sure I wasn't."

"OK, get a good rest after your long drive."

"Yes, Mom."

He laughed noisily and hung up.

I sat a while and watched the evening gather in the sky

above the sea, wondering why it's so much easier to be decisive about killing and destroying than it is about offering peace and creating life.

My bell rang and I opened the door to admit a young man in a burgundy uniform with a tray holding a bottle of Martini, Beefeater gin and a dish of olives. He mixed me a cocktail, I gave him twenty bucks and he left. I took my cocktail out to the terrace, sat and called Marni in Oxford.

"Lacklan... I didn't expect to hear from you."

"Everything OK with you?"

"Sure..." She was hesitant. "Why?"

"Just touching base."

There was a pause, then the hint of a smile in her voice. "It's nice to hear from you."

"How's life? Any news?"

"Like what?"

"Career, love life..." I let the words hang in the air and heard her laugh softly at the other end of the line.

"Well, since I gave Gibbons his marching orders, my career has been pretty much at a standstill, and since a certain party gave me *my* marching orders, my love life has been pretty much at a standstill too. So, no, no news to speak of."

I nodded, as though she could see me. "Well, sometimes no news is good news."

"Yeah, sometimes. Lacklan, why are you really calling?"

"I don't know. I'll have to ask my analyst." She laughed and I smiled, allowing it to show in my voice. "I might be going over to England in the next couple of days. I'd like to see you, if you're free."

She didn't answer straight away, but when she did, her voice was warm. "I'd like that."

"Marni?"

"Yes, Lacklan…"

I hesitated, indecisive. My head was crowded with things I wanted to say, but in the end I just said, "I have to go, but if anyone approaches you in the next few days, anyone who might come into your life, please treat them with caution."

"Oh…" Her voice had hardened. "Does that include you?"

"No."

"I thought you were touching base."

"I was—I am. I just don't want you to get hurt. I wouldn't be much of a friend if I didn't give you the heads up, would I?"

"So it's not over?"

"Apparently not."

"Lacklan, you can't keep on…"

"Not on the phone. I'll come and see you at Oxford. We'll talk about everything. But please, Marni, sometimes I feel it's enough for me to give you some advice for you to go right ahead and do the opposite."

"I guess we're more alike than we think."

"Maybe so, but I really need you to listen to me this time. Be careful, be smart. There are people out to hurt me, and…" I paused and sighed. "I guess you are my Achilles' heel. I don't know if they know that or not, but if they do, you're at risk. That was the real reason I was calling."

She was quiet for a long moment. Then she said, "I'm your Achilles' heel?"

"Look, don't…"

"Say it again." The smile had returned to her voice. I sighed. She repeated, "Say it again. What am I?"

"You're my Achilles' heel." I heard her giggling and stared up at the pink and powder blue sky. "Be serious, Marni."

"OK, I'll be serious and I will be cautious, I promise."

"Thank you."

There was an awkward silence for a few seconds. Then she said suddenly, "I was sorry to hear about you and Abi. I know you were…"

"It was for the best. She and Bat seem to be very close now. They seem happy."

"Bat?"

"Friend of mine from the Regiment."

"So you're alone now?"

I felt a bitter twist in my gut and tried to suppress it. "Yeah, it's the way I came in, it's the way I'm going out, and apparently it's the way I'm going to be in between too."

"I'm sorry."

"Listen, I'll see you in a couple of days. I'll drop you a line when I've booked my flight."

"Yeah…" We both hesitated, then she said, "Take care, Lacklan," and hung up.

I had a steak and salad sent up at seven thirty, then read for a couple of hours and had an early night. The next morning I rose at five-thirty, went for a run, trained for a couple of hours, showered and had a breakfast of bacon, pancakes and maple syrup, and at nine o'clock I was on Pier Two, smoking a Camel and looking like a tourist, scanning the area for Jim Redbeard. I didn't see him, but at ten past nine I saw a launch approaching through the mouth of the bite, and when I saw that, I noticed the white schooner anchored about a mile out of Big Shell Island. I smiled to myself. That was Jim all over, advising me that my silent, matte black Mustang was too conspicuous and showing up in a shiny, white, one hundred foot schooner.

Ten minutes later, I was sitting in the back of the launch and we were slapping over the small waves, with the gulls wheeling overhead under the blue dome of the morning. Soon the pitch of the engine dropped, we slowed and closed in on the steps that led down from the deck to the small boarding platform, just above the waves. Jim watched over the side, leaning on the gunwale, smoking a cigarette.

I swung up onto the ladder and he met me at the top with a warm handshake and an embrace.

"It's good to see you, Lacklan. You look well, I expected you to be heavier, putting on a spread now that you've settled as master of the manor. Glad to see I was wrong. You still looking lean and predatory."

"The war's not over yet, Jim."

He slapped me on the shoulder. "Come down to the lounge and have some coffee. Njal's down there."

"How is he? Last time I saw him, he was dying of a chest wound."

"That guy's an ox. He's indestructible."

We crossed the deck to a small structure that covered a flight of wooden steps, which led down into a space that looked more like an old world club than an oceangoing schooner. The walls were paneled in mahogany, there were chesterfields and Persian rugs, bookcases and even a bar. A short flight of steps led to an enclosed cockpit where there were two large, leather swivel chairs, a helm, and a bank of computers and electronic equipment.

Njal was sitting in one of the chesterfields, reading a book, and rose as we came in. He grinned at me, gripped my hand as though he were planning to Indian wrestle me and embraced me with his other arm.

"You still alive, huh? We thought maybe you died of middle-age boredom. What you doing now? You become a farmer or some shit, huh?"

I smiled. "Not dead, not a farmer. Just trying to stay out of trouble."

Jim laughed. "Don't go lookin' for trouble when trouble ain't lookin' to be looked for, huh? Only trouble *is* out lookin' for you, Lacklan. Come and sit down."

We sat around a mahogany coffee table as a door under the stairs to the cockpit opened and Mioko, Jim's Japanese companion, came out with a pot of coffee and three cups on a tray. She gave me a special smile, set down the tray and withdrew.

As Jim poured, I said, "So what's this about?"

Njal answered for him. "We don't know, but it stinks of Omega."

Jim handed me a cup. "It more than stinks, it is clearly Omega."

"You said that if I destroyed Omicron, Omega four and five would wither away."

He shrugged and handed Njal a cup. "Apparently I was wrong. Sometimes I am wrong. Not often, but sometimes."

"Good to know. So how wrong were you?"

Again it was Njal who answered. "We got two bits of

intel, with no obvious connection, until you dig a little deeper. First we got this building in the Northern Cape, on the border with Namibia. It is basically a pyramid the size of a skyscraper, on the Orange River, in the middle of fuckin' nowhere. It is in the desert. The nearest town of any size is Springbok, which has about twelve thousand people and is sixty miles away as the crow flies, but at least a hundred by road. Forty of those hundred miles are on dirt tracks through the desert."

"I get the idea. It's remote. But why connect it with Omega? It could be a secret government project."

Jim shook his head. "Wait and listen."

Njal continued. "Meanwhile, in parallel, almost simultaneous, we hear that Omega Four, who had been quiet for a long time, are arranging a summit. It's too much coincidence, right? So Omega Four covers all of Africa, Middle East—except for Israel, which fell under Omega One—Iran, Kazakhstan, Afghanistan..."

"I'm aware..."

"OK, right down to Pakistan and India."

"I was the one who gave you that information."

"Breathe, drink your coffee, chill, listen. Their areas of competence, what they specialized in, were Islam, mind control through indoctrination, the economy of war, unregulated research and development, especially in weaponry, biology and chemistry. So we were trying to get some idea: if this is the areas of special competence of Omega Four, what the fuck is this giant pyramid, right?"

I shrugged. "Right. And?"

"We still got no fuckin' idea, man. But, at the Omega Four summit, we got Pi and Ro, father and son, Ruud van

Dreiver and Jelle van Dreiver, both South African and both directors of the Van Dreiver Corporation. Ruud is the CEO, Jelle is his second in command. Then we got Sigma: Prince Mohamed bin Awad, resides between his Awadi palace, London and New York."

"I know him."

"Of course you do. Then we have Tau: Ameya Dabir, Brahmin woman of ancient lineage. If India was still a monarchy, she would be a princess. Her father was a very powerful industrialist, but she established her own business twenty years ago and made her way into the Forbes five hundred richest people on the planet. "And finally Upsilon, George da Silva, President of King Felipe, a small island republic in the Gulf of Guinea, between Cameroon and Nigeria, total population one hundred thousand inhabitants. All five of them are meeting in Knysna, South Africa, at the van Dreiver mansion on the Knysna lagoon, to eat fresh oysters and drink South African wine. What else they gonna do, we don't know. But it is the first time Omega Four have got together in a summit for over two years."

Jim drained his cup and set it down on the table. "I can't believe it is a coincidence that a hit man came looking for you at precisely this time."

"He was South African." I pulled his driver's license from my pocket and dropped it on the table. "It has his prints on it, I don't know if you can do anything with that."

"Yeah, we can."

"So you are making the assumption that their meeting is connected with this massive construction."

Jim nodded. "You're right. It is an assumption. Which is why we need to confirm it. We need to confirm it's an

Omega project, we need to confirm what kind of project it is, and then, if we are right about it, then we need to destroy it."

I laughed out loud. "You want to destroy a pyramid the size of a skyscraper? What do you plan to use, a tactical nuclear device?"

Njal was examining his thumbs. Jim watched me until I had finished laughing, then said, "If necessary, yes."

I stopped laughing. I studied his face and went cold inside. "You have access to that kind of hardware?"

"If necessary, yes. But the pyramid is not built yet. The point is, Lacklan, we may have to stop it ever being built. We may need to destroy it, whatever it is, and you need to find out if we do or we don't. Once that decision has been made, we'll find the way to do it."

I gave a single nod. "I shall consider myself told."

He smiled but without much humor. "We are defined by our limitations, Lacklan. But we also get to choose our limitations."

"Point taken. Don't quote your self-help books at me, Jim. So we are going on a recon mission to the Northern Cape. What about the summit in Knysna?"

Njal answered.

"That's in three weeks, the first weekend of September, from Friday through Monday. Ruud van Dreiver's mansion is on the southwest side of the lagoon, on a headland overlooking the Dylan Thomas Holiday Resort, half a mile away across the water. Security will be high and they will have a lot of well armed personnel. Knysna is the Western Cape, about three hundred and fifty miles east of Cape Town."

Jim took over. "We book you in to one of the log cabins

in the holiday resort. From there, you make the five hits. It will require fast planning and execution on the hoof. You may find that a bomb is your simplest option. That is your department and Njal's. However you decide to do it, you execute them, and then get out of there."

"That simple."

"Not at all. It will be anything but simple."

"That was irony, Jim. You are giving us three weeks in which to develop and execute two plans that are practically impossible."

He sighed. "Lacklan, how can I put this to you? Maybe you don't like the fact that the sky is blue, but it is blue. Maybe you don't like the fact that we are bound to the Earth by gravity, but we are. This pyramid has appeared on our radar and it could potentially signify an incalculable danger to us—*all* of us, and the Omega top brass have chosen this time to meet for the first time since you destroyed their American branch. I didn't choose for it to be that way. I only noticed it was happening. Now it is up to you to investigate and take action." He shrugged. "If you feel you are not up to it…"

"Untangle your panties, Jim, and get off your high horse. Maybe you should come along and show us how it's done before you start asking stupid questions about whether I'm up to it."

"Maybe I should, but my point is I don't choose the targets. I just spot them."

"OK, point taken. So we are going to need a lot of hardware for these jobs, and a lot of high explosive. How do we get that into South Africa? Or have you got suppliers there?"

He shook his head. "No, we'll deliver you by ship to Elizabeth Bay, in Namibia."

"How?"

"A tanker departing Cadiz in a few days' time. You'll take on supplies in Dakar, Senegal, including a couple of Land Rovers and other hardware that I am arranging. Then you'll proceed on to Namibia. In Elizabeth Bay there is an old, abandoned factory which still has a functional jetty where supplies were delivered and goods were loaded onto ships. You'll be put ashore there, with your Land Rovers and other cargo. From there you will drive to the South African border, about one hundred and fifty miles south. There are not many roads. Much of the time you'll be driving along desert tracks, but you shouldn't find it too difficult." He glanced at us each in turn, then went on. "You'll cross the River Orange at Oranjemund and pick up the R382 at Alexander Bay. What you do after that is for you and Njal to decide amongst yourselves."

I nodded. "What about the extraction?"

He shrugged. "First, decide how you are going to execute the operations, then tell me what you need for your extraction and I'll organize it."

I looked at Njal. "You got anything to add?"

He shook his head. "No. Until we know what's at the pyramid site, we don't know what we gonna need."

I thought a moment. "We may have to split up. We're on the clock and the time is short. You got maps?"

He smiled. "Yeah, we got maps. We also got satellite images and we got a printer."

Jim stood. "I am going to leave you guys to it. I'll talk to the master of the *Annie Rose* and give you a departure date. Meanwhile, start laying the foundations of your plan."

We worked all day, studying satellite imagery and maps, and digesting what little eyewitness information we had. In the end, we concluded that all we could do was hide the Land Rovers in the rocky hills that bordered the river and proceed on foot by night, until we had a visual on the construction site. If we couldn't make out what it was from watching it, then we would have to snatch an architect—or at least somebody at the site wearing a suit—and get them to tell us what the damn thing was. The workers, foremen and architects would have to be living either onsite or nearby in the small town of Steinkopf or the village of Goodhouse, so snatching them would not be impossible. Once we had that information, we would decide what to do next.

We played with a few alternative plans, left them as potentials to be developed, and, stretching and crunching our joints, we went up on deck and found Jim as the sun was turning to molten copper a few inches above the horizon. There, Njal presented him with the shopping list we had prepared. He examined it, sucking on his cigarette and trailing smoke from his nose.

"OK," he said, "you have four days. Put your affairs in order. You board the *Annie Rose* in Cadiz on Tuesday 20th. On the 23rd you will stop at Dakar to take on freight, including your two Land Rovers and the stuff on this list. A week after that, you will disembark at Elizabeth Bay."

"A week? That is one hell of a waste of time, Jim. That's nine or ten days sitting on our asses doing nothing."

He nodded. "I know, Lacklan, but what's the option? You want to fly military hardware into South Africa? Organizing such a thing would take months. And buying the kind of stuff you need in South Africa without Omega getting to hear about it…" He shook his head. "It's not realistic. You're on their radar. They are looking for you. Believe me. I have thought about it. It's the only way—and even so it is high risk."

"OK, I'll take your word for it."

"The skipper is a Norwegian…"

"Of course he is."

"His name is Daag Olafsen. He's a friend. He'll ignore you, like you're not there, unless you need help. But I can't see that you should. You eat on your own, don't get into conversation with the crew and they'll ignore you too; and stay in your cabins. I want you to be as invisible as possible."

He handed me a large manila envelope and another to Njal. I took mine and leaned against the gunwale to open it while he continued talking. "You have in there a passport and a driver's license which will pass muster in Spain when you board the ship. Lacklan, you are Richard Sinclair. Njal, you are Thomas Jansen. After you have crossed the border from Namibia into South Africa, Njal, I recommend you destroy them. You, Lacklan, will need yours for Knysna. But aside from that, once there you do not exist, you're just ghosts. If they find you, you're better off going down fighting than getting caught."

Njal sat at the table and Jim handed us each a slip of paper. "Memorize this number. It's a burner. You can use it once, then it will be destroyed. I'll have it with me at all times. You call me when you need to get out and I will arrange it, if I can."

I memorized the number, set fire to it with my Zippo and dropped the smoldering ash over the side.

"OK, I'm going." I turned to Njal. "I'll see you in Cadiz. Jim, I'll see you when I get back." I paused. "Thanks." I offered him my hand and we shook.

"Sure. Take care of yourself. I'll have José run you back."

———

I STOOD on the quay and watched the small lights of the launch disappear into the gathering dusk, heading back toward the yacht. Then I walked back to the apartment block and booked myself onto a British Airways midnight flight to London. After that, I had a shower and went down to the Nauti Mermaid to have some grilled shrimps and a burger, with a couple of martinis, dry.

At nine, I climbed in my car and took Route 41 to Miami, through the dark wilderness of the Big Cypress National Park. All the way, the tall trees made black walls on either side of the road, which loomed overhead and pressed in from the sides, like living walls. I ignored them and called Kenny.

"Good evening, sir."

"I'm going to be away for a couple of weeks, Kenny."

"I rather thought you might, sir."

"I need you to come down to Miami International Airport and collect the Zombie."

"Of course..." He hesitated a moment. "This won't be the last, will it, sir?"

"I don't know, Kenny. We thought after Mexico..."

"In Spanish they say that bad weeds never die."

"Yeah, I'm no philosopher, Kenny, but maybe that's why we're here. Maybe we're already in hell, and we need to work our way out."

"Perhaps you're right, sir. Stay safe, and I'll see you in a few hours."

"Yeah, you too, Kenny. Say hi to Rosalia for me."

I hung up and sped on through the pressing walls of the dark.

CHAPTER 3

I landed at Heathrow at one forty PM the next day, collected my rental car and drove north and west through warm, green fields under blue skies dotted with distant clouds, like Spanish galleons in full sail on an invisible ocean in the air.

It took me a little over an hour to get to Oxford. I parked at a meter outside Marni's apartment and rang on the bell. She buzzed me in and I climbed the narrow stairs to her door, remembering the last time I had been there, climbing those same stairs with a hot twist in my gut, to confront her with the fact that she had betrayed me, lied to me and passed secrets to my enemies. That had been then. Now things had changed.

I hoped.

I came to the landing and saw the door open at the top of the next flight. Her silhouette was in the doorway, backlit, looking down at me. I couldn't see her face or her expression. I heard her voice, disembodied.

"Hi."

It didn't tell me much, but I smiled and climbed the rest of the way. When I got to the top, I saw she was smiling too.

"How are you doing?"

She shrugged, leaning against the jamb. "Negotiating the challenges." She gave herself a little push off the doorframe. "Come on in. You want a beer?"

"Thanks."

She led me into her living room. She had tall, narrow windows open onto a small, cast iron balcony overlooking High Street. Wedges of warm sunshine were lying across the rugs on the bare boards, and drooping over her armchair like Dali clocks. On the floor by the sofa, she had a steel bucket full of ice, with half a dozen bottles of beer stuck in it. An open one stood on a lamp table beside her armchair.

She pointed at the bucket. "Help yourself."

I pulled out a bottle and cracked it with the opener she had hanging beside the bottles. She dropped into the chair and watched me. "You want some lunch?"

"I ate on the plane."

I sat and took a swig.

"Last time you were here, you were pretty mad at me."

I gave a small nod. "You could have got me killed. Not just me, but me and another guy who was with me."

"I apologized. I broke off all contact with Gibbons."

"I'm not here to bring that up again, Marni."

"Oh. Then why are you here?"

"I'm going to China."

She frowned. "What's in China?"

"One of the last two remaining chapters of Omega: Omega Five."

She sighed and closed her eyes. "You're going to kill them."

It wasn't a question, but I nodded and said, "Yes."

There was anger in her eyes when she opened them. "They are still human beings, Lacklan. I learned that from your father. I'm surprised you didn't. He was number three in the world, yet he came to realize that what he was doing was wrong. I killed him, and his murder will live on my conscience for the rest of my life. He was misguided, wrong about many things, but he was basically a good man, yet I robbed him of his life, and you of the chance of making peace with him. How do you live with all the men you're killing, all the children you've robbed of their fathers?"

I waited till she'd finished. "I came to talk to you, Marni, not to be lectured at by you."

She sighed. "I'm sorry. I just... I wish you would stop. I have lost the man I loved—the man I love—to a relentless, unforgiving need to kill. Stop, already, Lacklan. Please."

"They are coming after me. They sent a man to kill me. How do you suggest I deal with that threat? Call the cops? Or perhaps attempt a meaningful dialogue?"

"If you hadn't gone after them in the first place..."

"Seriously? We are going to have this conversation? Seriously? This is your new, enlightened philosophy of life? Back down in the face of despots and tyrants? Don't upset them and maybe, if you're lucky, they won't hurt you? And as for the men, women and children who *they* are murdering, torturing, enslaving and forcing to work on subsistence wages in mines, well, we'll form committees to talk about them, shall we?"

"Who's lecturing whom now, Lacklan?" She sighed. "Besides, you know that's not what I meant."

"What did you mean?"

Another sigh. "I don't know. But if there's anything in karma, you sure have a lot of blood on your hands. I just wish you'd start bringing some peace into the world, instead of violence."

"Yeah, I'd like that too, Marni. And if you ever come up with a way of doing that, that doesn't involve wishful thinking about sadists, murderers, drug traffickers and slave traders turning out to be nice guys at heart, I'd love to hear it. Can we start again, please?"

She stared at me for a moment. "Boy, you don't pull your punches, do you?"

I shook my head. "No. The last time I was here, I had lied to you about where I was going and what I was going to do. I was testing you because I believed you would tell Gibbons what I was going to do, and I was right. This time I am here for the opposite reason. I know you don't like what I am doing, but in spite of that I trust you. I want you to know where I am going, and what I am going to do. I am asking you not to tell anybody, least of all Gibbons. For the first time in years, perhaps in my life, I am trusting someone who is not a brother in the Regiment. That is hard for me. But I want to trust you, Marni. You were always the one person in the world I believed in. I want to believe in you again. I want to believe that you are true, and you have my back. If I am wrong, tell me and I'll leave."

She was quiet for a long time, gazing out the open windows at the cars and cyclists passing below in a lazy, desultory procession. After a while, she passed the heel of her hand across her eyes.

"You're not wrong, Lacklan. I'm wrong. I've been wrong about you for a long time. But I can't keep apologizing forever. At some point, you either have to accept my apology or tell me to go to hell."

"That's what I'm doing." I smiled. "Not telling you to go to hell, I am offering you my trust, Marni. I want you to know where I am going and what I am doing. I..." I hesitated. "I would like you to be more a part of my life."

She frowned. It was a small, confused frown. "You want me to be more a part of the killing?"

I gave a small laugh that wasn't very humorous. "Not exactly, no. There is more to my life than just killing people." I hesitated a moment. "There was a time when we were both devoted to bringing down Omega, remember? Now Omega is all but finished." I shrugged. "When they are gone, if I survive, I still want to have a life that has some meaning..."

"What are you saying?"

I stood, went to the window and leaned on the frame, looking down at the people milling in the street below, among those ancient stone temples to the human mind. What was I saying? I wasn't sure myself. I chewed my lip a while and turned to face her again.

"I guess what I am saying is, I'd like us to rebuild the trust we once had. More than that, we can't go back, but we can go forward and we can build a trust that is deeper and stronger than what we had before. And maybe, with time..." I shrugged. "I'd like you to be a part of my life, in some way..."

She gave a small sigh and stared at my belly for a

moment. She said, "That's nice, Lacklan." Then she looked down at her hands. "But you say this to me as you are about to embark on a journey to murder five people, in cold blood. I don't know how I am supposed to deal with that. You turn up and you say to me," she gestured at me with her open hand, "'Hi, Marni, I'm just off to kill a bunch of folk, but when I get back, I'd like you to be more involved in my life!' Neat."

I leaned on the jamb of the tall window, feeling the sun warm on my back, and smiled at her. "You're funny." I gave a small shrug. "Would it be different if this was 1945 and I was a pilot in the British Royal Air Force, and I was going on a bombing mission over Germany tonight? I'd be going to kill a bunch of people, many of them arguably less guilty than my targets in China, but when I got back, you would not see me as a killer; you'd see me as a hero fighting to protect his country."

"Come on, Lacklan, that's sophistry! It's totally different."

"No, Marni. Only the way you see it is different. Omega is real, as real as the Third Reich was. Hell! For all I know, they may be connected. Their aims are not so different. Omega murders and exploits and enslaves people every day, and if they ever achieve their ends, countless millions will die." I laughed, a harsh bark of a laugh. "It wouldn't be the first time a small elite wiped out millions of people to serve its own, peculiar vision of how the world ought to be, would it?"

"You're preaching to the choir, Lacklan. I know they exist."

"All I am doing, like that RAF pilot, is fighting them in

the only way I know how. You and Gibbons said my way was wrong. I should talk and reason and negotiate; but while you tried to do that, they grew in power until they were ready to plant a nuclear device at the United Nations, wipe out half of New York and slaughter a quarter of a million people. But now, because of those methods you disapproved of so much, New York is whole, those people did not die and Omega is almost finished. They are broken." I sighed and shook my head. "You label me a killer, Marni, but maybe you should think also about all the lives I've saved by killing these bastards and destroying their organization."

I put my bottle down on the lamp table. "I'm sorry, Marni, I am wasting your time. This was a mistake. I'll see you around."

I had gotten to the door when she said, "Lacklan, wait." I turned with my hand on the handle. "Please come back and finish your beer. Don't overreact. You want us to trust each other, so you should allow me to express my feelings, not just my opinions. They are not always the same, you know."

I walked back and sat on the arm of the sofa, looking at her. She met my gaze and went on.

"I know you hate what you do. I know it troubles you and it haunts you, and I know you left the SAS because you were tired of killing. So if you are conflicted about what you do, can't I be? For me, it isn't just the killing. If it were some anonymous entity killing these people, maybe I'd feel better about it. But it isn't. It's the man I love. We both knew it, Lacklan, from the time we were twelve, fourteen: it was us, *contra mundum*, you and me. And to think of you doing this stuff…" She shook her head. "It breaks my heart."

"I hadn't thought of it like that."

"Maybe we should talk more."

I raised an eyebrow at her. "Well, that was kind of what I was suggesting, if you recall."

She gave a snort that might have been a snigger. "Yeah, I guess it was, huh?"

I became serious. "When they are gone, then people like you and Cyndi McFarlane can talk your asses off, negotiate till you're blue in the face and find the way to make the world a better place. But before that, Omega has to be destroyed completely."

She wouldn't look at me. She just gazed out the window, with the sunlight on her face. "I know," she said at last. "I just wish it didn't have to be you."

"Yeah, well, on that at least, we can agree."

Now she looked at me. "I know. I know you feel the same."

She rose from her chair and came and sat on the sofa. I slid off the arm and dropped beside her, then put my arm across her shoulders and pulled her to me. "Do you ever think about going back to Weston?"

She slipped her arms around me and rested her head on my shoulder. "Sometimes I miss it. I remember playing in the woods with you, and our holidays in Colorado. Lately, I have found it hard to imagine going back, but I do miss it." She looked up at me. "And I love it here too."

"My mother lives near here."

"I know. I've visited her a few times."

My eyebrows told her I was surprised. "You have?"

"She asks after you. She says she gave up writing to you."

I stroked her cheek with the backs of my fingers. "Yeah. It's a long way back."

"What do you mean?"

"From where I am, to normality, to writing to your mom and visiting her, to visiting a country to see the architecture and the museums, or as she would say, the musea, and try the local cuisine, rather than toppling a regime or assassinating a drug lord. It's a long way back."

"Is it a journey you want to make, Lacklan?"

"You know it is, but I want to make it for a reason. Kenny and Rosalia are my family and I love them. But that house is so big and empty, and it still reeks of his pipe and his cigars, and the rooms still echo with his humiliating put-downs and insults. I need somebody to make the journey for. Otherwise…"

I left the words hanging and gazed out at the beautiful façade opposite.

"Otherwise what?"

"Otherwise I will probably follow Jim Redbeard and Njal, and my greatest ambition will be to fall in battle and get taken up to Valhalla by a Valkyrie, to spend the rest of eternity wenching, boozing and brawling."

"Wow, can I come?"

"No. You'd probably fall for one-eyed Odin and bear his children, and then I'd have to fight him too."

"Silly Lacklan."

"Will you be there, to help me come back?"

She nodded.

"Even though you know I must finish the job I started?"

She nodded again.

We stayed like that, talking quietly together, remembering the past and wondering about the future, watching the light turn to burnished copper on the ancient walls across the road, as the sky moved from blue to pink. Then the air seemed somehow to shift and turn grainy, and the sound of the traffic took on a nocturnal quality as the room slipped into darkness, and neither of us rose to switch on the light. Shortly after that, I picked her up in my arms and carried her to the bedroom.

In the morning, I rose at six and went for a run. When I got back at seven, she was up, making coffee in the kitchen. I showered and dressed and joined her at the table. She looked a little shy and that made me smile.

"We talked a lot last night," she said. "but it was all about feelings in the abstract. What did we actually conclude?"

I grunted a laugh. "Scientists! Always chasing facts…" I hesitated for a second, suddenly conflicted at having lied to her. "Let me do this job…" I held her eye a moment. "Marni, I…"

She shook her head. "Don't tell me anything about it, Lacklan. I don't want to know. Just come back alive and whole. And promise me this will be the last. And after that, you will leave this life behind."

I thought about it for a long moment, then nodded. "All right. I promise you that. I'll be away for a couple of weeks. When I get back, I'll come and see you, and then we'll talk in more concrete detail."

She grinned. It was a happy sight, and nice to see. "OK," she said. "I'll be waiting."

Twenty minutes later, I left and drove back south and east along the M40, toward London. There was somebody in East Acton I needed to see. It was a forty-five minute drive to his house on East Acton Lane, opposite the Alfayed Muslim School.

It was a classic, 1930s English semi-detached, with a front lawn and a big bow window. I parked my rental car in his driveway, blocking the exit for his TVR Cerbera, and rang on the bell. I hadn't phoned ahead, but I'd sent him a message saying I'd be shipping out in a couple of days, and he knew that meant I'd be showing up sometime soon.

He opened the door and looked at me without expression. He hadn't changed. He was short and wiry, his hair was grizzled and he had a mustache that would have looked more at home on the face of a Mongolian barbarian of the fourteenth century. When he spoke, the accent was Edinburgh: Scottish, but intelligible to the rest of the English speaking world.

"Look what the cat dragged in," he said. "By the looks of ye, you'll be needing a cup of tea."

"Hello, Ian. It's good to see you too."

"I never said it was good to see you. What have they been doing to you over in Wyoming? You look a mess. Come on in."

I stepped in and he closed the door, then slapped my shoulder with a hand like a girder. "How've you been, Lacklan? I heard you were fixin' fuckin' cars or some shit like that."

He led me past a living room and a dining room to a kitchen at the back of the house with a view of a large backyard with a lawn and a couple of vegetable patches.

"Tea or coffee?"

"Coffee. You settled down, huh?"

He grinned. "In a manner of speaking."

"You left the Regiment..."

He made a noise like sandpaper on petrified nicotine,

which was his way of laughing. "In a manner of speaking. I keep my hand in, unofficially. Know what I mean?"

"I know what you mean."

We were quiet while he spooned coffee into a percolator. "You see any of the lads?"

"Bat's over in the States."

"I heard. So what do you need?"

"I'm going to South Africa."

He put the percolator on the heat and pointed to a pine chair at a pine table. "Sit doon. You're not a fuckin' tree." I sat and he sat opposite. "You fixed for hardware?"

I nodded. "But I'm not sure about the route back."

He frowned at me like I'd spoken to him in classical Greek. "You're goin' in with no extraction plan? Tha's nuts."

"I know. That's why I'm here."

"I'm not followin' you, pal. How can I fix you up with an extraction?"

"You can't. And we're not without an extraction plan, I just don't much like the plan we have, so I'd like a plan B. Have we got any friends in Central Africa?"

"Guys?" He thought a moment, then nodded. "Aye, Billy. You remember Billy Beauchamp? Posh lad, Eton, dropped oot of Oxford, joined the Regiment. Nice lad, real gent."

"I remember him. He's in Africa now?"

"Aye, he got a job with the government, if you know what I mean. He's lookin' after some of Her Majesty's interests in Cameroon. You want me to get a message to him?"

I nodded. "We may have to pay him a visit on the way home."

"Who's we?"

"A pal. A good man."

"One of the guys?"

I shook my head. "No, but close enough."

"Can he be trusted, Lacklan?"

"I owe him my life several times over."

He made a face. "Good enough for me."

The coffee pot started to gurgle. He stood and made for the door, pointing at the pot. "Help yerself. There's some real whiskey in the cupboard, not that Irish muck you drink, real Scotch. I'll be back in a mo'."

I poured the coffee and laced it with Scotch, then stood at the back door, looking out at the lawn and the sycamore tree that shielded the backyard from the road at the back.

He returned five minutes later, as I was placing the empty cup in the sink. He picked up the pot and poured himself a cup.

"That's OK," he said. "He's given me a number for you to call if you're in trouble. He'll see you OK. But there's a problem."

"What's that?"

"I talked to Fido..."

"Major Crawley?"

Major Reginal 'Mad Dog' Crawley was affectionately known to the men as Fido. Ian nodded. "Aye."

"Why?"

"Because even though you're a Yankee bastard, you're a pal and I'd rather you didn't get killed. Your name has popped up on the bush telegraph a few times lately, and I thought I'd ask the major if he had any intel that might be useful to you. Seems Sgt. Bradley has been trying to get a hold of you in Wyoming, but nobody's had sight nor sound of you in a couple of years back there. What have you been up to?"

"Why was he looking for me?"

"Word is, there's a contract out on you. There's a price on your head, me old mucker."

Scan the QR code below to purchase KILL: FOUR.
Or go to: righthouse.com/kill-four

Printed in Dunstable, United Kingdom